The figure on the ground had certainly been hit repeatedly with cudgels, for there were lumps on his head and shoulders. Udolphus turned him over gently, under the uninterested eyes of the admiral's crew. Then one of the sailors cried in an indignant tone of voice, 'Why, it's only a young 'un. Not much older than a cabin jack, by the look—'

Udolphus gasped. 'It's Lucci, my apprentice.' He looked back towards the alley and saw a thin trail of blood being washed away by the rain. 'He's been dragged here and dumped. How could anyone do this to a youngster? How could they?' Udolphus's anguish came straight from the heart as he cradled Lucci's head in his paws.

'Perhaps we should ask *why*?' said the admiral, looking over his shoulder.

Udolphus ground his sharp otter's teeth together. 'I know why, signore. This was done as a warning to me.'

# The Silver Claw

## Garry Kilworth

Corgi Books

THE SILVER CLAW
A CORGI BOOK 0 552 55187 2

Published in Great Britain by Corgi Books,
an imprint of Random House Children's Books

This edition published 2005

1 3 5 7 9 10 8 6 4 2

Papers used by Random House Children's Books are natural,
recyclable products made from wood grown in sustainable forests.
The manufacturing processes conform to the environmental
regulations of the country of origin.

Set in 12/15 pt Sabon

Corgi Books are published by
Random House Children's Books,
61–63 Uxbridge Road, London W5 5SA,
a division of The Random House Group Ltd,
in Australia by Random House Australia (Pty) Ltd,
20 Alfred Street, Milsons Point, Sydney, NSW 2061, Australia,
in New Zealand by Random House New Zealand Ltd,
18 Poland Road, Glenfield, Auckland 10, New Zealand,
and in South Africa by Random House (Pty) Ltd,
Endulini, 5A Jubilee Road, Parktown 2193, South Africa

THE RANDOM HOUSE GROUP Limited Reg. No. 954009
www.kidsatrandomhouse.co.uk

A CIP catalogue record for this book
is available from the British Library.

Printed and bound in Great Britain by
Cox & Wyman Ltd, Reading, Berkshire

*To my friend Andrew Hall*
*'Venice' is synonymous with 'Paradise'*
*He motivated this story*
*with his infectious enthusiasm*

# Author's Note

Vequince, an island city of canals, is inhabited by water voles. We commonly refer to them as 'water rats' due to the fact that they're of a similar size to black and brown rats. Otters we simply call otters, which is just as well really, because Udolphus Beck would not wish to be known as anything else. The mammals in this story wear clothes, drink coffee and sail tall ships, much as we do. They're civilized. If you think of the otters and water rats we know now as Stone Age mammals, then you'll see that it's going to take at least 3 million years for an Udolphus or Lucci to come along. It might be worth the wait.

# Chapter One

Udolphus Beck was an unraveller. Not so long ago he had been a shoemaker for the otters of Geranium. Udolphus had followed his father into a cobbler's trade, but his heart was not in the work. Oh, he was *good* at shoemaking, of course: Geranium otters always applied themselves to their jobs. But he found the work lacked flair and imagination. He was a youthful otter who burned to do great things. It was fortunate that the other talent he had was for solving mysteries. Unravelling puzzles.

Once shoemakers have mastered their work they have a great deal of time for thinking. While they are cutting the leather, shaping the sole and heel, stitching, hammering in the small bright nails, their minds wander. So it was that the lively-minded Udolphus Beck became an unraveller. He thought about things, turned them over in his mind, picked away at them with his sharp intellect.

This he excelled at and, now that his father had passed away and he no longer had to make shoes, he was able to earn his living at it. Mammals brought him tangled problems and he sought the ends, found them, untangled the knotted ball. In fact, his fame as an unraveller had spread far and wide after the King of Geranium's daughter had been found alive and well. It was Udolphus whose intellect had tracked her movements to a log cabin in the Dense Forest, after unravelling all the clues to her kidnapping by a lovesick woodsman. The king had rewarded him very handsomely, of course, and now Udolphus was a wealthy otter.

'Interesting, how very interesting,' he said over a breakfast tray in bed one morning as he read a letter propped against the salt pot. 'Vequince! The island city in the sea! Now there's a place I've *always* wanted to visit. Magnificent architecture, I'm told. Wonderful works of art in the churches and the public buildings. A colourful population . . .'

The letter itself was strange enough. The carrier, too, had been unusual: a mute pine marten. A small purse of silver bezants accompanied the note – Udolphus's fare to Vequince, should he take the job. This indicated that the courier had been well paid or he might well have absconded with this money. There was also the promise of a large fee – *a Vequincian carnival mask of pure gold* – if he should solve the mystery; a smaller fee in coin if he took on the work but failed.

The writer was almost certainly a water rat, for it was this species of mammal that inhabited the island of Vequince, which lay over the mountains, to the south of Geranium. It was part of a country which on the map looked like a fisherjack's boot – a shape which had Udolphus's fond approval. Vequince nestled in the corner of a crook in the mainland's coastline. Its sheltered position gave it ideal harbours and its trade had flourished until Vequince was a very rich city, full of very rich water rats, and growing richer all the time.

'How very peculiar,' muttered Udolphus. 'How wonderfully mysterious.'

He stared at his bedroom ceiling. This had been painted a subtle shade of night, a very dark blue. In this night blueness Udolphus had nailed the bright nails left over from his shoemaking. Caught in lamplight, these nails twinkled like stars. Indeed, Udolphus had not just hammered them in randomly. Like the bright, clever otter he was, he had made an exact copy of the heavens.

Each nail represented a particular star and was precisely in the right place. There was the Belt of Orion, and over here Sirius, and down there in the corner Ursa Major, or the Big Bear. The solar system and all the constellations and galaxies were present. He derived great pleasure and much inspiration from his ceiling. Under its benign influence he could concentrate his thoughts and bend his mind to the complex problems he needed to solve.

'So,' he said, not without a sigh, 'do I do this thing or not? If I went now I would be in time for Carnival. I've been told it's a magnificent spectacle.'

He stared again at the letter. It was signed, very bizarrely, by someone calling themselves *The Silver*

*Claw*. (Clearly the author needed a false name in case the letter was intercepted by his enemies.) The note asked Udolphus to make his way to Vequince, there to reside until he had uncovered a conspiracy to bring down – possibly even to assassinate – every member of the government. The writer went on:

> *I have no doubt that the infamous Mudditchis, rulers of the city of Florion, are part of this plot. As rivals in art, architecture and trade, they have nothing to lose by supporting rebellious and ambitious elements in our society. The Mudditchis are a cunning and greedy family. He who promises the Mudditchis a share of Vequince's trade I am sure will receive all the support he needs. If any such plotters are gullible enough to invite the Florion army to attack on their behalf, however, I doubt the invaders will leave the city of Vequince without plundering it of much of its wealth. If you shake paws with a Mudditchi, you always check your purse afterwards.*

The idea that Vequince's dazzling palazzo, its tall campaniles and its opulent churches, should be robbed was too awful to contemplate. Udolphus was aware of the great rivalry between the two ruling families of the two great cities: the Mudditchis of Florion and the Voleccis of Vequince had been deadly rivals and enemies since the first bird heralded in the first day on Earth. Perhaps neither family could be trusted when it came to the other, but the invasion of a city state was a thing which needed to be stopped. Invasions, as the writer had said, tend to lead to chaos.

The writer had ended by saying that if Udolphus took up his offer, he should go to Vequince, where he would be contacted by the Silver Claw.

'I shall do it. I shall take the stagecoach,' Udolphus said to himself, as he removed the special sock that kept his tail warm at night, 'as far as the border. There I shall have to proceed on foot over the mountains. The journey will be an adventure in itself, I have no doubt. I shall need all the proper clothing and equipment' – like most Geraniums, Udolphus was very correct about such things – 'including a stout walking staff with a tasteful number of badges on it, a good hat with a neat little feather, and a knapsack to keep out the weather. Good solid boots. Spare socks, shirt and drawers. Sandwiches. Plenty of sausage sandwiches.'

Once he was dressed and had breakfasted, his whiskers oiled and his fur brushed to that brilliant sheen which only healthy otters achieve, Udolphus set about the enjoyable task of preparing for the journey. There is a great deal of pleasure to be had from buying necessities. Frivolous purchases always worried him, which took away the enjoyment somewhat. But things he *needed* were a different matter. Such purchases were most satisfying. He knew just the shops for the right kind of walking hat, suit and cloak. The walking boots, of course, he made himself. He still had his awl, his hammer, his cutting tools and leftover leather. Nails were a different matter; he was only one short and was loath to buy a whole new packet.

He borrowed the star of Sirius from his ceiling, promising himself that he would replace it later.

One week later, 22nd March 1777 Anno Melliferous, the young Geranium unraveller was standing on the slopes of a mountain, looking down at the ocean. There, caught in a bay as sharp as an otter's elbow, lay the island of Vequince, its inshore waters sprinkled with colourful boats and ships. Several other smaller islands were scattered around it, but even from this distance Udolphus could see that the canalled city glittered with grand and beautiful architecture. Glass domes, tall square campaniles, green cupolas, red roofs, golden fascias, basilicas with colonnaded atriums, rotundas: all were spread before him as food at a banquet. And feast with his eyes he did. The island city sparkled like a gem-encrusted brooch pinned to a blue-green cloak. It took his breath away, this wonderful sight, and his approval was evident in the way he stood and nodded his head, a humming noise in his throat.

He carried on down the slopes to a town a little less blessed. Here in this bustling port – for the wealth of Vequince spilled over onto mainland shores – he sought transport. Udolphus crossed the lagoon on a black craft and eventually disembarked on the quay of the Piazza San Arvicola.

There he had to pass through a series of barriers

and undergo an assault course of clerks with quills at the ready. These able scribes were taking down the details of all visitors. Vequincians were suspicious mammals and they lived in suspicious times. Their bureaucracy was second only to that of Geranium, whose citizens loved bits of paper covered in signatures and seals. Here in Vequince all foreigners were regarded with narrow eyes and narrow minds. Udolphus gave the clerks his details, provided such proof of his identity as they required, and was allowed to pass into the square beyond, where he was left alone.

For a few moments he simply regarded the hurrying populace of dark brown water rats with their distinctive little rounded ears and blunt noses. Now that he was standing on Vequincian soil – or rather the fabulous marble which formed the promenade – he was alert for danger. He was not foolish enough to think that the plotters would not know he was here. Udolphus was a renowned unraveller after all. It was best to assume they did know and to keep them guessing as to why.

He gradually became aware that he was being stared at. Even rich cities – *especially* rich cities – have their poor and abandoned ones. There was a small group of waifs standing in the shadow of a magnificent palace that must have cost hundreds of thousands of bezants to build. They seemed cheerful enough, but it was clear to Udolphus that they had not had the fortunate upbringing of a shoemaker's son. A ragged youngster moved away from his friends and walked towards Udolphus, nodding at him.

Udolphus tried to ignore the urchin, but the little water rat spoke.

'I'm not a beggar,' he said. 'I wouldn't beg if you paid me.' He seemed unaware of the irony of his words. 'It's work I want. I'll carry your suitcase for you, signore. I'll do that all right, if you pay me.'

Udolphus liked the youngster's forthright manner. 'It just so happens I was looking for a carrier for my luggage.'

'Then that's me,' replied the urchin, brightening. He stepped forward, swishing his long tail, his two front teeth overlapping his lower lip. 'I'm the best luggage-carrier in the whole of Vequince.'

Udolphus put a friendly paw on the scruffy head before him, aware that it was probably swarming with fleas. 'Then you shall carry my case to the nearest restaurant, where we shall eat our fill. Then I must seek accommodation.'

The light that came to the urchin's face might have outshone the smile of God's most favoured cherubim. The youngster led Udolphus through the thronging crowds, across a campo, over a charming little white bridge which spanned a canal, and into a narrow alley. Outside a restaurant the urchin looked up and said, 'I shall wait here, signore, if you would be so kind as to bring me your leftovers, when you leave.'

'I shall do nothing of the kind,' said Udolphus grimly. 'I don't share my food with the homeless from the streets.' He paused, realizing he was framing his words badly and that the youngster's bottom lip was trembling below his two visible front teeth. 'What I mean to say is, you, my young guide, will accompany me within and partake of your own meal. You will have to forgive my rough manners though, for I am unused to eating in company. I tend to bolt my food, shovel it down, so to speak, as would a gannet.'

'Oh, that's all right, signore,' cried the youngster, beaming again, 'for I employ the same method of eating.'

'Really?' the otter said, smiling. 'I would never have thought it. I feel we will do very well together then, don't you?'

He led the way into the eating house, only to have the landlord stop the urchin at the door.

'Out!' cried the landlord. 'No guttersnipes in here.'

'The young rat is with me,' growled Udolphus, flashing a gold coin. 'Please show us to a window table where I may watch the gondolas go by on the canal.'

The gondolas of Vequince were painted all the colours of the rainbow and brightened the scene enormously.

'Yes, signore!' cried the landlord, whipping the white napkin from his forelimb and dusting a seat in a bow window. 'And your little friend too.'

Udolphus ordered fried sparrows' wings and cabbage. He found he could not have his favourite potatoes – there were none in Vequince – and made do with pasta instead. The urchin went through the menu five times before deciding upon spaghetti and meat balls. While they were waiting to be served, Udolphus spoke to the youngster.

At first he did not find it easy conversing with his new friend, not because the water rat was of a different species, but because he was young with a bubbling personality. Udolphus was reasonably young himself, of course, only a few years senior to the scruffy rat before him. But he was from a country which boasted solid citizens. There were right ways and wrong ways of doing everything in Geranium, and if one were to be respected one always did the former. His raiment had always been sober, sombre even, and of a cut designed not to cause offence. Browns were the colours he wore, and blacks, and the occasional flighty beige when he was feeling particularly roguish. Geranium had its fashion rebels, of course, and eccentric characters, but Udolphus Beck was not one of them. He knew it and he blamed his mother, who had brought him up very strictly.

Udolphus was supposed to find hilarity vulgar, but underneath he was full of humour. There was a great sense of fun in there just waiting for the opportunity to burst out.

'What's your name, young rat?' he asked while they waited. 'You do have a name, I take it?'

'Oh, yes, signore, it's Lucci.'

'Well, Lucci, I suppose you were born here?' And not much further back than yesterday, he thought, as he studied the youngster's face.

'Born here, raised here.'

'And your parents?'

'Both dead, sir. My padre was killed in a riot and my madre died of a fever.'

'A riot? Does that happen often?'

'Only when there's no oranges, sir.'

'Oh, I see. By the way, you must call me Udolphus. That's my name. And you have no other relatives?'

'An uncle who hates me and a cousin on the mainland somewhere. Those are the only two I know, master. The rest are on the Isle of the Dead, out there on the water, cold as you like. Oh, here's the food! Last one to finish is a salted herring . . .'

Udolphus found himself having to bolt his food as he had claimed he always did – quite a difficult task for one whose table manners were normally impeccable. Lucci beat him, which was to be expected. Then they ordered ice cream and fruit for Lucci, while Udolphus had coffee, cheese and biscuits.

'Now then, young rat,' Udolphus said, taking a long, noisy sip of coffee, 'we need some accommodation. I'm going to be in this city for quite a while and, being a complete stranger, I shall need the help of one who knows its streets and ways. How would you like to work for me, become my assistant, my guide and informant? I pay' – he considered what would be appropriate – 'two bezants on the twenty-eighth day of every month. One month in advance.' The youngster stared at him with wide, disbelieving eyes. 'Of course,' he continued, as he crunched away on a brittle wafer, the shards scattering over the tablecloth, 'there will be expenses too. If you have to take a ferry on an errand, that sort of thing, fares will be reimbursed. Now, are you my apprentice unraveller, or do I look elsewhere?'

'A un-what, signore— master?'

'Unraveller.' The otter leaned forward as one of the other diners, a water rat with a patch over one eye and an unhealthy pallor to his pelt, seemed to have an ear tuned to their table. Udolphus spoke in low tones. 'My work involves the solving of puzzles and mysteries, unravelling them so to speak. What we shall do, in the course of the next few weeks, is to walk about the city, listening, watching, taking note.'

Udolphus stared at the waif for a few moments, wondering whether it was too early to reveal secrets, but he had always been a good judge of character. It was not only unlikely, but most improbable that this scruffy tyke was involved in a conspiracy. Udolphus needed allies fast. He decided to trust Lucci from the outset. He lowered his voice to a whisper.

'There is a plot afoot, young Lucci, which threatens all who live here. You and I are going to solve that plot, uncover a conspiracy and prevent a catastrophe.'

'Wow!'

'Indeed, wow.' Udolphus leaned back again. 'You have ice cream on your whiskers. Wipe! That's better. Now, the first thing *you* have to do, to earn your bezants, is to find us some good, dependable, comfortable lodgings. Nothing too expensive, but not cheap either. We want no cockroaches in the soup, but we do not wish to pay the earth. Nothing below the waterline, which I'm sure would be damp and cause rheumatism. I expect you know of such a hostelry? Two rooms, mind. I'm not used to sharing my

12

quarters with anyone, let alone a young rodent with adenoids who probably snores—'

'I don't snore,' said Lucci indignantly.

'– and a bath somewhere in the establishment. I do so detest public baths, don't you? All those bodies with flabby rolls of fur emerging from the steam, bellies barely keeping the towel aloft.' Udolphus gave a little shudder. 'You, my young friend, could benefit from some soap and water *straight* away. Well then, let's be about our lawful business. Lead on. Lead on. I shall pay the landlord as we leave.'

They passed the suspicious-looking water rat on the way out, but he did not even glance at Udolphus. Lucci led the way: Udolphus discovered that Vequince was a maze of narrow streets, canals, alleys and tiny courtyards. In just a few moments he was lost, with no idea where he was going or how to get back again. Without a Lucci such as the one he had been fortunate enough to find, you might disappear in this tangled city, never to be heard of again, especially if you were an Udolphus from Geranium, a place of wide streets, open avenues and parks the size of small countries.

The walls and stones along the tiny walkways were worn shiny by the shoulders of furry mammals. They were old walls, ancient stones, touched by distant antiquity. There was wonderful architecture in this city, astounding buildings of great magnificence, but here in the confines of the alleyways there were only cold stones and iron grilles. Udolphus passed rusting gates, some half below the waterline; wooden doors ragged with rot; paving bricks which had been

13

hollowed by a million boot soles. The city closed in on you as you went deeper into its heart. It rose up and leaned over, blocking out much of the heavens. Up there were blue canals of sky, mirror images of those beside which he walked.

Finally Lucci stopped and pointed to a doorway. It looked much like any of the other doors they had passed, its paint peeling and its bottom edge ravaged by damp. A single worn step led upwards. There was an iron ring for a knocker, which Udolphus lifted and dropped. Some minutes later the door was wrenched open on its rusty hinges. A female water rat stood there in billowing skirts and a mob cap. She had a severe but not unkindly look about her, of which Udolphus approved.

'Madam, er, signora,' he said, 'I understand from my friend here that you rent accommodations?'

'That's true.' She folded her forelimbs over her breast. 'Five bezants a month. Well-swept rooms with no dirt to speak of, even under the beds. Meals served on request. Baths extra.'

'That sounds very reasonable. We'll take two.'

'Two?' Her eyes opened wider as she bobbed and tried to look over Udolphus's shoulder for the second mammal. 'Two separate rooms?'

'Yes, one for me and the other for Lucci here, who would also like a bath laced with a strong anti-lice embrocation.'

'What?' said Lucci, not really understanding that he was going into a rat-dip, but not liking the sound of the words. 'Not me?'

'Yes indeed,' said his master, 'followed by a lubrication with cedarwood and sandalwood oils. We must turn you into a civilized water rat, young Lucci, if you are to work with me. A rat who doesn't smell like a sewer during a plague of dysentery. A rat that is not a refuge for fleas.'

The landlady stared at the street urchin, her mouth twisted and her whiskers pointing at every compass bearing. 'Him? Work for you?'

'He has been hired as my new apprentice.'

She shrugged and stepped aside for them to enter. As the new apprentice passed her, she hissed quietly in his ear, 'Don't think I'm paying you for bringing this one, Signor Uppity, not if he's already given you something.'

'Signora,' Lucci said in a normal voice, 'I have no need of your grudged copper coins. I am in full employment and paid in silver.'

That first evening Lucci took his new master out for a stroll. Udolphus had only been in the city for a few hours and already he had the feeling that he was being followed. Shadowy characters drifted along behind them and seemed to fade into the stonework whenever Udolphus turned round. It was possible these stalkers came from the Silver Claw, but perhaps his enemies were already on the case and it was they who were the pursuers? Udolphus was used to being tailed – it went with the work – and he was adept at pretending he did not see those who trod in his pawprints.

The pair walked along the promenade looking out

at the lagoon, dark-blue in the fading light. The lamps swinging on the prows of the gondolas created bouncing reflections on the surface of the water. Above, the wonderful, reliable stars were in their places: the bright eyes of Heaven.

Udolphus asked his apprentice, 'Where would one find the Silver Claw? Where would I find him – or her?'

'Eh?' exclaimed the urchin. 'Where would you find him, master? The silver claw's not a him, it's an *it*. It's to do with the choosing of the Duce.'

'Oh, really? How does it—?' Udolphus broke off to say, in the hushed, reverent tones one might use in church, 'Look! Cards!'

There was a group of water rats gambling under the covering of an arcade. In the light of some lamps they were playing cards. All creatures on this earth have a weakness of some kind, otherwise they would not be mammal. Udolphus was no exception. His weakness was for cards. He knew it was unseemly. He knew his mother would have disapproved. But he could not help himself. There was a mystique to cards which drew him to them. When he saw a pack of playing cards with their different suits – oak-leaves, elm-leaves, pine-needles and sycamore-seeds; the pips coloured gold, red, green and brown – something stirred inside him. It was the Devil lodged in his heart, poking the coals of his red-hot passion for wagering with cards. To other forms of gambling he was immune: dice left him cold; beetle-racing brought on the yawns; hoop-la was for idiots. But the cards? Oh,

16

my, the cards were magic. They made his blood race.

'What's the name of this game, gentlejacks?' he said, sitting down on a spare orange box. 'Can anyone play?'

'Anyone with bezants in his pocket,' replied a water rat with a rather faded floppy velvet cap. 'The name of the game is Seven Seasons.'

Udolphus rubbed his paws together, his eyes glittering. 'Seven Seasons? Ah yes, I have played once or twice.'

'Master,' murmured Lucci, tugging at Udolphus's sleeve, 'do not play with these creatures. They will take all your money. They would fleece a dormouse while he slept. They're card sharps, master.'

Udolphus removed the young rat's claw from his garment. 'Lucci, I am a past master at cards. We shall be as rich as Crowsus by morning.'

Lucci shrugged and went to sit in a corner of the arcade to watch the moths batting around the lamps, while Udolphus chortled, an otter in his element, loving every minute and every turn of the card.

At two o'clock in the morning Udolphus rose from the game and woke Lucci. He was feeling immensely guilty. How had he managed so soon after arriving to forget his mission here? Such a dangerous thing to do in the circumstances. How alluring those cards were, but he must in future ignore all such games and keep his mind on his work. If he did not he would surely soon be floating away on a morning tide, stiff with rigor mortis.

'Come, young fellow. We must be on our way

home. Our landlady will have gone to bed, I hope, and we must go too.'

Lucci sat up and rubbed his eyes with his paws, bending his whiskers in the process. 'How much did we win?' he asked, yawning.

Udolphus's mouth set in a hard line. 'The cards were stacked against us, Lucci. Jill Fortune was not with us tonight. I thought for one minute with that last hand . . . but it was the seven of oak-leaves and not the seven of sycamore-seeds. The light was bad. I blame it on the poor light and my confounded luck.' He sighed and nodded at Lucci. 'Next time, young Lucci. Next time we'll take them to the cleaner's.'

Lucci nodded, but thought to himself, This rich otter I've found myself has a sickness. I've seen it before in other mammals. And so the little fellow resolved to keep his master away from gambling dens and card sharps. He suspected, quite rightly, that though Udolphus believed himself a wizard at cards, the otter was actually terrible at them. Lucci knew where all the dens were: he might have been an urchin but he was king of the streets. He knew everything that went on, in every corner of Vequince. He also knew an addiction to a vice when he saw it. He realized that if Udolphus so much as glimpsed a game of cards, the otter would be in there, throwing his money to the four winds.

# Chapter Two

The room was indeed comfortable, with a good hard bed and dark, heavy furniture, which you could hit with a hammer without denting. It was just to Udolphus's austere northern taste. What was more, Signora Nelli – for that was the landlady's name – kept a clean house. It was not as spotless as a Geranium house, of course, but then the cleanliness of the Geranium hausfrau is legendary. Nelli had been told you could eat off a Geranium floor, but this did not impress her, since she had a cupboard full of crockery. 'Why would you want to?' she asked her Geranium guests. 'We have plates for that in Vequince.'

All in all, Udolphus Beck felt he was going to be very much at home in Nelli's house. A canal ran right beneath his window. In fact, if you turned left when leaving the front door you would fall into it. The view of the canal, and the lagoon beyond, was a source of enjoyment to him: he could watch the coloured gondolas go back and forth.

More importantly, he could also hear and see any

craft approaching the house from the lagoon. On the other side the window overlooked the street in front of the only land entrance. The otter knew that at some time he might be under attack from those who wished to stop him from unravelling their secrets and it was wise to cover as many approaches as possible. Those shadowy creatures from the previous evening might just have been common thieves following a visitor, but Udolphus took nothing for granted.

Lucci had a room on the other side of the arch that joined the two parts of the house. It was smaller than Udolphus's, but then Lucci was a smaller creature.

'Well now,' said Udolphus, over their first breakfast together, 'today I want you to familiarize me with the city.' There was no mention of the card game the previous evening, nor would there ever be. 'Let us just walk through its streets, visit its wonderful buildings. At the end of the day I want to have a picture in my head of Vequince.' He lowered his voice to explain. 'I do not want to find myself in a blind alley, the exit blocked by a gang of thugs. Fairly soon I need to know which streets to avoid and where my escape routes might lie.'

He paused again, before adding, 'I know one day is not going to give me an infallible mental map, but I want at least to get a good general *feel* of the place . . . Infallible? Oh, it means without errors. So let's just stroll around, take in the brisk sea airs, meet with the populace.'

'Yes, signore – but you mentioned a plot.'

Udolphus leaned forward so that Nelli, in the

adjoining room, could not hear what he said. 'Yes, your government is under threat from unknown villains. We – you and I, Lucci – must thwart their aims.'

Thus they set out along the cobbled streets and crooked passageways which wound this way and that. Vequince was truly a twisting, turning, magical city. There was nowhere else like it in the world. Lucci took his master over the Bridge of Braggarts, by the Ca' d'Oro, the House of Gold, across the Canal of Mercy, into the Ducal Palace, through the Alley of Arrowsmiths, over the Campo San Paolo, with its warm-looking red-brick paving. They finally ended up at the top of one of the campaniles, those obelisk-shaped bell towers that pierced the sky from every part of the city, looking down onto the Beach of the Seven Martyrs.

From here they could see the ocean-going ships. Stately galleons plied their trade to every corner of the earth. The older established merchants' vessels would often change from canvas to silk sails when they came into port, in order to display their wealth. They were like red, blue and yellow banners clustered on the waters, a scene to take a mammal's breath away. Udolphus could not but be impressed, though as a Geranium he disliked vulgar show. The Vequincians had no such reservations, and their galleons hove in and out of port blooming with billowing silk sails. They went with holds full of Merino glass, marbled paper, sheet music and other Vequincian products. They returned to the great city bursting with scarlet feathers, indigo dye, gold, silver, perfumes, oils, nutmeg from the spice islands, sandalwood and Tartary silk.

Udolphus got down to business at once. 'Now, today I must meet someone who knows how the city works: who is officially in charge; who is *un*officially in charge – that sort of thing. Do you know of anyone trustworthy who might help us, young Lucci?'

'My uncle, Septimi?'

'But your uncle hates you – so you said.'

'I don't know anyone else except my orphan friends— Ow!'

Udolphus was gripping Lucci by the shoulder, which made the water rat yell. 'I'm sorry,' he hissed, 'but Lucci, who is that creature who has been following us for the last twenty minutes? Quickly, look behind me. Do you see him? He wears a black hat with a red feather.'

Lucci peered around Udolphus's right hip. 'I know him not, signore— Ah, he approaches. He's one of those dandies, master. He's all decked out in fancy clothes and high heels.'

'Armed?'

'He wears a rapier at his side. It's a very pretty one with a ribbon fluttering from the pommel.'

Udolphus's paw went straight to a pistol in his pocket, but he smiled as he turned towards the stranger. 'Do you want something?' he asked of the mincing macaroni who stood before him. 'Do I know you?'

'No, thignore,' lisped the fop, 'but I have been told

to find you and give you thith card. By your leave, thignore, and a thouthand apologieth.'

The water rat bowed low, his tail swishing the air behind him, and he swept out his paw in a graceful flourish. Udolphus bowed curtly. The other then straightened, took out a snuffbox, opened it delicately and removed a white card, which he gave to the otter. He then took a pinch of mustard-yellow snuff and inhaled it up his nostrils. His whiskers quivered violently as his nose received the snuff, then he minced away.

The card read: *Meet me on the Arcade Bridge – The Silver Claw*.

'The Arcade Bridge, Lucci,' said Udolphus. 'I know the direction, but not the exact route. Lead on.'

Lucci guided his new master through the winding streets once more, past architecture so fantastic it astonished the eye. And within those buildings were priceless religious murals by the thousand and precious artefacts valuable enough to purchase a hundred kings. When they reached the Arcade, they found it crowded with market stalls and shoppers. There on the steps to the bridge sat a very elderly water rat; the rest of the populace was hurrying up and down the steps, with no time to look around.

Udolphus eyed the old rat, who nodded slowly.

'Signore,' said the otter, sitting down on the steps himself, in the midst of the rodent traffic that swept across the bridge, 'my name is Udolphus Beck and I am from Geranium. Do you wish to speak with me?'

Watery eyes were turned on the otter. 'I would love

to gossip with a young otter from beyond this city. No one here is interested in what I have say any more and they don't seem to have the time to tell me about themselves. Look at them, hurrying this way and that. Half of them don't know where they're going or what to do once they get there. It wasn't like that in my day, otter. Oh no. I can enthral you with my reminiscences, I'm sure. Now, back in 1634 – or was it '38? – I always get my even numbers mixed up. Anyway, there was a coup . . .'

Udolphus let the water rat rattle on for a long while, wondering whether he had indeed got the right rat. Then the other lowered his voice a little. 'You are thinking to yourself,' he said, 'that you are being played like a fiddle by a madjack.'

'Signore,' said Udolphus patiently, 'what I *think* is not as important as what I *know*. What I know is that you have a very young voice for one who looks antique.'

'Quite right,' confessed the other. 'I'm not old.'

'Then you are in disguise. And the reason must be that you don't wish to be seen talking to me.' Udolphus glanced at the populace rushing by them. 'I can see why you chose this spot to talk. This is a crowded city. In any other place we might be overheard, but this mass of water rats is in such a hurry they will catch nothing but the odd word. Now, you know who I am. May I know who you are?'

The other glanced quickly at Lucci, who was idly tossing pebbles into the Grand Canal below. Satisfied that the waif could not hear him, he replied, 'You are

24

entitled to that. My name is Roma Volecci. I'm a member of the governing council. It was I who sent for you. I am the Silver Claw.'

'Why do you call yourself that?'

Roma Volecci shrugged. 'The name is significant, as you will learn later, but also anonymous. Now, let me explain why I asked you to come here. A few weeks ago a youngster came to me in fear of her life with a report of rebellion on the wind. This is a city of intrigue. There are always rumours and whispers, but this one struck a chord with me. I set a spy to work to try to find out more. My fellow discovered that there was indeed a plot in progress, but before he could make the conspirators known to me, he was murdered.'

Udolphus tweaked his own silky whiskers, a sign that he was not a little shocked. 'Murdered?'

'Poisoned and then stabbed, before being thrown into the lagoon. All I learned from him was that there's a small group who wish to take get rid of the government and place themselves in power as dictators. Their plan is to assassinate the governing council, and perhaps the Duce at the same time, then call on the Florions to invade before the populace rises against them. Once the city has been subdued by the Florions, this small group of plotters will take over, rewarding the invaders for their assistance.'

'Have you any names at all?' asked the otter, as some casual passer-by almost trod on his paw.

'The policing in Vequince is done by thieftakers. The head of these thieftakers, the Thieftaker General, is a rat called Rotzi di Coporoni. I believe he may be implicated, but I have no proof. It's simply a strong guess on my part—'

Roma Volecci stopped in mid-sentence. Lucci had obviously struck someone below with a pebble because there was a very loud shout and he quickly ducked down behind the parapet. Lucci looked back at Udolphus and, seeing a frown, protested, 'It was an accident, master.'

'Who is that ragamuffin?' asked Roma.

'My new assistant. But do go on. I would be grateful if you would tell me exactly how things are run here. For example, is the Duce all-powerful, or does he answer to the citizens?'

Roma chuckled. 'All-powerful? I should say not. Once upon a time perhaps, but now he's merely a figurehead. The office is associated with authority and splendour – it's a mystery shrouded in pomp and ceremony – but in truth the Duce has little influence on the city. Of course, there are some things over which he still has control, like promotions in the navy, which give him certain powers. We once had a Duce who was thrown in jail for taking bribes from young captains who wanted to be admirals.'

'There is corruption, then?'

'Of course. All cities have their criminals. But the Council are beginning to deal with it very severely. In the old days you couldn't get anything done without a backpaw payment, but things are different now.'

'Then who does run things?'

Udolphus learned that the rulers were an elected

body called the Council of Ten. Their sumptuous meeting hall, bizarrely, was in the same building as the prison: the floor below the dungeons, in fact. A metre above the heads of the rulers walked the filthy bare soles of malefactors. Prisoners were tried in the Duce's Palace and crossed the Bridge of Lost Souls to the top-floor prison. Udolphus found this very strange, coming from a city where the jail and parliament were kept as far away from each other as space would allow.

'. . . at the moment six of the Council of Ten are from my family, the Voleccis – uncles, sisters, brothers – we are one of the most powerful families Vequince has ever known. Merchants by profession. We rule with an iron claw – believe me, Herr Beck, it is necessary in such a hotbed of intrigue – but since the city prospers by the day the citizens don't mind.'

Udolphus was extremely grateful for the information. 'I thank you, signore, for your explanations. I hope my questions were not too tedious?'

'Not at all,' replied Roma. 'A delight as well as a duty. Remember, young otter, this city is based on a thousand ceremonies, all full of mystery and grandeur. Intrigue abounds. Where there is great wealth, there is envy and greed. A shadow here might mean your death. Be careful, stranger. We had better leave each other now. Think about what I have said and return here tomorrow. You may have more questions for me. Then, I think, we had better not meet again under the same circumstances. If we're being watched, a third meeting is when they will strike. Once arouses suspicion. Twice confirms that suspicion. Three times is plain foolishness.'

'How will you get away now?'

'By gondola. Who can follow a gondola out onto the lagoon without being seen? They have to be careful too, you know. Now I urge you also to be vigilant and watchful for your own safety.'

Udolphus indeed meant to be careful – very careful.

One of the things that Udolphus loved about unravelling mysteries was the fact that he had to study lists. Udolphus loved lists. In the ordinary way of things he made laundry lists, shopping lists, lists of things to do, lists of his property, the objects in his house, his socks, shirts and cravats: all sorts of mundane lists. While investigating a mystery, however, he collected other lists, such as cargo lists, lists of buildings, lists of boats, passenger lists, even lists of lists. These he went through thoroughly, not missing an object or a name, building some sort of picture in his mind of the kind of society he was in, as well as looking for deviants.

Deviants were not madmammals or demons but simply names or objects that looked out of place, unusual. By the evening he had collected lists from several government and private sources and now began to go through them by the light of his bedside candle. Outside, a horned moon, accompanied by the evening star, was shining on the water and Udolphus could see gondolas and other craft drifting by his window. Finding it hard to concentrate in such a tranquil pleasant atmosphere, he allowed himself to become distracted.

'I wonder,' he mused, 'if there is any real difference between sun-made shadows and moon-made shadows? Are moonshadows separate scientific entities, or formed of a similar substance to sunshadows? An interesting study, I would think.'

He sighed. There was really no time for luxuries such as lying back and contemplating the strangeness of natural phenomena. He had other mysteries to unravel. He sorted through his pieces of paper. The one list he was really interested in he kept until last, so that he could give it his whole attention. He was halfway through it when Signora Nelli knocked on his door and then entered with a cup of hot chocolate.

'I do so love hot chocolate,' said Udolphus, as she placed it on his bedside table. 'It really settles the mind before sleep.'

'Have you been taking a hammer to my furniture?' muttered Nelli. 'What's that mark on the leg of my chair?'

'Ah,' replied the embarrassed otter, 'I did just test it with the toe of my boot. I wanted to see if it was as sturdy as Geranium furniture. I shall pay for any damage of course.'

'Do you always kick furniture? Fortunately you've only scuffed it. A good hard polish will get it off.' She folded her forelimbs over her breast. 'And how did you find it?'

'Most satisfactory,' he replied. 'Every bit as hard.'

'Glad to hear it. Hmmm. I'll thank you, Herr Beck,

not to kick things in future. I don't know what you otters do in Geranium, but here in Vequince we respect other mammals' property.'

'I am most dreadfully sorry and not a little ashamed of myself, Signora Nelli. Please forgive me and add another bezant to the rent.'

'That won't be necessary,' she replied in haughty tones. 'Just don't do it again.'

Once she had gone Udolphus went back to his list of visitors and returning citizens who had arrived in Vequince. It was entirely possible that the conspirators might need to use outside expertise. The otter was aware that new inventive ways of assassination were less likely to be uncovered than those already used in the past. The city's bureaucracy was fortunately very efficient. When he had finished going through the list he had come up with the names of six characters with unusual occupations. So absorbed had he been in his list, Udolphus had not realized that he himself was one of the names.

*U. Beck*, read the entry, *Geranium ex-shoemaker, now an investigator of abnormal occurrences. Otter* (lutra lutra). *Purpose of visit: to attend Carnival.*

'Lutra lutra, lala lala,' grumbled Udolphus. 'Them and their Latin.'

He was annoyed they had not called him an *unraveller of mysteries*. It sounded so much more exotic than an *investigator*.

He crossed out his own name, glad to be left with only five.

The rest of the list went as follows:

*Stanley Rigwiddie, Albion musket-maker. Stoat (mustela erminea). Purpose of visit: to sell firearms.*

*Banda Rambutan, Mulaysian embalmer of insects. Mongoose (herpestes). Purpose of visit: to collect Vequincian cockroaches.*

*Yumi Horishma, Joponic learned cleric and origami master [paper folding]. Vole (unknown species). Purpose of visit: to attend Carnival.*

*Crome de Boile, Gaulic knife-thrower. Otter (lutra lutra). Purpose of visit: to seek employment.*

*Potsdam Rich, Czachlander water wrestler. Marten (martes martes). Purpose of visit: sightseeing and entertaining.*

Well, there it was: the list whittled down to five names. Apart from the gun-maker and the knife-thrower they seemed to have rather harmless occupations. Yet even the gun-maker would not have put down his profession as such unless he were there to do honourable trade. If he meant to foment rebellion or was implicated in this devious plot to overthrow the government, the Albion stoat would have called himself a schoolteacher or seed-seller. Following that line of reasoning, the water wrestler, for example, might not be into wrestling at all, but into poisons, or explosives, or something equally violent and ugly.

'I shall have to keep these visitors in mind,' Udolphus said, putting the list aside, 'and see if there is any connection with them or their professions.'

He heard a gentle splashing sound from outside and was immediately alert for unwelcome visitors. His paw went to the loaded pistol by his bed. But it was a large rubbish-collecting craft which was passing by his window. Its stench wafted in. The shadow of the boat clung to its plimsoll line, as if the solid wood were dragging the dark shade reluctantly along with it. Once the craft reached the end of the canal it cruised out into the calm moonlit waters of the lagoon beyond. Out there were many more craft, galleons and the like, throwing their own moon-made shadows on the water.

'I wonder if those shadows *are* any different to those made by the sun?' murmured Udolphus. 'They look blacker and much more exotic, but surely that is due to the humours of the night? When all is peaceful and there is a backdrop of blackness studded with stars, things only appear different, only *seem* more entrancing. See how they ripple, like black velvet shaken loose from a roll by a fabric seller! Deep creatures, those moonshadows. Deep and soft. Yet, if they *appear* different, then they must indeed not be the same, for appearances are all we have to define the world . . .'

Happily he fell asleep before this flawed philosophy started revealing its cracks to his enquiring mind.

The next day there was a cold snap. Overhead the sky was a clear light blue, with not a cloud to be seen; the waters of the lagoon a chilled green with occasional white ruffs to the eddies. Udolphus wore a thick black woollen cloak, which he wrapped around his body, turning himself into a walking cocoon. On his head went a dark tricorn hat, with no adornments. Finally a grey scarf was wound thrice round his neck, the final turn covering his mouth to protect his lungs from the freezing air. Walking briskly, he returned to the Arcade Bridge to talk with Roma.

The disguised rat was sitting on the same top step.

'Will you join me, signore, in a cup of hot coffee?' Udolphus asked him. 'It's not appropriate to be sitting on cold stone in these temperatures without a warm drink. I don't like them in my own city and I don't like them here. They are bad for the bones and coagulate the blood.'

'Delighted,' said Roma, signalling a nearby coffee stall and sticking up two claws. 'Here, join me.'

Udolphus took off his cloak to cushion his furry bottom on the stone step. The coffee came and they sipped it gratefully.

Then, without further pleasantries, the otter asked who were the most important mammals after the Duce and the Council of Ten. Who held the unofficial power in the city and were they dangerous?

'The guilds,' replied Roma without hesitation. 'of which of course there are many. The three most powerful are the Guild of Maskmakers, the Guild of Apothecaries and the Alchemists' Guild . . .'

Roma paused while a street-hawker tried to sell Udolphus a religious icon, a painting on wood of San

Meliferus, the Hole Vole who slept in the straw of Jesus' crib and kept his feet warm during the cold night.

'Only three bezants,' insisted the hawker. 'It's a genuine Leonardi, painted by the great artist hisself. Don't ask me how I came by it, 'cause I'll have to lie to you, and I promised me mother I wouldn't tell fibs. Let's just say it fell out of some cardinal's pocket. Take this back to Geranium and you'll get twice what I'm askin', if you want to sell it on.'

'How did you know I come from Geranium?'

The hawker sniggered. So did Roma Volecci.

'I see – that obvious, is it? Well, I don't want your wares, signore, and would be grateful to be left alone. If you please?'

'Hoity-toity,' muttered the hawker, but he moved on, accosting two female water rats.

'So,' said Udolphus, 'you were saying? The guilds – where do they have their headquarters?'

At that moment the morning sun struck the front of the Ca' d'Oro, the House of Gold, on the far side of the Grand Canal, and flecked Roma's eyes with golden spots. The water rat put his paw up to shield his face from the blinding light. Udolphus, with his back to the house, sensed the golden glow behind him. The beauty of the Ca' d'Oro's facade and its balconies was lost in the brilliance and they had to move into the shade of a shop to save Roma's sight from further punishment.

Roma Volecci then spoke in a grave tone. 'You are right to ask questions of the guildmasters and mistresses. The guilds are being investigated at the moment by government officials. For malpractice and other misdemeanours. The guilds have their various headquarters, friend otter, but you would do better to find the guildmasters at the shops where they work, if you are going to question them.'

'Indeed, I intend to – among others.'

Roma stared into his eyes and then finally gave him a faint smile. He stroked his chin with his claws, nodding as he did so. 'The guilds are always on the edge of the law, being powerful in their own right. The apothecaries, for example, are not above producing special poisons for those who wish to murder their victims without being discovered. Then alchemists dilute their gold and silver with copper, making an alloy, which is then sold as the pure metal. Both these practices are illegal, of course.

'The Council of Ten has been concerned for a long time about the power of the guilds and their leaders – Dropsi of the Apothecaries, Botcchio of the Maskmakers and Malacite of the Alchemists. These guildmasters know that their time is limited. Very soon the Council will clamp down on their criminal activities. But first we have to get rid of Rotzi di Coporoni.'

'Ah, the renegade Thieftaker General.'

'As I said, we have no police, as such. What we have is a private force of watchmammals organized by a thieftaker general. Citizens who are robbed go straight to di Coporoni, who miraculously finds their goods for them and returns them – for a large fee.

Shops and houses are also protected by di Coporoni's watchmammals, otherwise they catch fire.'

'From what you are saying, am I to understand that di Coporoni's own watchmammals are the robbers and arsonists?'

The water rat nodded slowly. 'My friend, you catch on very quickly.'

'And this Rotzi di Coporoni is in the pay of the guildmasters?'

'Another source of revenue for the Thieftaker General. The Council are just waiting for him to slip up, so that they can put him on trial for dozens of offences. At the moment they have no proof, and those rich citizens whose houses the thieftaker's mammals protect need to be reassured that once di Coporoni has gone their property won't be left unguarded. Many ordinary mammals believe di Coporoni when he says he's honest. They fear that if he's thrown in jail there will be anarchy in Vequince. They say there will be no one to control the mobs, that there'll be looting and burning without Coporoni's private army to prevent it.'

'Whereas in fact, it is Coporoni's watchmammals who are more likely to go on the rampage? Is that correct?'

'Exactly. So the Council has to tread carefully. They're waiting to catch the thieftaker red-clawed, so that they can say to the citizens of Vequince, Here is your thief*maker*, not your thief*taker*.'

Udolphus nodded. 'Now, I must leave, signore. By the way, may I congratulate you on a marvellous pair of sandals. I was once a shoemaker by trade and I know a good pair of middle-eastern sandals when I see them.'

'Thank you,' replied Roma. 'They were a present from the Holy Land.'

'Well, thank you for the information.' Udolphus got up to leave. 'As you said yesterday, this must be our last meeting in such circumstances. I shall leave it to you to contact me and meet me at a future date in a different disguise, in a different place. Now, where is my cloak . . . ?' The otter looked back to where he had been sitting before they had moved to the shadow of the shop. He had left his cloak on the step.

But the cloak had gone. His warm woollen cloak!

'Someone has stolen it,' said the dismayed otter. 'Now I shall have to walk back in the cold without it.'

'If I were you,' Roma suggested, 'I would go straight to the Thieftaker General. Rotzi di Coporoni will know where to lay his claws on your cloak, I'll be bound.'

Later, when Udolphus returned shivering to his lodgings, he found Lucci waiting for him.

'Lucci, my young water rat, why did you not tell me of Rotzi di Coporoni?'

The urchin's eyes went big and round, and he hunched his head into his shoulders. 'Signore,' he whispered, 'do not speak of the Devil.'

'Ah, but I must. I must know of any unusual citizen of this city of Vequince.'

37

'Then you wish to know *everyone*, signore, for we are all different in our ways.'

Udolphus looked sternly at the youngster. 'You know what I mean. I'm prepared to believe this city of yours is unique, but there certain creatures who inhabit it who mean to do it harm.'

# Chapter Three

That evening Udolphus heard a slight noise in the street below his window and glanced out. A visitor, coming in by the front door. Udolphus put his loaded pistol in the pocket of his dressing gown. Since he had arrived in the city he had taken the precaution of wearing a protective chain-mail vest, but he did not wear this to bed. It was hanging in his wardrobe. He left it there, having no time to put it on, since he had already snuffed his lamp.

There was a knock on his door. The room was in darkness but Udolphus was familiar with it by now. He navigated his way around the furniture using both memory and instinct. When he opened the door Signora Nelli was standing there, candle in paw, with a large, menacing figure just a metre or two down the hall. Young Lucci had also been woken by the knock and he appeared at his door, rubbing his sleepy eyes.

'Go back to bed, Lucci,' said Udolphus. 'And wear that nightcap I gave you. Do you want to catch a cold? Yes, Signora Nelli? It is very late. I had retired.'

39

'You have a visitor, signore,' Nelli said, a tremble in her voice. 'It's – it's the general.'

A long sharp nose preceded a large rafter rat as the creature stepped forward into the light thrown by the wavering candle flame. There were glittering eyes behind the nose, which changed from red to pink as the candle flame waxed and waned. The rat was dressed to brave the cold, damp Vequincian night: a many-layered coat bulked his form; an outsized three-cornered hat had been rammed on his head. On his feet was a pair of highly polished boots. The leather creaked, proudly broadcasting their newness, as the thieftaker strode into the room.

'Signor Rotzi di Coporoni, I presume?' said Udolphus, hiding his feelings of alarm. The rat put out a claw and Udolphus shook it with his own. 'It's very late, but won't you come in?'

Di Coporoni took the candle from Nelli's paw and stepped into Udolphus's room. He shut the door in Nelli's face, leaving her on the dark landing outside. Udolphus lit one of his own candles and opened the door. Nelli was still standing on the same spot in some distress. He gave her the candle and closed the door quietly again, hearing her slippers pad down the hallway.

'Quite the gentleman, Herr Beck,' sneered the thieftaker, slumping into one of the chairs. He pulled up the hem of his coat and the brown boots shone in the flickering candlelight. It was only now that Udolphus noticed di Coporoni had a bundle under his forelimb, enveloped by the folds in his coat. 'Here' – he tossed it at Udolphus's feet – 'this is yours, I believe.'

The whole atmosphere in the room was affected by the presence of the thieftaker. His body contained an enormous amount of compacted strength: Udolphus had experienced that power when they had shaken paws. Moreover, di Coporoni had *wanted* him to feel it, as if he were saying, *Now you know I could crush your head like a rotten tomato, if I so wished.* The thieftaker also glowed with malevolence. You sensed that if he ever used his strength to hurt you, he would enjoy it.

What was less obvious about him, but was more alarming than his physical power and his evil intent, was his insecurity. Udolphus saw through the protective layers to this personality flaw beneath and it concerned him. There is nothing so unpredictable and dangerous as an insecure rat.

The black bundle hit the floor and unrolled. Udolphus gasped. It was his own woollen cloak, the one which had been stolen on the steps. What upset him was not the mud and filth on the garment, but the fact that there were holes in it, rimmed with blood. Whoever had been wearing it at the time had been stabbed repeatedly by a sharp implement.

'What are you thinking?' asked Rotzi di Coporoni with an amused smile. 'That you're a lucky otter? That it could have been you in that cloak when the wearer was attacked? I wondered about that too. Perhaps you have had a narrow escape, Herr Beck. If I were you, I would not stay in Vequince very much longer. It is so easy to kill someone here and get rid of the body. A sword in the back and slip the corpse into the lagoon to be washed away by the outgoing tides. So easy.'

'Ah, I see.' Udolphus picked up the cloak and poked a claw through one of the holes. 'Nasty. Very nasty. And the wearer?'

'A street seller. We found fake religious icons in his pockets.'

'The hawker by the coffee stall,' murmured Udolphus.

'You knew the creature?'

'He tried to sell me one of those icons this morning. Obviously it was he who stole the cloak.'

'Obviously.' Di Coporoni nodded, his sharp nose going up and down. 'Well now, our meeting is rather fortuitous. I've been meaning to come and see you. I understand you're a snooper by trade?'

'An unraveller of mysteries.'

'As I said, a snooper. You pry into things you shouldn't.' Rotzi di Coporoni's eyes glittered in the candlelight. 'Let me warn you, this is a dangerous occupation in Vequince. There are those who like visitors to mind their own business.' He glanced at the cloak. 'You could take that as a warning.'

'The killing might have been random – just some robber taking advantage of a lonely walker in the dark. I myself am not here on business. I am here for Carnival.'

'There are those who might believe you, and those who don't.'

'Don't?'

'Me for one. *I* think you're here for a reason. Carnival? No, no. Something other than Carnival brought you here.'

Udolphus sighed, as if caught out. 'Ah, there's no fooling a thieftaker, is there? Well, Signor di Coporoni, you have me dead to rights. I am here on a mission. I must ask you to keep this information strictly private. What I am about to tell you involves the government. It is a delicate matter, a secret they wish uncovered, and it would not do to let it get about.'

Di Coporoni's eyes became intense. 'You'd better tell me.'

Udolphus went to the door and opened it, peering outside as if to make sure no one was eavesdropping. 'I'm here for Carnival,' he said at last, as if giving away a deep secret. 'I'm here to enjoy the fun.'

The thieftaker looked doubtful. 'You expect me to believe that?'

'My dear signore, you may believe what you like. Your beliefs are your own affair, but let me assure you Geraniums do not dissemble like Vequincians.'

'Huh. Well, be warned, otter, we don't like creatures who sneak around looking for things, especially at the behest of the government. You might not be so lucky the next time.' Di Coporoni spread his paws. 'I shall do my best to protect you, of course, as I do all visitors to our lovely city. But I can't be every-where at once. I shall bid you good night.' He rose heavily from the chair. 'I have work to do. The streets are not safe during the dark hours.'

'Clearly not.'

Without another word the rat picked up the candleholder and took the light with him when he left, leaving Udolphus standing in the darkness. The otter heard the front door slam. He moved to the window and saw di Coporoni walking away under the dim light of the stars, noticing that the thieftaker was joined by two figures almost as bulky as himself. His bodyguards, without a doubt. Soon the street was empty.

Udolphus lit another candle, surprised to find that his paw was shaking. Rotzi di Coporoni was indeed a frightening creature. Was he responsible for the death of that poor hawker? Udolphus could not say, but he would not rule it out. Perhaps the thieftaker had set out to kill Udolphus, having been told of the otter's conversations with a strange old water rat on the Arcade Bridge? No doubt the thieftaker had spies all over the place. It was certain that very little went on that he did not know about.

There was a light rap on the door. Udolphus's heart began to beat faster again, but after a moment the door opened and Lucci's blunt water rat's nose poked round the jamb.

'Has the Devil gone yet?' whispered the urchin.

'Lucci, go back to bed.'

Seeing that there was no one in the room but Udolphus, the young water rat entered. 'If he tries anything,' he growled, shaking a clenched claw, 'I shall challenge him to a duel.'

'Thank you, Lucci, but that won't be necessary.

Now go back to bed. And *where* is that nightcap?'

Lucci rubbed his pate. 'It itches.'

'Never mind – it itches, you wear it. You'll catch your death without it in these damp conditions. Off with you now. I'll see you in the morning.'

'Yes, signore.'

'My name is Udolphus.'

The urchin scuttled away, saying, 'That's a *long* name, longer than an eel. I'll *never* get it right. I prefer signore – or master.'

Udolphus spent the next hour cleaning his cloak as best he could and sewing up the holes. He had no other outdoor garment and this one was so warm and comfortable he was loath to buy another. Back in Geranium he would have cast it aside, for there appearances were everything. But here in Vequince no one seemed to worry too much if you walked about in rags. They admired rich attire, beautiful raiment, but they did not scorn those who could not afford to look the height of fashion. They were short on disapproval, the Vequincians, but long on craftiness, intrigue and conspiratorial manners. Each to his own, thought Udolphus.

Udolphus was wearing his patched and mended cloak the following morning when Signora Nelli stopped him on the stairs. She hardly even glanced at it; Nelli was not concerned by mere appearances.

'Signore, about last night—'

'I do apologize for that,' said Udolphus, reaching into his pocket and producing a shiny silver bezant.

He pressed it into her paw. 'That was not my fault and I'll endeavour to make sure it doesn't happen again.'

She looked down at the bezant, shrugged and put it into her apron pocket. 'It wasn't that, signore. I wanted to ask you to be careful. That – that creature is not to be trusted. You have business with him?'

'None at all. Someone stole my cloak. He recovered it. That was the sole reason for his visit.'

'He probably had it stolen himself. It's a trick of his.'

'So I understand. Thank you, Signora Nelli, I do appreciate your concern.' Udolphus was warming by the moment to his Vequincian landlady. 'And your kindness. But you need not worry. I am simply here to enjoy the Carnival, when it comes. I'm not looking for any trouble.'

'Stay away from the general,' she murmured. 'No good can come of *that* association.'

'I believe you. Tell me, signora, does he often leave the city?'

She looked a little startled by this remark. 'The Thieftaker General? He wouldn't dare. If they ever found out he'd left, he'd never get back in again. The Council would see to that, I'm sure. They're just looking for an excuse, so the rumours have it, to rid themselves of him.'

'Oh, my mistake. Well then, I bid you good day, signora.' Lucci was now hovering at his heels. 'We must be off on another sightseeing tour of your wonderful island city.'

As they walked along the street an inquisitive wind

was gusting this way and that, lifting gowns and long coats, revealing ankles – some clad in silk, some in wool or cotton, a few bare of any hosiery. Overhead a weak sun was struggling to emerge from behind some grey streaky clouds. It was a bitter, gnawing coldness, persistent in its labours. One thing about Vequince: the wintriness in the stones, beautiful as their arrangements were, penetrated to the very marrow of one's skeleton.

The other constant in this city, Udolphus reflected, was the threat to his life, which he knew was very real after that visit from di Coporoni. He had little doubt he was being followed wherever he went. Shadows drifted behind, merged with those of buildings, appeared again. Were they simply waiting for him to make a move or were they awaiting an opportunity to attack him?

He also needed to be aware of the danger to young Lucci, though Udolphus believed his foes would realize there was little to gain by harming the urchin. Still, the pistol in his pocket was there to protect them both. He had tried to get Lucci to wear protection under his clothes, but the young rat was as reluctant to wear a protective vest as he was to wear his nightcap. Lucci hated uncomfortable clothes and it was the one area where Udolphus's authority was firmly ignored.

'Why did you say that?' asked Lucci. 'Why did you ask her if the Devil had left the city? You think he did, don't you?'

'Lucci,' said Udolphus, looking down on the young water rat, 'you are fast becoming my star pupil!'

'I am your *only* pupil, signore!' Lucci was indignant.

'Yes, you are, and I'm very pleased with your progress. I do believe the thieftaker has been out of the city – obviously in secret since it does not appear to be general knowledge. He must have slipped away and returned unnoticed by any of his enemies. Now, you will wish me to tell you how I know all this?'

'Yes, of course.'

'The boots he was wearing. They were made in the city of Florion. I recognized the style of stitching instantly. Those who have not been shoemakers would simply see good workmanship, but I know Florion boots when I see them. Rotzi di Coporoni has been to that city recently.'

'Really?' cried Lucci. 'You think he is plotting with the Florions?'

'That I do not know, but can only guess and fear.'

They walked on further, passed by creatures holding onto their hats and scarves in case they blew away. Udolphus's eyes were everywhere, though no one would have thought it. He seemed for all the world like a visitor, only interested in the architecture and the statues.

Lucci said, 'How do you know, signore, that he did not *send* for the boots?'

'Ah, good question, young rat. I have to say because they fitted him perfectly. No shoemaker produces his best from a piece of paper bearing measurements. I have to say those boots were exquisite, though my admiration is mingled with envy.

Of course he might have been there at some other time, bought the boots, and put them away until now, but I don't think so. He was too proud of them. Too eager to show them off. No, they were a new acquisition.'

'He might have had some others made once and then sent *those* back to be copied.'

'Very good, very good. Or used the same measurements as before. But then paws change – they spread with age, grow bunions and corns, the pads harden and flatten. No, those boots were *perfect*. You could see how comfortable they were. Custom made, without doubt, with the wearer there for several fittings. I'm never wrong about footwear. Now, will you take me to the workshops of a Signor Botcchio? I understand he is the head of the Guild of Maskmakers.'

'Yes, he is, signore.'

'Then let us meet him. And I will need a mask for Carnival, will I not?'

'Yes, master, nearly everyone wears masks at Carnival.'

However, when they reached the shop, the thick doors with their brass studs and massive locks were closed. Udolphus used the huge knocker, a representation of the Pestilence Doctor mask, with its long white nose and spectacles. Still there was no answer. He stepped back and looked up. Over his head was a swinging sign, buffeted by the wind. On it was a painting of another traditional mask, the Mattaccino, above the word BOTCCHIO. The mask was black with large eyeholes, a long black nose, and a magnificent military-looking golden moustache which swept around the cheekbones.

'Is there no one in?' he called to the upstairs window. 'It is not yet siesta.'

At that moment three mammals came round the corner. Two were heavy fellows wearing rapiers and with large pistols in their belts. The middle one was a short, barrel-chested water rat. This fellow was wearing plain black, like Udolphus himself, but with a silk trim to the hems and edges. He walked slowly and was panting heavily, as if he had great difficulty in breathing. There was something strange about his centre of gravity. It was lower and more leaden than those of his companions, as if his torso were pressing downwards into the earth.

All three creatures stopped on seeing Udolphus and Lucci standing outside the shop. After a minute they came nearer, presumably judging the situation as harmless.

'Are you waiting for me?' wheezed the sturdy one. 'Just a moment while I get the keys.' His breath whistled in and out of his mouth as he fumbled inside his garments, eventually producing a ring of heavy iron keys. With these he proceeded to unlock the shop. The doors were flung open and everyone trooped inside. An oil lamp was already burning within, which threw a mellow light over the whole workshop and serving counter. There were masks everywhere, some partly finished, others complete. The whole room was dripping with them. In the first instant it was their ghoulish appearance which caught

Udolphus's attention, but a moment later his eyes had turned down towards the floor.

The unraveller was startled to see a whole host of gleaming beetles scuttling across the flagstones and under the benches. It was only after careful observation that he realized these were not gilded cockroaches but very thin shavings of gold leaf, blown across the floor by the draught from outside. Once the doors were closed, the shavings came to rest. There was a fine layer of golden dust too on the benches and other furniture. This precious powder glistened under the light of the lamp like a thin covering of yellow frost.

'Good day,' said Udolphus, gathering his wits. 'Am I addressing Signor Botcchio, the owner of this establishment?'

'You are indeed,' wheezed the fat water rat. 'Are you a trader or a private purchaser?'

The two large rats had melted into the shadows at the back of the workshop, one sitting on a stool, the other standing by a lit stove. Both kept an eye on Udolphus and Lucci, however. Clearly they were guarding their employer, alert to any sudden or suspicious moves.

'A private purchaser, a visitor from Geranium. I'm interested in buying a mask for Carnival. You, I am led to understand, are the best maskmaker in Vequince.'

'You could be right, but I'm not the cheapest.'

'No, no, I realize that. Expense is not a great issue. Obviously I want value for money, but that's a different thing. Could you show me some masks? Perhaps you could match one to my personality? You must have had great experience in your years as an artisan. Do mammals instinctively choose the mask that suits their character? Or do you assist them in that choice?'

'Both. Let me look at you under the light. Yes, Geranium – anyone would have guessed it. Sober, respectable and, sad to say, a little dull in appearance. No gold and scarlet for you, my friend. No silver and blue, either. A single colour. Black, or white, perhaps? And something not too outlandish. Definitely not outlandish. You want to remain inconspicuous, of course, being a Geranium. Something unlikely to excite the imagination.'

'Is it that bad?'

'I'm afraid so. I think the most common of masks – very traditional and acceptable to all carnival-goers. The Bauta. Plain white, half-face. A ghost-like face. I make them of pressed lace, though you may get a less expensive one from another maskmaker. You wear the mask with a horned black hat and black cloak.' He looked Udolphus up and down, before adding, 'Which would suit your present mode of dress.'

Udolphus pointed to a bronze-coloured mask with a longish nose. 'I rather saw myself as that one.'

'The Captain? You can wear what you like, but I would hardly put you down as a swashbuckling type. You might be challenged in that mask. There are always ruffians willing to test their mettle against the

Captain. If you wear that mask, don't go abroad without wearing a sword – that's my advice.'

A snigger from one of the burly rats in the shadows.

'What do you think, Lucci?' asked Udolphus of his protégé. 'The Captain or the Bauta?'

'The Bauta – definitely.'

'Perhaps you're right. Why invite trouble? Bauta it is then.'

Botcchio wheezed, 'That will be seventy bezants.'

Udolphus sucked in his breath, but nodded.

Botcchio began wrapping the mask in tissue paper, explaining, 'This is not just a purchase, it's an investment. Some of my earlier masks are now worth hundreds. I'm not just a craftsman, I'm an artist.'

'The mask is indeed a work of genius.'

'Thank you, friend.'

Udolphus took out his purse and passed over the money, then he leaned forward. 'Signore, may I venture to ask a personal question?'

'You've just given me seventy bezants – you can ask what you like, Geranium.'

'I can't help noticing you seem to have difficulty in breathing. Do you have some sort of respiratory disease? Is it something that can be cured? Where I come from – what with our dense woodlands and deep valley meadows – they have had great success with natural remedies. Perhaps I can help in some way?'

Botcchio grinned and glanced back at his guards. 'No, nothing that can be cured. You see, I have been decorating masks all my life, ever since I was that urchin's age. It is surely obvious to you that I use fine gold leaf and gold dust – *real* gold – for my designs. Over the years I have inhaled that dust. Now my lungs are lined with solid gold. They hang so heavy in my chest they rest upon my lower ribs like two leaden balloons. Apart from the ill health they give me, I need to be guarded night and day. My lungs are very precious. I carry a fortune in my chest. There are those who would murder me and cut them out, to enrich themselves. Thus these two, and others, watch me wherever I go, ready for assassins.'

'Precious lungs!' cried Udolphus. 'How very strange.'

Botcchio gave a coughing laugh. 'When I die they'll fight over my body like scavengers. I've been told the state has a team ready to claim my corpse the moment it falls to the ground. My own relatives have me followed, waiting for the fatal hour, watching for the mortal moment. A walking treasure house, that's what I am. But I'm not going yet. I'll be damned if I am. They have a long wait, those jackals. But what about you, signore? What is your trade or line of work?'

'I have been – am still on occasion – a shoemaker. Not so romantic an occupation as a maskmaker, but it has its artistic moments.'

'Indeed yes,' whistled Botcchio. 'A good pair of shoes is worth a king's ransom. I'm heavy on shoes.'

'You do not surprise me, given your condition.'

Another husky laugh. 'No? But you said *on*

*occasion.* Is that not now your main source of income, friend?'

'Now? Now I am an *unraveller*, signore. I solve mysteries by untangling them to get at their centres.' He leaned forward again. 'I'm here to seek out those who would plot against the Council of Ten.' Udolphus tapped his nose with a claw. 'Already I have my suspicions. Very soon I shall make my report.'

'Oh?' Botcchio had suddenly gone very frosty. 'A spy. Well, had I known, I might not have sold you a mask. We don't like snoops in here, do we?'

The two bodyguards emerged from the shadows and looked down on Udolphus and Lucci with unpitying eyes.

'Do you then,' asked Udolphus, 'have reason to be alarmed?'

Botcchio's breathing became more rapid. 'Be very careful whom you accuse,' hissed the maskmaker. 'This is a small, contained city. You can be found very easily, Geranium.'

'Ah! A threat! Do I call the police?'

Botcchio coughed harshly and spat on the floor: sparkling sputum flecked with gold. 'What? That bastard Rotzi? Call him.'

Lucci was pulling urgently on the edge of Udolphus's cloak. He heeded the warning of his pupil. 'Come, Lucci,' he said. 'We're clearly not wanted here. I'm sorry to have inflamed passions so quickly.'

Udolphus looked around the gloomy workshop, at the hundreds of masks hanging from racks above their heads, all with hollow eye-sockets. There were noses, long and short, and cheeks decorated with precious-metal paints, scored swirls and centripetals and all kinds of designs. All manner of masks: grotesque, absurd, beautiful, ugly, bizarre, horrible, nightmarish. They were clearly wonderful works of great genius. Botcchio was indeed a craftsman of immense worth and Udolphus regretted having enraged the maskmaker. But he had needed to anger him to test his honesty.

However, Udolphus was still not sure of Botcchio. He sensed that Botcchio's passionate outburst might stem from a normal distrust of governments and spies, but that did not mean he was innocent. Botcchio remained on Udolphus's list of suspects. It had been useful meeting the creature and assessing him. Unravelling was a careful business and Udolphus was not going to hurry his conclusions for the sake of speed.

Udolphus and Lucci left the shop, parcel in paw. Shadows drifted in their wake.

# Chapter Four

The day after their visit to the maskmaker the
weather improved. A bright sun came out and
once again the city glistened. White marble and quartz
provided spangled walkways. Udolphus's heart lifted.
He roamed the streets again with Lucci, admiring the
gilt facades and mosaic fronts of some of the buildings. It was difficult for him to imagine that there was
something dark and unwholesome in this city of
intrigue on such a wonderful day, and it irked him to
have to look over his shoulder. Yet such was the case:
one eye on beauty, the other alert for evil. I must never
relax my vigilance, he kept telling himself, while
surreptitiously scanning the area for stalkers.

He was a great lover of Baroque and Byzantine
architecture, was Udolphus Beck, and he tried to
interest Lucci in the different styles. Lucci, however,
had grown up with 'all these old places' and he took
them for granted. The Basilica of Santa Magenta della
Martes was but one of a hundred beautiful churches
which stunned Udolphus. It had been built to mark
the end of the last plague which had ravaged

Vequince. Apart from the architect's talent, a dozen sculptors had created masterpieces to adorn both interior and exterior. Paintings, any one of which would have purchased a small country, adorned the interior walls, along with marvellous tapestries and altar trappings to enrich the poorest mind and bleakest spirit.

'Yes, it's fine,' said Lucci dutifully, as Udolphus pointed out the church's merits, 'but can we ride on a gondola today?'

The young, thought Udolphus with a sigh, have no yearning spirit, no aching soul. He too had been much the same at that age, quite uninterested in anything but pleasurable activities like boating. It was proof to the unraveller that souls actually developed as one got older. One day this young rat would be drooling over the same old bricks, Udolphus was sure.

'I'm not sure I'm ready to go on a boat yet,' said Udolphus, looking doubtfully at the cold-looking waters of a canal, where craft of all kind drifted up and down. 'Look, the bridges are dripping moisture onto those who go beneath them! Do you really want to get wet?'

'Master, I can't believe you mean that. You're an *otter*. Otters *love* the water. You just don't want to spend the time, do you? You can't come to Vequince and not go on a gondola,' protested the urchin. He struck at his master with a double-edged blade. 'The buildings look *much* more beautiful from the canals. You wait and see. You'll be going "Ooooohhhh" and "Aaaaahhhhhhh" much more often.'

'I do not ooohhh and aaahhh. And while Neanderthal Otter might have enjoyed a swim in freezing water, Modern Otter does not. All right then, I see I shall get no peace until we take to the boats.'

It will be an opportunity to throw off any stalkers, Udolphus thought. As Roma Volecci had pointed out, they themselves would need a boat to follow him and they might not risk going onto open water where he could identify them.

He and Lucci took their gondola ride in a bright green vessel through the Grand Canal, and various others, despite the dripping bridges. Udolphus did indeed make appreciative noises, but he was now rather self-conscious about ooohhing and aaahhing. Lucci persuaded the gondolier to let him propel and steer the craft. This almost resulted in disaster when they headed towards a huge barge and a collision was only narrowly avoided. On the whole though, the experience for Udolphus was a good one. The city did indeed come alive in a different way when viewed from the water.

'Stop the craft here,' ordered Udolphus suddenly, as they bumped against the bank of the canal. 'Lucci, we'll get out now. Quickly, quickly. Let's get into these narrow streets.'

Udolphus knew that by acting impetuously, he would escape any stalkers who might have spotted them from the banks. He and Lucci now set out to visit the head of the Guild of Apothecaries, a female called Dropsi, a vole very much in demand by conspirators, plotters and common murderers.

Signora Dropsi knew all the poisons in all the books and many more besides. It was only because of the desperate need for apothecaries and their remedies during plagues that the guild had been allowed to survive at all. After all, what were one or two murders weighed against the whole population dying of horrible sores?

As the pair made their way along a narrow winding alley, the sunlight still striking glass windows and blinding passers-by, they met someone who was almost more important to Vequince than the Duce: Viporatti! The great musician! The red rat of Vequince!

Udolphus recognized him from the miniature portraits he had seen on cameos dangling around female necks. Viporatti was adored by jills from every land for his flamboyant style of dress and his devastatingly handsome looks. Males would have hated him, if it had not been for his music, which enchanted even the most envious of macaronis and dandies.

Today Viporatti was wearing a scarlet satin coat which the Vequincians called a *velada*: a tight-waisted garment with flared skirts. It was worn open, not because it was not a cool day, but to allow full view of the richly decorated waistcoat. On his head he wore a white hat with a long red feather. Skin-tight red breeches ran down to his knees, where they met white silk stockings. His shoes were black, with bright buckles studded with diamonds. The laugh that came from his mouth was as musical as birdsong, as he replied to greetings, waving a lace handkerchief. As he approached, his sparkling eyes rested on Udolphus and Lucci.

'Signore,' said Udolphus, removing his hat, 'may I be permitted to say that your music has lifted my soul and carried it away on many occasions. Your *Concert for the Prince of Furland* is a work of great genius.'

'Ah, you do not like the more popular *Four Winds*, I take it?'

'I *like* it, of course,' replied Udolphus in measured tones, 'but it does not soar and reach the heights of your less obvious works.'

Viporatti laughed. 'Well countered, otter. Might I be permitted to know your name? Are you visiting our great city from Geranium?'

'Ah, you guessed my origins. Everyone here seems to. Yes, I'm here for Carnival. My name is Udolphus Beck . . .'

Viporatti took a step backwards and pointed with a triumphant claw. 'Ha! The marvellous unraveller! The mystery solver.'

'You've heard of me?' murmured the modest otter. 'I'm very flattered.'

'Why, Herr Beck, you're almost as famous as I am,' cried the zesty composer. 'We are mirror images, you and I. You are an unraveller of puzzles and I am a raveller of music. You take the knotted cords of weaving gone wrong and unpick it. I take scattered musical notes and ravel them into beautiful tapestries of sound. How opposite we are, yet how alike in our endeavours to reach perfection. Would that we could change places for a single day and appreciate each other's talents!'

'Oh, I could never compose music. I can't even play.' Udolphus laughed lightly. 'The only thing I play well is cards. You don't indulge, I suppose?' Udolphus's tone was wistful.

'Cards? No. But I could teach you to play an instrument in an instant,' said the great master, snapping his claws. 'You' – he stroked his whiskers as he studied the otter very carefully, assessing him – 'you, I think, could play the hog-horn, or perhaps the snake-flute.' Viporatti had invented a set of instruments that resembled animals in their shapes. 'No, no, I take those back. You are definitely a student of the bird-violin. Yes, I am settled on that. If you are here long enough, I suggest you purchase one.'

'What am I?' cried Lucci. 'Am I something?'

'You, my dear street urchin, are most emphatically a penny worm-whistle! I can hear your delightful trilling now, in my head.' Viporatti took a small note-book encased in silver from a pocket in his embroidered waistcoat. A silver pencil was withdrawn from the spine. He flipped the notebook open, scribbled some musical notes fantastically fast, and then flipped it shut again.

'We must see more of each other, Herr Beck,' he said. 'You must allow me to play for you.'

'My dear Signor Viporatti,' replied Udolphus, over-whelmed, 'nothing would give me greater pleasure than to listen to you play. When could that be?'

'Well, I have to give a private concert for the

Fabulous Beast tonight, or I would say then.' Viporatti leaned forward and said in a low voice, 'Between you and me, Herr Beck, he doesn't appreciate my music, or any high music for that matter. He is a very *young*, if enchanting, creature, after all, the Fabulous Beast. The young, they love their popular songs, their street serenades, but to sit through a whole concert! You must know what I mean.'

'The Fabulous Beast?' repeated Udolphus in awed tones. 'I'd forgotten you have a strange unrecognizable being in Vequince.'

'Lives in the Great White Palace, at the end of the island,' confirmed Lucci, who had been listening to every word. 'They keep it there.'

'It stays of its own accord,' said Viporatti, with a stern glance at Udolphus's pupil. 'It wandered in one day, crossed the lagoon on its own, and asked to be given a home. We Vequincians are a generous nation. Of course we said yes, it could stay. Now it is an institution. If the Beast ever leaves Vequince . . . but it will not. It loves us.'

'Are there any more that you know of?' asked Udolphus. 'What about the city of Florion?'

Viporatti gave Udolphus a withering look and shuddered. '*That* rabble? Why would a fabulous creature go to them? No, no other that I have ever heard of. Not anywhere else in the world, not like our Beast. Of course,' he conceded, 'I have not travelled widely. But our sailors have and would report any other such creature, if they came across one. Even so, could it be unique? No one knows. You should endeavour to visit the Fabulous Beast while you're here. Do something for the Council of Ten. They control access to the creature. Do them a favour and they will do likewise. I shall be in touch, Herr Beck, with a suitable time for us both. *Ciao!*'

Udolphus gave Viporatti one of his cards and received the other mammal's card in reply.

They had not long parted when Udolphus became aware that something unusual was happening around his feet. When he looked down he saw that the campo they were crossing was awash with water. It seemed to be bubbling up through the drains. But then the Geranium visitor saw that the bulk of the water was flowing from one of the entrances to the lagoon. Soon he and Lucci were knee-deep in freezing sea water. It was as if they were in a ship which had been shot full of holes.

'We're sinking!' cried Udolphus. 'Someone's pulled the island's plug and we're going down.'

'No,' said a calm Lucci, 'the water is coming up.'

'You know about this?' asked Udolphus. 'It's happened before?'

'Do not alarm yourself, master. It happens ten times a year at least,' said the young water rat. He pulled on Udolphus's cloak to guide him to the steps of the Scuola San Rocco. Here they stood on the base of a pilaster, letting the water swill around their feet. 'That's why there're planks and bags of sand around to put at the bottoms of the doorways.'

'But what is causing such an inundation?'

'An in-what?'

'The flood, the attack from the sea, Lucci.'

Lucci shrugged. 'I don't know, signore, but we call it the *acqua alta*. I think it's got something to do with the tides.'

'Ah!' Udolphus stared up at the heavens. 'It must be the moon, pulling the waters up. I read about this in Coppernickel's book, when I was studying his celestial maps for my bedroom ceiling. Yes, of course, a high tide and a full moon, perhaps even a rising wind from the sea? The *acqua alta*, you say? If it's the tide, it won't go down for quite a while yet. We shall get very tired standing here on this ledge.'

'It's only water, master. We could find a higher place.'

'So we could. So we could. Fascinating.' Udolphus looked about him at the rising water, aware that the lagoon was washing over the floor of the city. 'Vequince becomes part of the sea again. The ocean reclaims its own. Now we are at the same level as the mid-Atlantic. We could be gulls, or boobies, or albatrosses, standing on water. On then, Lucci. Let us send out our ravens and doves to find higher ground.'

Lucci looked mystified. 'Ravens and doves?' Was his master going mad?

'It was a figure of speech, my dear Lucci, nothing more. I was recalling the story of Nobah and the flood. We have no such birds, of course. It's simply my Geranium sense of humour.'

'Geraniums *have* a sense of humour?'

'Don't be cheeky.'

They went forth and sought higher ground. Not far away was a chocolate-drinking house with a second storey. It was much more pleasant waiting out the *acqua alta* with a cup of drinking chocolate than it was standing on the base of a pillar. In fact it gave Udolphus the chance to discuss herbs and spices with the young rat. Lucci was amazed by the price put on such things as saffron and nutmeg. He knew they came from far away, that for the most part they smelled and tasted nice, but he could not come to terms with their value. After all, he argued, you could not keep them for ever, like diamonds. You ended up eating them, or sniffing them through your nose, or sprinkling them on furniture to make it smell nice.

'Why does nutmeg, for instance, cost so much?' he asked. 'I've heard that with just a pinch in your pocket you could be rich for ever.'

'It wards off the plague, so I'm told,' said Udolphus. 'You can't put a price on life. A rich mammal will pay anything to protect himself from the plague. Ah, the mysteries of the Orient, my dear Lucci,' he went on. 'Do you not find they excite your blood? Out there are dark jungles and forests, hidden valleys and mountain meadows, harbouring many secrets. We have found the cocoa leaf, the nutmeg, the autumn crocus, but there must be many more which remain beyond our knowledge. One day someone will find new ones and the world will go into a frenzy again, trying to harvest this plant or that nut or that piece of bark, and huge fortunes will be made.'

'I would like to be the finder,' Lucci agreed, 'but I

would *give* it all away, so that everyone could have some.'

'That is called being philanthropic, Lucci, which is a good thing for the spirit. No, no, I heartily approve. It means you do something for the good of your fellow mammals without seeking any kind of reward.' He sighed. 'Unfortunately there are others out there who will try to prevent you. Just because you find something doesn't mean you have sole control over its distribution. Others will wrest it from you, bring in armies to protect their interests, force you out. In any case, one often finds that such plants are very rare and there's not enough to go around. *That's* what makes them so valuable in the end. The scarcity, the rarity of the thing.'

The flood eventually subsided and the pair once again set forth to visit the apothecary, Signora Dropsi. They found her in a shop with bull's-eye window-panes and dozens of jars on display. The contents of the jars looked unpleasant, being a dirty yellow or oily grey colour. Some of them were simply herbs and had names like 'Wolfsbane' or 'Bladderwort' on the label, but many were concoctions, the recipe known only to Dropsi herself. The shop smelled of horrible stale things and Lucci had difficulty in keeping his stomach in order.

'Signora,' Udolphus said to Dropsi, who was standing in the dim depths of her shop, 'do you have something for an ache in the head?'

'I have a powder or a pill.'

'The powder, if you please? And the price?'

'You cannot have a very bad headache if you ask the price,' said Dropsi astutely. 'I know I would pay anything to get rid of such a pain when I have it.'

Clever, thought Udolphus, but said, 'I don't have the headache at the moment, but I know one will come. I suffer from them all the time and have run out of my own prescription, which I brought from—'

'Geranium. Yes, yes. We all know where you come from.'

'You know who I am?'

She cackled. 'No, I said I know where you come from.'

'Ah.' He looked down. 'My mode of dress.'

'Your dull appearance, your manner, your stolid features, your clumping walk, your humourless face, everything about you.'

'Humourless face? Clumping walk? I am offended, signora.' And he was.

'Forgive me, signore, forgive me. I am so old I speak my mind where others would filter truth through politeness. I have come to believe the years entitle me to say what I feel. I have lost the art of civility and good manners. I ask your pardon.'

She had still not taken back what she had said about him. What she had done was tell him that it was all true but that she was not prepared to sugar it with nice words. Udolphus was wise enough to proceed with his investigation, rather than worrying about his wounded feelings.

Dropsi moved forward into the moted light coming through the thick windowpanes. She was an ancient old vole with a wall eye and shrivelled features. Her bones showed through her fur like broken twigs. Beneath her forelimbs, her skin sagged and hung in flaps. Her dry, staring pelt was patchy, shedding fur in clumps. It would not have surprised Udolphus to learn that she had been locked in a dark, dusty attic for the last ten years.

She really was a most grotesque-looking water rat, but Udolphus knew better than to judge a creature on its looks alone. Character was what counted with him and he would not pass any comment on her, even to himself, before he learned what she was like as a mammal. She might look like a witch – she might indeed *be* a sorceress – but until any such state was confirmed Udolphus would treat her like any other water rat.

'You are wondering,' said Dropsi, her voice like crackling paper, 'how old is this crone? Has she seen a century? Or even two?' She was weighing some white powder on a pair of very small brass scales and though she spoke her attention was wholly on her work.

'It had crossed my mind, yes,' said Udolphus.

'I keep myself alive with my own secret potions.'

'An elixir!' cried Udolphus. 'You can prolong life?

'Heh! Prolong it, yes. I can keep this dried-out corpse still on its feet, walking around. But in here' – she tapped her skull – 'is a great weariness, a dearth of joy, a lack of any vitality. And though I can dull the aches and pains, they still trouble me. Who can shrink arthritic joints? Not I. Who can turn dreary sludge into sweet young blood again? Not I. Who can make supple those brittle muscles, those dried tendons? Not I.' She shook her walnut-wrinkled head. 'All I can do is keep the heart beating, the brain pulsing, the legs moving. The rest have broken down.'

Satisfied as to the weight, she poured the white powder from the scale pan onto a flat piece of paper. Then she folded the paper inwards, into a packet, with the powder inside. This she placed on the counter that stood between her and her two customers. 'One half-bezant.'

Udolphus reached into his purse and took out the copper coin. He reached forward to put it into her paw. Dropsi swiftly drew back, her paw withdrawn. 'Don't touch me!' she cried.

'I'm sorry, signora,' replied Udolphus, shocked by her reaction. 'I was going to do nothing untoward.'

Lucci put his paws on the counter and looked up at his master. 'It's not that,' he said. 'She's poison.'

'Poisonous,' corrected Udolphus, without thinking. Then he added, 'But you must not be so ill-mannered, Lucci.'

'No, no,' cried Dropsi, 'the urchin is right. I have been working with such plants as hemlock and monkshood for so long, my fur and whiskers are saturated with deadly residues. What's more, the poisons have mingled. Nux vomica with aconite with upas sap. The result is that I carry on my fur a poison so toxic there is no antidote. Brush against me and you will fall sick and die. Touch me and belladonna will seep through your pores and into your blood.

70

You will go out convulsing horribly. Your eyes will start from your head, your breath will quicken, your heart stop dead. Put the coin into the dish full of vinegar in front of you. I shall retrieve it.'

'Indeed, I shall keep myself to myself,' replied Udolphus, his claws trembling a little as the coin splashed into the vinegar. 'I am sorry for you, signora.'

At that moment a young female water rat came through a doorway at the back of the shop. Lucci, whose eyes and nose were just above the counter, let out a little sigh of deep approval. She was indeed a pretty creature, with large brown eyes and sleek fur. The young jill saw the young jack staring at her and she dipped her head shyly.

'Gramma,' she said, 'I have come to remind you that you need to take your evening pills.'

Signora Dropsi turned, but before she did so Udolphus noticed a gleam of fondness come to her eyes. 'Thank you, Sophia. I shall do so in a moment.'

Lucci let out another loud, involuntary sigh, his attentions completely engaged by young Sophia, whose name he now knew. He was eternally grateful to Signora Dropsi for that name, which would now haunt his dreams and waking hours alike. Sophia. Sophia. Sophia.

'I believe the urchin has been smitten,' cackled Dropsi, jerking Lucci back to the real world. 'Poor soul.'

'I have not,' growled Lucci indignantly. Then, with a glance at Sophia, who had heard this fierce denial, added, 'Not *too* much, anyway.'

Sophia stuck her nose up in a haughty manner. *She* did not care what this jack thought of her. *She* did not give a fig for his approval.

'That'll be all, Sophia,' said the grandmother. 'I shall be back with you in a moment.'

Sophia left. A yearning look appeared on Lucci's face. He looked down, pretending to be interested in the shape of his own feet.

Dropsi said to Udolphus, 'You see? I can't even hug my own family. I can't cuddle her, as a normal gramma would.'

'I feel for you, signora. I have one last question to ask. I understand that like one or two other guilds, you are under investigation by the authorities.'

Her eyes narrowed. 'Possibly.'

'So if there was a plot to bring down the government, you would benefit by it?'

As Dropsi answered this question, spittle flew from her mouth, and both Lucci and Udolphus leaped backwards to avoid the venomous spray. The Lord knew, it might burn through their skin like acid, or soak through the pores and enter their hearts by osmosis to stop them dead.

'I'm a loyal citizen,' spat Dropsi. 'Ask anyone! I would never join any plot to destroy my own government.'

'I thank you for your time,' said a nervous Udolphus, leaving quickly. 'A long life to you, signora.'

'I've already got that – what I need is respect.'

Udolphus had learned a lot about Dropsi in that

short period in the shop. Random killing was not on her agenda, that much was certain. And she loved her own. However, this did not mean that she was not a conspirator. He had no doubt she could be a formidable enemy when threatened. The means to do harm was there, in great force. All she had to do was reach out and touch her foes and they would fall to the ground stone-dead.

Roma Volecci had told him that the Council of Ten intended to make public the individual ingredients of the various potions sold by apothecaries. They thought it time that the public knew what they were taking in the form of medicine. Some creatures might be allergic to aspirin or fennel or poppyseed. Udolphus had heard the rumours in the coffee shops. Such a law would make known to all any secret remedies the individual apothecaries owned. Thus *anyone* would be able to make them and the apothecary family who owned the secrets would lose their customers.

'She and her guild might feel strongly enough about such a move to try to prevent it, even to the point of betraying Vequince to the Florions,' muttered Udolphus to himself, as he and Lucci hurried along. 'I know if my whole livelihood were threatened, I would feel very aggrieved and wish to do *something* about it.'

He looked at the small fold of paper he still held in his paw. Who knew what was in this powder and what it would do to him? It would be wise not to take the remedy and he threw it into the canal.

'What's that, master?' asked Lucci.

'Nothing, nothing – and Lucci, I wish you wouldn't call me "master" – it makes you sound like some sort of slave.'

'But you are the master and I the apprentice.'

'I suppose that's true. Oh, well, if you must. Now look at the sky. Nimbus clouds are forming. It's going to rain. We must get back to our lodgings. I've been wet already at the bottom today. I would prefer to keep the top half of my body dry.'

As they hurried along the sharply turning alleys and narrow streets, Lucci spoke to Udolphus, asking for advice. Udolphus was more interested in who might be following them than in young Lucci's chatterings, but he listened anyway, since it seemed important to the waif.

'If you really liked someone,' said his apprentice; 'really, really liked them – how would you get them to like you back?'

'This wouldn't have anything to do with that young female we just left behind in the shop, would it? Of course not. Well, I would send them a note saying how nice it was to meet them and that I hoped we should meet again sometime in the future.'

'Just that?' muttered a dubious Lucci. 'Wouldn't you say your heart was bursting in your chest and your stomach felt like melting butter?'

'I would save those poetic words for the future. You wouldn't want to scare this new friend away, would you? And you will, if you go thundering in with bursting hearts and buttery stomachs. Take my advice, Lucci. Slowly and carefully, so nothing breaks. Treat it delicately. The second time you meet, you might tell her you admire her dress, or something of that nature. Speak sincerely, but not too enthusiastically.'

'Are you sure I shouldn't say that her eyes destroy me?'

'Perfectly sure,' sighed the otter. 'Believe me, I know.'

Lucci was quiet for a while, then he said, 'You've never had a friend like that, have you? A jill otter?'

'No, but don't make the mistake of thinking I don't know what I'm talking about. I was young once too. I was as smitten as you are now. But I went blundering in. I'm giving you good advice – advice that would have saved me from a broken heart, Lucci. They scare easily, these jills. Slowly and surely, with gentle steps. That's the way to do it.'

# Chapter Five

Udolphus needed to inspect the carcass of the cloak-stealer, to ascertain how he had been killed. The unraveller wished to know whether this death was merely a warning to him, or whether the assassins had actually tried to kill *him*, Udolphus Beck. If it was a warning it meant they merely suspected he *might* be after them. If they thought it was Udolphus in the cloak, it meant they were *sure* he was after them.

The morgue was on the Isle of the Dead. This was, you might say, satisfactory, since the whole island was the only graveyard for the mammals of Vequince. It meant that once the embalmers had done their jobs the bodies could go straight into their allotted tombs. Embalmers were kept in constant work, even though they were an expensive addition to funeral expenses. Corpses tend to sag and collapse in on themselves after death. Wealthy relatives often wished to put on a good show for the mourners as they trooped through the chapel of rest. It was the duty of the embalmers to plump them up as one would cushions; oil their fur to give it back some lifelike gloss; stiffen the whiskers with scented wax; fluff up the tummy hair and draw back the gums to produce a smile (actually, the smile produced was often ghastly; certainly it did not present the face of a creature happy to pass on to everlasting life).

Udolphus had told Lucci on the journey over, 'The body might give us some clues as to how he was killed and whether those who murdered him knew who it was they were killing.'

When they arrived at the morgue he was still a little seasick after the boat ride over the choppy lagoon. 'Is the corpse available for viewing?' he said to the water rat mortician. 'I wonder if I might be permitted to examine it?'

'Are you a relative of the deceased?' he was asked. 'Or do you have a permit from the correct department?'

'A permit,' said Udolphus, pressing a gold coin into the creature's paw.

'Ah, yes, of course. Signed by the undersecretary himself,' said the mortician, smirking. 'This way, please.'

Udolphus was shown into a room in which stood a marble table, a slab with two supports, on which lay a corpse. It was indeed the body of the street hawker who had bothered Udolphus near the coffee stall. Udolphus approached the remains and looked down on them, while Lucci remained in the doorway, shaking a little.

'So, my friend,' murmured Udolphus, addressing the dead water rat, 'here are the rewards of thieving.'

There were a number of wounds on the corpse. Two of them were to the head. Udolphus now took off his cloak and looked at the hood, which he rarely wore up. There were no tears in the hood. He nodded.

'Whoever killed you, my friend, knew you were not me. Indeed, your head and face were exposed to view. There was no mistaken identity. Now, let's have a look at these wounds.'

Udolphus took out one of the long thick needles he had once used for sewing leather, when he was a shoemaker. He poked around in one of the holes in the corpse. The metal needle grated against something still in the wound. It did not take long to prise out the object. It was a slim sliver of glass. He poked again, in another wound. Again he found a spike of glass. A third wound revealed a similar object. Udolphus had his gloves on, so he picked up the three spikes and carried them to a water pump in the corner, where he washed them clean of blood and gore.

Lucci was still hovering in the doorway, looking grey with unease.

'There's nothing to fear in here, Lucci,' said Udolphus. 'Dead mammals can't hurt you.'

Lucci crept in, going to his master's side. Udolphus showed him the glass spikes. 'Do you know what these are?' he asked.

'No, signore,' said Lucci. 'Can we go now?'

At that moment the greasy-looking mortician entered the chamber, rubbing his paws together. 'Signore, you have had quite a long time—'

'We are about to leave, but first let me show you something.'

Udolphus stretched forth his paw and revealed the glass spikes. As he had hoped, he got an immediate reaction from the mortician. The creature drew back with hiss and looked upset.

Udolphus said, 'You know what these are?'

'No, no – I – no, signore. They mean nothing to me. What are they? Pieces of windowpane? I must wonder, did the victim fall through a shop window?'

Another gold coin leaped to the tips of Udolphus's claws.

'Perhaps this will help you remember what they are?'

Still the mortician looked frightened. He glanced over his shoulder twice, licked his lips when he looked at the coin, then seemed about to shake his head again. Udolphus added a second gold piece to the first. Now the mortician was his. The coins were snatched from his claws.

'Merino daggers,' hissed the mortician. 'Blades of Merino daggers.'

Udolphus was still in the dark. 'What are Merino daggers?'

'Glass weapons, slim-bladed knives, made in the glass-blowing factories on the island of Merino. They're illegal, signore, of course. What you do is stab your victim and twist the dagger violently to one side or the other. This action causes the hilt to snap off. The blade remains in the wound, of course, preventing the cut from sealing itself. Bleeding is therefore profuse. The user then smashes the dagger handle on the ground. Thus the murder weapon is destroyed.' The mortician was quite shaken by his own description. 'As I say, these are highly illegal. Anyone found carrying a Merino dagger is in very serious trouble.'

'So, who in your society would dare carry such a heinous implement?'

'I could not say. Truly, signore, I could not say.'

The mortician stared out of the one small window at the white tombs littering the island. There were gravestones of every description out there, some upright and new, others skewed by time and weather. Clearly the creature was thinking that if he said any more he might end up under one of those white headstones sooner than he expected.

'I know who would carry such daggers,' cried Lucci. 'Rotzi di Coporoni. They say that big coat of his has many sheaths sewn into the lining, where he keeps weapons. There's no one really who would have the courage to stop the Thieftaker General, master.'

'Well, well. So what do we deduce from this piece of unravelling?'

'The thieftaker thought he was killing you, when he stabbed the hawker?' said Lucci.

'No. I believe di Coporoni killed the hawker on purpose. He knew who it was and, guessing I would inspect the body for clues, he used the Merino daggers to frighten me.' Udolphus was a little disturbed by his own deductions, realizing that he was dealing with a clever opponent who knew the value of mind games. 'The death of a vagrant street seller does not warrant great official concern. The murder of a distinguished visitor like me, however, would excite attention. The ambassador of Geranium would become involved; the Council of Ten would ask questions about the safety of visitors to their city; di Coporoni himself would be criticized for the lack of protection. Ergo – that means *therefore*, young rat – he wanted to chase me away from Vequince without causing any fuss in government circles.'

'And are you frightened, master?'

'I would be foolish not to be,' admitted Udolphus truthfully. 'I think any sensible mammal needs to be frightened by such ruthlessness. Here we have this loose cannon, the Thieftaker General, rolling around the streets in a semi-official role, answerable to no one in particular. Rotzi di Coporoni has obviously got something to hide and he thinks I'm here to find out what it is. Yes, the idea that I'm a target of this Thieftaker General certainly does scare me. I shall watch my back with a keen eye.'

The mortician wound the corpse up in its shroud. 'If I were you, signore, I'd go back to Geranium as fast as my legs would carry me.'

After leaving the mortuary, Udolphus and his apprentice took a walk around the island. There was not a great deal to see there, but both needed some fresh air after spending time with a corpse. They found one gravestone on which was written: HE THOUGHT HE HAD WON THE GAME WITH HIS ACE, BUT HE WAS PLAYING WITH A PAIR OF KNAVES.

'What a strange epitaph,' muttered Udolphus. 'I do believe I know what it means.'

'So do I,' said Lucci in a prim voice. 'It means if you gamble with cards you're likely to meet some murderous characters.'

'Cards is a gentlejack's game,' sniffed Udolphus.

'I expect he thought that too. And look where it got him.'

Lucci then showed his master where his mother and father were buried, in a pauper's grave with a cross of rotten wood. 'It's the first time I've been here,' he admitted, scraping moss from the cross. 'I couldn't afford the boat fare before you came, signore.'

'Doesn't your uncle bring you here?'

'No, signore, my uncle is very wicked. I was told my father had left some money with my uncle in trust for me, but he always turns me away from his door when I seek him out. He says there was nothing; that the funeral and the tombstones of my parents were expensive; that all the money was eaten up. Yet my uncle lives in a nice house and seems to have all that he needs, while I was cast out onto the streets to fend for myself.'

'I think it's time we went to see your uncle Septimi.'

'Oh – oh, no, signore,' cried Lucci suddenly in alarm. 'Please. He will cause you great trouble and you will have to leave Vequince.'

'Will he now? We'll see about that.'

The otter made his way back to the jetty, to await the next boat. Lucci remained for a short time longer in the company of his parents, then rejoined his master. They crossed the lagoon again. Today the sea was a blue so vivid it might have been squeezed from lapis lazuli. Udolphus was always amazed by the ability of the lagoon to change its colour. One day a deep sea-green, the next a summer-sky blue. It was difficult to believe it was the same water. One might have been forgiven for thinking that God poured different inks into the lagoon before everyone awoke each morning.

'The address,' said Udolphus as stepped gratefully onto the quay. 'Quickly please.'

Lucci had been hoping that his master had forgotten about visiting his uncle. Nevertheless he gave the otter the street and house name.

'Show me the way, if you please,' demanded Udolphus. 'The sooner we get this over with, the better.'

Lucci did as he was told, leading his master past a great shipyard and military arsenal to a row of pretty houses on the waterfront. Septimi's was a tall thirteenth-century house not far from the Campo San Leo, and was in the Vequincian-Byzantine style. The windows were narrow but elegant, in two rows of four. They had rounded arches at the top and were supported by side pillars. The whole ground floor had obviously been built for commercial use and consisted of a windowless warehouse.

Udolphus climbed some external stairs to reach a door above and to the side of the warehouse. He rang the gleaming copper bell. Within a short time a timid female water rat answered the door.

'Yes, signore?'

'Is Signor Septimi at home please? Could you tell him that Herr Udolphus Beck would like a word with him?'

The maid, for that was what she seemed to be, disappeared into the interior of the house. A while later a male water rat appeared. He was dressed in a velvet jacket, a pillbox hat with a tassel dangling from the top and a pair of satin breeches. This fellow looked down his long nose at Udolphus, unable for a moment to see Lucci cowering behind his master.

'Herr Beck?' said the rat. 'I am Septimi.'

'Then you,' Udolphus said, turning and grasping the head of his protégé, 'are the uncle of this young rat?'

Septimi's eyes narrowed. 'You! What's he done now, the little hobbledehoy? Should be thrown in the dungeons. Nothin' but wasters and scroungers—'

'Perhaps,' murmured Udolphus, hardly able to contain his temper, 'he would not be forced to scrounge if his uncle took responsibility for him.'

Septimi's head went back and his eyes narrowed. 'What's that supposed to mean?'

'That you, as his relative, should look after him. He has no parents and I'm told that his father – your brother – was quite well off. Did he not leave the youth any money? Most fathers would ensure their offspring were cared for, once they departed this life. I feel certain that young Lucci here must have been due a bequest.'

The tone was hostile now. 'What're you? Some kind of lawyer?'

'Not a lawyer, but certainly a well-respected citizen of Geranium.'

'Well why don't you go back there? Why don't you go home? We don't want your kind in Vequince.'

'And what kind is that?'

'The kind that pokes their snouts into others' business.'

Septimi tried to slam the door in Udolphus's face, but the otter reached out with his paw and firmly held it open.

'Now you listen to me, you worm-ridden excuse for a mammal,' snarled Udolphus as Septimi frantically tried to push the door shut. 'The care of the young is a universal responsibility. If any grown mammal sees or hears of a youngling being abused, then they have a duty to bring the perpetrator to justice. I shall bring all my powers to bear on you, signore, so do not be surprised to receive a visit from my friend Rotzi di Coporoni. As Thieftaker General he would be obliged to look into this affair, especially since we are distant cousins. Be well warned. Be ready with your excuses.'

'Rotzi di Coporoni?' cried Septimi. 'I – I don't—'

'You don't believe me? Good, all the better. The shock of my cousin kicking down your door will be that much greater, won't it?'

Septimi was shaking so much now that he let go of the door. 'What am I supposed to do?' he wailed. 'Take the urchin into my home? I have no room.'

'There are about eight bedrooms to this house and many other rooms beside. But in fact Lucci doesn't want to come here, so that won't be necessary. However, I expect you to find Lucci's father's last will and testament, and to meet the terms of that will. Lucci wants neither more nor less than what his father left him. You, signore, have had that money in your possession for some time now. You will have made profits from it, which you will keep, though you have behaved in a reprehensible manner. The capital itself belongs to this youth. We will expect a call from you soon.'

A shudder went through Septimi. 'I – I can't find that sort of money just like that. It takes time—'

'Soon,' snapped Udolphus. 'If we do not see it within the month, then the Thieftaker General will be here to take your soul. I will personally see you shackled to the punishment wall and the pelt flayed from your back to your bones. What's left will hang on a gibbet for the crows to peck. You disgust me, signore. To take advantage of one so young as this? You should be ashamed of yourself. I would cringe if I were in your shoes – which incidentally were not worth the money you paid for them, for I recognize them as fakes. You believe them to be Pershan originals, but they are actually copies shipped from the Orient in their thousands.' Udolphus, having been sidetracked, gathered his breath and finished with, 'We shall be back to collect the young rat's inheritance.'

Udolphus turned and climbed down the wooden stairs, while Lucci scrambled after him.

'You just want the money for yourself,' yelled Septimi, becoming bolder with every step that Udolphus took. 'Lucci, he just wants your money. He's not interested in helping you. I – I've been investing your share of the will. When you are of age, it'll be here for you. I haven't forgotten it's yours. Di Coporoni? Bah! I don't think you know him at all.'

Lucci spoke to his uncle for the first and last time. 'Oh yes he does, Uncle, as you'll soon find out.'

Septimi stared at his nephew for a few minutes, then shut the door with a loud bang.

'Cousin?' asked Lucci, trotting beside his master as they walked by the lagoon. 'How do you make that out? An otter and a rafter rat?'

'Why, we are all cousins, if you go back far enough,' said Udolphus, smiling. 'We are all of one family.'

Out in the lagoon the ships were coming and going as usual. Those with silk sails came proudly into port, their rigging decorated with excited sailors. On the quays the unloaders waited with the ship owners, to see what sort of cargo their captains had brought them. If you looked down upon the scene from the air, a bird's-eye view, you would have seen ships clustering like butterflies at every dock and jetty. Bales, packets and crates were being ferried back and forth to and from warehouses – jewels, jam rolls and Jamacky rum. In and out of lighters carrying goods wove the pretty gondolas with their passengers. Mammals with fine turbans, bedecked in gems and richly embroidered gowns, sat in the passenger seats.

Vequince was the richest city in the world, boasted the finest architecture, the most beautiful churches, the most talented painters and sculptors. The whole city was one huge crown of gemstones standing in an aquamarine sea.

'Don't you feel elevated to be a Vequincian?' asked Udolphus, finding the walk along the waterfront breathtaking. 'Doesn't it fill you with pride?'

'I shouldn't be so vain,' replied Lucci, 'for being born in any city, in any land, is but an accident. One should only be proud of one's own achievements, otherwise one is an empty swankpot.'

Udolphus was taken aback by Lucci's reply. 'Why,' he said, 'I do believe I'm being put in my place. Bravo, young Lucci, bravo. I was becoming carried away with the scene, but you kept your head and remained true to yourself. I am the pupil and you the teacher.'

They said no more on the subject, but Udolphus was profoundly impressed by his apprentice. Lucci had not been learning his master's values by rote; he had done better than that. He had absorbed the substance and formed his own views on the subject. That was indeed value for teaching. The general philosophy had soaked into the pupil, not meaningless words repeated word for word. Udolphus had never directly spoken about *pride* to Lucci, yet Lucci's ethics on the subject mirrored his own.

'Where are we going?' asked Lucci, suddenly aware that his master was taking him into a shop. 'What's this place?'

*This place* was a shop where tombstones could be purchased. Here was a craftsjack who carved marble headstones and cut the letters and numbers into the surface. When they stood before the craftsjack, in his leather apron, hammer and chisel one in each paw, Udolphus told Lucci to order a tombstone for his mother and father.

'We would like your best marble, signore. Tell the carver their names,' said Udolphus to Lucci, 'and, if you can remember them, the dates of their births and deaths. Put some nice words on the stone. *Sacred to the Memory of My Beloved Parents.* That sort of thing. *Who took with them from this world the best of all that is to be found in the next.*'

'Does that make sense?' asked Lucci dubiously. 'Those last words?'

'Certainly,' said the carver, who charged by the letter. 'A nice epitaph like that shows love and respect for the departed.'

However, to Udolphus's slight disappointment, Lucci chose another epitaph out of the carver's book, not quite as long and wordy as that suggested by Udolphus, rather more sentimental: *They had souls as soft as sable.* But the marble Lucci picked was of the very best: pink marble from the quarry of San Sealsian. Not only was it wonderful to work with, Udolphus believed the finished stone would be worthy enough to stand in any cathedral in the land. Lucci wanted it shaped like a bell, because he knew his mother had loved the bells which rang in the campaniles. Udolphus drew the carver a map of the Isle of the Dead, to show the location of the wooden cross which the stone would replace.

'Please send a note to this address,' he said as he finished his business with the carver, 'when you have completed the task, so that we may go and inspect your work, which I am certain will be of the highest order.'

'I am the best carver of tombstones in all Vequince,' murmured the carver, pocketing money. 'You will be amazed.'

The pair left the shop to fluff their fur in the breeze. Lucci, walking beside his master, could not believe that a mere few days previously he had been fighting the crows in the gutters for cabbage stalks. Now his whole life had been changed. I must not get above myself, he thought, for my fortunes might change back again tomorrow.

To Udolphus he said, 'When my uncle gives me the money he owes me, I shall pay you for the tombstone, signore.'

'Please, it was my pleasure.'

'Yes, but master, they were *my* parents.'

'This is true. This is true.' Udolphus wanted to pat his pupil on the head, but did not do so, for that would be patronizing him. Instead he was satisfied with the glow that warmed his heart.

At that moment they came across a crowd of feral waifs. Lucci knew them, and hailed them.

'Here is my new master,' he said, introducing his scruffy, dirty friends to Udolphus. 'He has been very kind to me. Master, this is Poggio, this ragged fellow

Broccoli, and this Noccolo, and that small one hiding behind Carla is Puccio Pucci. Where are you going, my friends?'

'Have you not heard?' said the one called Poggio. 'There is to be a new Duce crowned tomorrow, as the old one has died.'

Udolphus wondered whether the plot had already been set in motion while he was occupied on the Isle of the Dead. 'Died, or been killed?' he snapped. 'Tell me quickly, young jack.'

Poggio looked a bit taken aback by the otter's sharpness. 'His heart stopped in the night,' he said. 'That's all I know, signore.'

Udolphus realized he had upset the young rat and he apologized, asking, 'Can they do a ceremony like this so quickly?'

'In an emergency, yes, master,' explained his apprentice. 'The last Duce was only crowned a few weeks ago. It's very bad luck for the city to have no Duce in place, for one normally takes over from the other leaving no gap. They will have rushed around today, sending out heralds through the streets, proclaiming that there is to be a new ceremony. We were on the Isle of the Dead, so we didn't hear them.'

'And why do you wish to be there?' Udolphus asked the urchins. 'Do they throw sweets to the younglings on such occasions?'

'No, signore,' cried little Puccio Pucci. 'One of us gets chosen to count the wax balls and whoever it is becomes the new page to the Duce. We want to be first there, so we'll sleep in the piazza until morning.'

Lucci explained. Coloured wax balls were dropped into an urn by the heads of all the leading Vequincian families. Each colour represented a candidate for the post of Duce, the King of Vequince. Some of these wax balls were removed from the urn by an orphan picked at random from the populace. This youngster, male or female, was always a foundling. He or she was known in the old language as *Il Scegliere*, or the chooser, and wore a rigid hollow silver glove with a pointing claw. With this silver claw the chooser dipped into the urn and removed seven of the wax balls, thus ensuring no duplicity. There were always only six candidates, so at least two or more of the balls were of the same colour. If, say, there were three red balls, one blue, two yellow and a green, then the candidate whose colour was red became the next Duce and was crowned. *Il Scegliere*, the choosing youngster, became his page for the period that he sat upon the throne.

'We will of course attend the ceremony,' said Udolphus when the chattering waifs and strays had gone their own way, 'even though the danger increases for us, young Lucci. We must be ever wary. If you wish, you may leave my service now, for I don't want any harm to come to you. I would hope they would not hurt a youngster like you, who has nothing to offer them, but I can't be sure. Di Coporoni and his cronies seem very ruthless.'

'Master,' explained Lucci, 'if you had left me on the streets I would have been in just as much danger there. Who cares what happens to a homeless foundling? No one. Urchins die of disease or get killed all the time, some in accidents, some by bad mammals. I wish to stay with you. If anything happens to me, it will be fate's, not your fault.'

'We can choose our fate.'

'Not me, master. Not a foundling.'

Udolphus was troubled. 'I feel the danger is growing by the hour. As one responsible, I should send you away.'

'And then I would come back,' replied Lucci cheerfully. 'You do not own me, signore. I must choose my own path, as you said. No one should choose for me. Now, do you know what will happen tomorrow?'

'Unique rituals?'

'Yes, some of those,' said Lucci, rather unsure of what his master was talking about, but reluctant to seem ignorant. 'Oh, I remember, I told you about it, didn't I? So you know.'

Udolphus said, 'You did indeed. It sounds like a magnificent ceremony. We shall certainly go and watch. How are the candidates chosen?'

'Well, they put themselves forward, of course. Every citizen votes to get fifty candidates. Then they vote on the fifty and whittle it down to twenty. Finally they vote out all those they feel are unsuitable, until there are ten candidates left. These ten vote on each other, until there are but seven – for the seven colours of the rainbow.'

'A most complex system. Will the new Duce be a Volecci?'

'All the important Voleccis are on the Council,

unless you want an infant Duce. There is one three-year-old in the care of a nurse. Anyway, an important Volecci would rather be on the Council, which is more powerful than being the Duce. There are some less important Voleccis, small-time merchants, traders and bankers for the most part – it's an old and large Vequincian family – oh, and I think there's one who is an artist.'

'Hurrah for the artist. Well, perhaps one of your young friends will be picked for the chooser?' suggested Udolphus. 'That would be one less ruffian on the streets of Vequince.'

'Now, signore,' admonished Lucci, 'you know you don't mean that last remark.'

Udolphus sighed. 'No, I don't. I say such things to hide my guilt. I wish I could take care of all you waifs, Lucci, but I am only one otter. I can't feed the whole world.'

'Master,' said Lucci, 'if everyone were like you and did something for just one of us, the streets would be empty of orphans for good.'

# Chapter Six

The ceremony was indeed a grand affair. It seemed that all of Vequince was there to see the new Duce in. The crown and robe of office were on a throne at the top of the steps to the Duce's Palace, along with sceptres and orbs. These precious objects glistered in the sunlight. All around were gathered noblejacks and noblejills in fine clothes.

The heads of the guilds were there too: the squat and heavy Botcchio of the Maskmakers; the burned, tattered and torn figure of Malacite the Alchemist; and the guildmistress of the Apothecaries: the shrivelled, odious husk known as Dropsi, around whom was a ring of space, for none dared touch even the hem of her garment for fear of poison.

The crowds pressed forward, eager to see what was happening at the front. Here were gathered the seven candidates for the Ducedom, dressed in bright colours. They too came in all shapes and sizes, but were mostly fat. Coming as they did from aristocratic families, they were all wealthy merchants or bankers. Vequince was not a place where noble and royal families despised trade. Indeed, there was little chance they would be noble without having been lifted out of the masses by their handling of commerce and business. They all owned ships which carried their goods over the seven seas. They did not consider the accumulation of wealth to be crass. Buildings, warehouses and ships were what counted on an island where there were no landowners, no vast estates as there were in Britannica or Geranium.

Udolphus and Lucci had managed to get a place at the front of the multitude, despite the fact that others had slept the night in the square. The unraveller was careful to note who was close to him in the crowd. He did not want a knife in the back, despite his protective vest. He chose a spot amongst a group of burly females obviously just out of the steaming wash house, where they laundered citizens' clothes for a zint an item. They were all red-eyed and limp-furred, but a cheerful bunch.

Udolphus was keen to see everything that went on.

'Still here, Beck?' called a harsh voice from behind the washerjills. 'I expected to see you gone before now.'

Udolphus turned to see Rotzi di Coporoni sneering at him and a tingle of fear went through the otter. Even from there the thieftaker's breath smelled of dead fish. Udolphus tried not to wince when the creature exhaled in his direction. Then the unraveller noticed someone at the thieftaker's side: a well-dressed rat in plain but expensive clothes.

This youngish water rat was rather disconcerting to look at. The hair on his head and face had, it seemed, turned prematurely grey. Even his whiskers had a more ghostly hue about them. This, coupled with his wishy-washy eyes, gave the rat a spectral air. Udolphus had heard that a sudden shock could cause the pigments of one's pelt to turn pale.

'Ah,' said di Coporoni, noticing his gaze, 'allow me to introduce you. Signor Pavolo, Herr Beck.' The thieftaker turned to Signor Pavolo. 'Herr Beck is of course from Geranium, an ex-shoemaker, here on a short visit.'

Pavolo seemed bored. 'And the purpose of your visit, shoemaker?'

'Ex-shoemaker. I intend staying for Carnival,' said Udolphus, studying this friend of Rotzi di Coporoni. 'I have already purchased my mask. It would be a pity to miss the opportunity to use it.'

Pavolo said nothing, but briefly inclined his head in answer. He remained standing there, his claws clasped behind his back. He evidently wished to remain aloof from the proceedings. His lazy, bored-looking eyes soon left Udolphus's features and began roaming over the exterior of the basilica, the campanile, the Zecca, and the arcades and loggias of the Libreria. It was as if he had seen it all before and even the dirty brown sparrows watching from the surrounding buildings were more interesting than this overblown ceremony. He did at one point raise a forelimb and point to something.

Udolphus, always observant, noticed that Pavolo's

paw was covered in small neat cuts, which the unraveller recognized instantly.

'Signor Pavolo,' said Udolphus, 'seems unimpressed.'

Di Coporoni looked annoyed, more with Udolphus than with his companion. 'You just be careful that your tadpole here doesn't get snatched up for a Duce's page, Beck.'

With that the pair moved off towards one of the side streets. Soon they were in deep discussion. Pavolo kept nodding, while di Coporoni was rattling on, using his paws to emphasize a point.

But at that moment a loud shout went up as a stunning-looking craft appeared out of the mouth of the Grand Canal. As soon as he saw it Udolphus knew this was the magnificent *Bucintoro*, the royal golden barque which was used by the Duce on state occasions. The prow, which extended several metres from the front of the barque, was decorated with a winged golden lion, crouched as if ready to spring. Behind this, on the covered decks, were gilt carvings of cherubs and seraphs and mythical beasts. Indeed, the whole craft was carved with figures from stem to stern: a tremendous work of art that must have taken a hundred artisans years to complete.

Banners and flags flew from its decks and decorated the gilded roof. Such a splendid vessel, with its thrones and canopies, all of shining gold, must have been a treasure worth several small provincial kingdoms. Liveried servants stood proudly on its decks, while rows of hidden oarjacks propelled the craft forward at a solemn pace, appropriate to its status as the royal barque.

The *Bucintoro* came to rest amongst the forest of gondola mooring poles off the quay, ready to receive the new Duce. Udolphus said in hushed tones, 'Cloplatipus of Aegipt could not have owned such a vessel. It is the most beautiful craft I have ever had the fortune to see with my own eyes. I shall die happy knowing I have seen the first wonder of the civilized world.'

'You are dying?' cried young Lucci. 'You did not tell me.'

'No, no, infant. It's merely an expression, a figure of speech. I wanted to express my utter admiration for the royal barque.'

Udolphus then saw, out of the corner of his eye, that the thieftaker and his mysterious friend had returned. Far from looking bored, Signor Pavolo was now looking intently at the *Bucintoro*. Had he not seen this sight before? And if he had not, why was his face not registering wonder and amazement, rather than a studied expression? Udolphus had no further time to consider, for the choosing ceremony had begun. His attention returned to what was happening on the steps of the palace.

Young water rats pressed forward, forming a small sea of youth in front of the unseeing official. Lucci's friends were all there, standing in anticipation, and Udolphus indicated that Lucci himself might like to join them, but Lucci shook his head.

Then the chosen foundling was led out of the

crowd and up onto the steps of the palace. A shout of great joy went up from the rest of the street urchins, who clustered below.

'It's Noccolo!' cried an excited Lucci. 'Noccolo has been chosen.'

Noccolo, who until now had been a ragamuffin, was thrust forward by an official bearing a magnificent silver rod. Another official appeared with a kind of glove, a silver claw, on a satin cushion. The great urn bearing all the wax balls stood by a pillar, ready for the Chosen One to plunge into. First the silver claw (Udolphus had not forgotten this was the signature on the bottom of his letter!) had to be fitted. Noccolo seemed a little hesitant at first and held up the silver claw to look inside it. Udolphus wondered what was wrong and asked Lucci.

'Recently,' said Lucci, 'a Chosen One refused to put on the silver claw. There was a story about a poisoned needle inside the finger.'

'What happened to him – or her?'

'You can't refuse, master – it's forbidden. They had to postpone the ceremony until the next day, when they chose another foundling. I think they arrested her – it was someone I didn't know – a jill from the docks on the north side of the island – they threw her in prison. They made an example of her. Of course, the next Chosen One didn't hesitate, but nothing happened to him or her. The prison here is a horrible place – just stone cells covered in dirty straw. Once you're thrown in there, they seem to forget you.'

'Prisons are awful places anywhere, but let's watch the ceremony . . .'

'Oh yes – and look – Noccolo has put on the silver claw. He's going to the urn to take the first ball. Yellow! It's yellow. See how the yellow candidate is smiling. Oh, the smile has gone, as a red one comes out. It has flitted like a fickle butterfly to his neighbour's face. The red candidate laughs and turns to another in excitement, but that one wears blue and looks grumpy. No blue balls have emerged. Yes, there is one. Hope springs to blue eyes. Now come gleeful sneers. Another yellow. There are beams from that quarter again. Yet a green one emerges. And another green. Oh my, the final ball is . . . green again! How fortunes change in an instant, master.'

Joy and sorrow. They were both there in abundance on the steps of the Duce's Palace. The candidates wearing the wrong colours were thrust aside as if they were now cabbage sellers. The wearer of green was hailed, hastily robed and crowned, his rivals now ignored.

'The noblejack Alphonso Rossi replaces the noblejack Mereccino Tomassi as the new Duce,' cried the herald.

Cheers floated about the Duce's head and rose petals under his feet. He was smiling, smiling, smiling, buoyed up, floating on a tide of pleasure. The other candidates-in-waiting had been important citizens up until a few seconds ago. Now they were ordinary again, for there was only one important being on those steps: the chosen Duce.

Gloria in excelsis! Gloria rex!

There were further lengthy rituals, none of which made very much sense, falling as welcome gentle waves upon the watching multitude, until finally the oiled and perfumed Duce, encrusted with jewels and weighed down by heavy embroidered clothes, was carried to the golden *Bucintoro* on a golden palanquin. Gold on gold. Everything shone with the colour of the sun.

Once the ceremony was over Udolphus and Lucci went to find the public record office. There Udolphus checked the list of names he carried – to wit: Stanley Rigwiddie, the gun-maker; Banda Rambutan, the insect embalmer; Yumi Horishma, cleric and origami master; Crome de Boile, knife-thrower; Potsdam Rich, water wrestler. He studied these names and occupations with a focused eye, trying to see through them to what lay behind. Udolphus had learned that behind all surface information lies a great mass of other material, some of which is relevant, some not.

'What do you say to watching some water wrestling one evening?' asked Udolphus of Lucci. 'I'm not sure what water wrestling is, but it sounds as if it could be a spectacle.'

'I've seen it. It's all right. But once you've seen it . . .'

'I take it you're not all that enthusiastic.'

Lucci shrugged. 'Not really.'

'What about knife-throwing?'

Lucci perked up at this. 'That sounds better. I should like to see a knife-thrower.'

'Well, it's possible we shall, for M. Crome de Boile

is here to seek employment. If we find him we might ask him for a demonstration. In the meantime' – Udolphus slammed the file shut – 'I'm hungry. Let's go and find somewhere to eat. Would you be so kind as to give this file to the clerk at the desk over there, Lucci? I must visit the toilet.'

'You're always going to the toilet.'

'Otters do, I'm afraid. It stems from the time when we were water creatures and could go without thinking. The habit is there.'

Over the meal in a nearby restaurant the eager Lucci asked his master whether they were visiting the Guild of Alchemists next: '. . . as you said we would do.'

'I think not, young Lucci. Not yet. There is another place close by which has become important in my mind. I understand they make something called marbled paper in Vequince. I should like to see where it is made and sold. Are you familiar with marbled paper?'

'What a funny way you have of saying things, master,' said Lucci, stuffing lasagne into his mouth. 'I suppose you could say I'm *familiar* with marbled paper. I know where it's made and sold, anyway.'

'Then you shall take me there, immediately after you have devoured that pasta dish. So, the marbled paper shop first, but soon – as soon as possible – we need to visit the prison.'

Lucci almost choked on his pasta. 'The prison?' he croaked.

'Yes, I realize you dislike the place. One should. But

your story about the jill who refused to wear the silver claw has revealed a new thread end in our un-ravellings. We must pick away at it, until it becomes loose. We must apply for permission to visit the prison, for I imagine it's not easy to get inside without the right papers and permits. The dungeons are above the halls where the Council of Ten meet, I understand. They won't let mammals in there without good reason.'

'But the prison, master! Sometimes they never let you out.'

'Oh, visitors? Surely.'

'Sometimes.'

'Well, we shall have to risk it. Now, to the marbled paper.'

Marbled paper was new to Vequince, having come originally from the Far Eastern islands of Jopon, reaching Vequince itself by way of Persha. There was one big factory fronted by an enormous shop which was almost always full of customers. Udolphus and Lucci entered the shop just as one of the staff was explaining to an interested group of clients the technique of marbling paper.

'. . . ordinary paper is normally dipped in water and left pegged up to dry, but we use *gum*. Each sheet of paper is entirely unique. Here you see mortar and pestle for pounding the colours to powder, and the various brushes and combs used to apply the colours. One ingredient, wasp gall, is very important. The second and subsequent colours must carry more wasp gall in them, so as to push the earlier colours aside and float on them . . .'

The water rat droned on. Udolphus had visited many factories and workshops in his time – weavers, carpet makers, foundries – and all were fascinating for the period of the talk, yet if he was asked to recall his knowledge later he found himself entirely at a loss.

'Come, Lucci,' he said, 'let us look at some of the sheets of finished paper.'

The sheets were in some instances very large – as big as living-room carpets. The colours were wonderful, of course, and the unique patterns fascinating to the eye. Udolphus was more interested in recent purchasers though, and he questioned one of the staff about buyers.

'Has anyone bought any vast quantities of your stock lately?'

The store clerk stroked his chin. 'Why, we ship lots of it out every day, to other countries.'

'But local buyers? Anyone locally?'

'Not that I can think of.'

'What about visitors? I suppose visitors buy it to take back with them. Any large quantities in that direction?'

The clerk thought hard and then his face lit up. 'Oh yes, there was one gentlemammal, from the Orient—'

'Still snooping?' interrupted a harsh voice which made Lucci jump. 'What're you doing in here?'

The clerk's eyes had gone pale with fear on seeing the Thieftaker General creep up behind the otter. He drifted away to the far corner of the shop, looking for real customers. The heavy-coated Rotzi di Coporoni stood in front of Udolphus, a snarl on his lips.

'I was thinking,' replied Udolphus in a calm voice, 'of purchasing some marbled paper.'

'For what purpose?' barked the thieftaker.

'A paper chase,' came the smart reply. 'You are familiar with paper chases? It's where the runner leaves a trail which the pack follows. The idea is one of pursuit. The runner is eventually doomed, of course, to be caught by the pursuer. It's simply a matter of *when*. I'm hoping to involve the Fabulous Beast in such a game, since I've been asked by the government to try to solve the mystery of the Beast, while I'm here. I am, after all, a famous unraveller, as you well know. There are not many mysteries which cannot be solved by applying a little intelligence.'

'The Fabulous Beast – they asked you to do that?'

Di Coporoni's eyes narrowed and his wetted fangs dripped angry spittle on the floor. He was intelligent enough to read the implication behind the otter's description of a paper chase. He of course was the 'runner' and Beck the 'pursuer', the trail of paper being the clues which the unraveller picked up.

'I understand the metaphor,' he growled. 'But you may find that in the end, the hunter becomes the hunted.'

'You're brighter than you look, di Coporoni,' snapped back Udolphus.

A claw came out of the sleeve of the coat and pointed into Udolphus's face. 'You, shoemaker, will soon have cause to regret ever coming to Vequince.

Whatever happens, it will be your fault – you understand that? All the responsibility is yours.'

'Is that a threat to my person? I'll have you know I can boast a good friend in a very prominent citizen. Signor Septimi, who lives just beyond the arsenal, will have something to say about this. If anything happens to me, he will certainly go to the government and report it.'

'Will he now?'

'I'm sure of it. We're very close.'

'Well I'm shaking in my shoes.'

'Boots,' murmured Udolphus, looking down. 'Florion-made boots. By the way, where's Signor Pavolo at the moment? Buying paper?'

For the very first time Rotzi di Coporoni looked taken aback. His eyes widened and he whipped round quickly in case anyone had heard the remark. However, he quickly recovered his composure. Quite soon he was hissing into Udolphus's face again: this time the threats were not as veiled.

'I'll see you in the ground, otter. I understand you visited the Isle of the Dead recently. Well, you'll be paying a second visit, but I don't think you'll need a return ticket on the ferry.'

'Well, that's certainly plain enough,' said Udolphus. 'Now if you'll excuse us, we wish to enjoy these premises for what they are, makers of marbled paper.'

Udolphus left the thieftaker staring at his back. Lucci trotted by his side, whispering, 'The Devil is still looking at us . . .'

Udolphus sought out the clerk again. This time he

seemed a little less forthcoming, but Udolphus calmed his fears by saying, 'Did you enjoy that little joke from my friend the Thieftaker General? He has such a wit, does he not? We laugh together all the time.'

'It – it was a joke?'

'Of course,' cried Udolphus, laughing. 'Oh Lord, see how he glares at us from across the room. He takes a joke too far, that one. Rotzi,' Udolphus called, 'you're frightening the staff. Go away, signore, go away. Leave us and buy some new boots, for heaven's sake. Those will get you into trouble if the weather turns nasty, as it surely will. The forecast is bad.'

Di Coporoni frowned at this, glanced down at his feet, then left the shop quickly.

'Such a wag,' said Udolphus, grinning, 'but not a great dresser, I'm afraid. I keep telling him those Florion boots are out of fashion – I'm a shoemaker by trade – but he won't listen. They look well enough to the untrained eye, but the leather's not strong. It wears through too quickly. One day our beloved Thieftaker General is going to find himself in the middle of an *acqua alta* and those boots will let in water. He'll catch cold, which will turn to pneumonia, and he will expire and die – probably painfully – and all because of vanity, vanity, vanity. All because he chose to shop for his footwear in the wrong city.'

The clerk was looking stunned, but at least he remained to answer Udolphus's question.

'Signore,' said the unraveller, 'could you show me a

similar pattern to the paper that was purchased by the foreign gentlemammal of whom you spoke earlier, before my friend Rotzi so rudely interrupted with his poorly timed jest? If you would be so kind?'

The clerk, still in a kind of daze, did as he was asked. 'It's not exactly like the other one, of course,' he said. 'All sheets are different.'

'I understand that,' murmured Udolphus, 'but thank you.'

He examined the paper and then told Lucci they were leaving.

Outside the shop, Lucci said, 'Ha! The clerk said the Orient, didn't he? I know, you think the purchaser was that Banda Rambutan, the insect embalmer. He is from the Orient, isn't he?'

'I do believe he is,' replied Udolphus. 'Ah, here's our lodgings. Oh dear, what's wrong now?'

Signora Nelli was standing on the top of her well-scrubbed step. 'Oh, signore,' she cried, all of a flutter, 'someone's been here.'

Lucci shuddered, clearly thinking that someone was the thieftaker or his uncle Septimi, but Udolphus knew it was neither. Nelli was clearly in transports of delight. She spoke with a quaver in her voice. The *someone* was a mammal who filled her not with loathing or fear, but with awe.

'He left a card,' she said, her trembling claws passing the object to Udolphus, 'after writin' something on the back.'

The card simply read:

```
┌─────────────────────────────────────┐
│                                     │
│   Viporatti                         │
│   Composer of Music                 │
│   1 Campo de Adagio                 │
│   Vequince                          │
│                                     │
└─────────────────────────────────────┘
```

On the back, in perfect copperplate longhand, were the words, *9 o'clock tonight? Dinner followed by a recital. The address is overleaf.*

'I've been invited to Viporatti's for dinner,' murmured Udolphus. 'How gratifying.'

'Yes, I know,' trebled Nelli. 'Just think. Viporatti!'

'Am I going?' asked Lucci, trying to get a look at the card. 'Does it say me too?'

'I'm afraid not, young rat,' replied his master. 'But you'd only be bored anyway, with all the adult talk and the music. I shall give you some money and you can take all your street friends – who was it? – Noccolo, Poggio, Carla and the rest? You can treat them all to a hot meal. How's that?'

'Noccolo is now the Duce's page,' Lucci reminded him, 'but I know the others would love to fill their bellies.'

'Then that's what you shall do while I am otherwise engaged. Fill your bellies, as you so delicately put it. I shall give you enough to fill them to bursting.'

110

'Thank you, master.'

'Think nothing of it, apprentice.'

'Viporatti!' trilled Nelli, determined not to be left out of the excitement. 'The great composer.'

'I wonder if I should wear red, as a sort of compliment – or do I mean complement?' said Udolphus, almost as excited as Nelli. 'That was a joke, you two. You're supposed to laugh. A very sophisticated joke. A very Britannic joke, since it was a play on words. I don't hear you laughing . . .'

They laughed false laughs, just to please him.

At eight-thirty Udolphus set out for the house of Viporatti with a lamp in his paw. When he had dressed that evening he had of course put on his special vest. It was padded with goose-down and was lined with chain mail. He had made the vest himself. It was light to wear, extremely strong and tough enough to stop a bullet penetrating, so long as it was not fired at point-blank range. Udolphus had made quite a few enemies now.

The night was cool and fresh. He walked by the lagoon, then turned in, following the canals to his destination. The horned moon was like a gilded gondola floating on an ocean of darkness. He breathed the sea air, thinking how good it was for his lungs. In the narrow back streets it was quite dark, though there were mammals about, some like him carrying square lamps, the naked flames shielded from the breeze by metal screens. Thin beams of light came from the front of the lamps and these were directed at steps and bridges, and other potential obstacles. Udolphus trod carefully, not only because of the stone and wooden hazards which might be in his path, but also because he was wary of shapes that lurked in the shadows.

If Rotzi di Coporoni is going to get me, he thought, it'll be on a night like tonight.

Udolphus knew that three or four burly water rats could do him a great injury, perhaps even a mortal one. He had in his cloak pocket a flintlock pistol, loaded and ready to fire. The otter was actually a very good shot with such a weapon. He had an unerring eye trained by years of striking nails on their heads. A shoemaker who wastes nails by hitting them wrongly and bending them can soon go out of business. Udolphus had learned from the start to concentrate, focus hard on the bright head of the nail, and strike with precision. He used the same techniques when he shot at a target. He concentrated on the point to which the bullet was to be delivered and squeezed the trigger. The shoemaker could take the spot out of the middle of an ace of oaks from twenty-five paces.

Of course, a pistol only has one shot, and he was not as good with the rapier at his side as some might be. However, he could probably use it well enough to defend himself against common footpads and thugs. A gentlejack practised in the science of fencing might be a different proposition, but why would a gentlejack wish to attack a Geranium otter in the street?

Thankfully, Udolphus had no need of any such skills, for he arrived at Viporatti's house without incident.

A maid took his cloak at the door. 'Signor Viporatti awaits you in the dining room,' she said. 'All the other guests are here.'

He was concerned. 'Oh really? Am I late?'

She smiled. 'No, signor, it's just that Signor Viporatti is *always* impatient when it comes to food. Others know of it. You could not. You are most punctual.'

The second that Udolphus's bottom touched the seat of his chair, Viporatti's fork went into the roasted sparrow on his plate.

'Welcome!' cried the composer. 'Welcome. Welcome. Forgive me for speaking with a full mouth, but I am *famished*.'

There were seventeen guests, who tucked into their meals at the same time as Viporatti. Udolphus was urged to do the same. In true Vequincian style everyone was speaking at once, chattering loudly into the face of their opposite neighbour.

'You must do the same,' said the creature immediately to his left, a water rat in a bright yellow waistcoat embroidered with dandelions. 'Talk, talk, don't listen to anyone else. If you stop to listen, you'll be lost. You'll drown in the words flowing from the mouths of others. You must talk and keep on talking, pausing only to take a bite. That's the way of the Vequincian. No one is saying anything of any importance, anyway, so you won't be missing anything.'

So Udolphus joined in the mêlée, happy to be a Vequincian, an evening of beautiful music to look forward to.

\* \* \*

Out on the streets, the music was of a darker mood.

Lucci, hurrying to meet his friends, took a short cut across a campo where the moonshadows dropped across each other, forming black, fathomless pools. Not being of a superstitious mind, Lucci did not trouble to avoid these lakes of darkness, some of them bordered on two sides by the walls of dank buildings with no visible exits. So it was that while Udolphus was leaning back in a red-satin chair, listening in bliss to the hippopotamus-harpsichord plinking, Lucci was suddenly and viciously attacked. Those splashes of moonshadow did not contain supernatural beings: but disguised in black cloaks and black hats, hidden within the night, were very real and dangerous monsters born of ordinary folk.

# Chapter Seven

Udolphus was left drained and breathless by the passion in Viporatti's final viper-cello solo. The musician was certainly a genius of a very high order. The ex-shoemaker did not have the words to express his emotions, which had been filled to the brim, sapped by the dramatic pauses, then filled again to overflowing. He wanted to laugh, he wanted to cry, he wanted to go somewhere quiet and just sit with his feelings. Such music was surely passed down from angels! Viporatti's creativity came directly from Heaven: it had to. No earthly source could be responsible for such uplifting melodies and such sorrowful tunes, all woven together by the clever claws of a composer the like of which the world had never seen before.

Yet, even while he was lost in the music, Udolphus was working at unravelling the conspiracy to bring down the government. Carnival was approaching and already some of the high society were wearing masks. There was the head of the Spadoria, the Swordsmiths' Guild, who had on the mask of the Tartaglia character. The mask covered half his face, with small eyeholes over which he wore a pair of thick-rimmed spectacles. And one from the Frezzerie, the Arrowsmiths' Guild, with an edited affair of a mask: nothing more than the black eye mask worn by highway robbers. Several of Viporatti's guests were wearing these brief disguises. Secretly Udolphus began inspecting the forepaws of all the water rats around him. He was looking for marks – small cuts on the pads. One of the masked guests, Udolphus noted, was wearing blue satin gloves and the mask covered his whole head. The unraveller found this interesting, as it was anything but cold in the room. In fact, it was quite warm.

'Pavolo,' he murmured to himself, satisfied he was right. 'Covering up the hoary visage and disguising those paper cuts on his paws.'

He kept an eye on Pavolo to see who he spoke to. But Pavolo seemed very sociable and moved about the room, chatting with almost everyone. At one point he passed nearby and murmured under his breath, 'Take warning by tonight's events.' Udolphus was puzzled by this. He wondered if Pavolo were speaking to him or simply muttering to himself.

Udolphus heard the words 'Roma Volecci' and turned to see the elegant noblejack dressed in a silver coat and silver shoes, with a sky-blue waistcoat. His companion was also very expensively dressed, but did not carry his clothes as well. His fashionable coat and breeches looked less imposing on his figure, which was thin and brittle, with sharp elbows and knees.

There was something lacking in Roma's companion – Sparkle? Charisma? Bearing? – something which left him looking more like an accountant's clerk than a noblejack, especially since he was wearing grey.

'Who is that with the one called Signor Roma Volecci?' asked Udolphus of another guest. 'The fellow in the dull clothes?'

The guest, another lean water rat, stepped languidly away from Udolphus and looked him up and down with a lorgnette. He peered hard at him through the gold-rimmed lenses, wearing a pinched expression, as if to say, *Who are you calling dull, you provincially clothed otter?*

'The rat with the nasty sore on his neck? That is Signor Chapaquida, another member of the Council of Ten.'

'Ah. That's why they're together?'

'Oh,' said the lorgnette wielder, 'are they together? No, they're just passing a few words, as civil guests are wont to do. Then moving on, see? Now I must do the same, or everyone will think *we're* together . . .' He drifted off, mouthing the words, 'Perish the thought.'

Roma came over to Udolphus, but all he said was, 'Ah, a visitor to our city. Such a profound face. Welcome, signore. Have a wonderful stay and don't forget to enjoy Carnival.'

He then moved on to be polite somewhere else in the room, pausing to speak to a beautiful jill wearing a voluminous dress which would have provided enough sailcloth for a thousand galleons, should the merchant marines ever need them.

117

'Magnificent,' Udolphus murmured to his host when Viporatti had finished playing. 'Simply wonderful.'

'Not a bad bit of ravelling, eh?' cried Viporatti, delighted with himself and with the compliments. 'I'll wager even you would have trouble untangling that one, Herr Beck.'

'I would not wish to – it was perfect.'

The red composer let out a tinkling laugh. Tonight he was wearing a crimson velada with a dun waistcoat. The buttons on the waistcoat were black toggles in the shapes of musical notes. His breeches matched the colour of his coat and his stockings followed his waistcoat. On his head he wore a wig fashioned from the mane of a palomino horse of a golden-white that hurt the eyes with its sheen. At the back of the clubbed wig sat a huge floppy satin bow. His whiskers had been dyed the same hue as his velada. There was nothing inconspicuous about the Red Rat of Vequince. Viporatti leaned over the chair on which his guest was sitting and whispered, 'So, how is your unravelling going? Have you been lurking in our secret gardens, in our walled courtyards? Are you meeting with success?'

'Somewhat, somewhat,' replied Udolphus, aware of the other guests in the room. None seemed to be listening, but he did not want to draw attention to himself. Unlike the composer, of course, Udolphus was a pleasantly brown mammal, mellow and easy on the eyes. So far he had hardly been noticed and that was the way he liked it. 'Things are developing.'

'Good. Good. I hope you're successful. I wish this city rid of plots, intrigues and conspiracies.' Then in a louder voice, Viporatti cried, 'Come, Herr Beck, meet Count Crome de Boile. The count is as talented with knives as I am with music. Monsieur de Boile is an otter like yourself, though from the regions of Gaul.'

The count, a taller otter than Udolphus, was 'enchanted' to meet the world's greatest unraveller.

'I wish my apprentice were here,' said Udolphus. 'He showed a desire to see your artistry.'

'Why,' cried the count, 'I shall give you a performance and you can recount it to him!'

'Bravo!' said Viporatti, as excited as Lucci would have been. 'Never mind any damage. Pick a guest and let us see you miss him by the thickness of a shadow . . .'

'There's one there,' murmured Udolphus, seeing that the masked Pavolo was leaving and was almost at the door. 'I'm sure he won't mind.'

De Boile whipped open his coat to reveal a dozen throwing knives in a belt on his waist.

'Hi!' he yelled, to attract Pavolo's attention. 'Stand very still, signore. Very very still. We are about to perform together.'

Pavolo, his claw on the door knob, turned. The eyes behind the mask opened wide as the first knife flew towards him and missed him by a fraction, sticking in a door panel above his head. Before he could recover, more knives came thick and fast to thud into the woodwork around him, each blade flashing through the air and, indeed, missing him by the thickness of a shadow. He was left trembling and shaken, as de Boile took his bow and everyone else in the room burst into applause.

Pavolo squealed, 'You – you *idiot*.'

A silence followed, and then murmurs of, 'Shame. Shame.'

Roma Volecci called out, 'Signore, you forget yourself. Where are your manners? It was only a performance. You were in no danger.'

But by this time Pavolo had opened the door, still bristling with knives, and left.

The count recovered his knives and someone put an ace of oak-leaves on the door and challenged the knife-thrower to 'hit the pip'. Indeed, de Boile tried, but failed every time. Udolphus was not as astonished as the rest of the guests and it was he who explained it to them.

'The count,' he said, 'has trained all his life to *miss* things, not to hit them.' De Boile acknowledged this with a little bow towards Udolphus, who realized he could cross the count off his list. A knife-thrower who was adept at missing things but hopeless at hitting them, was hardly a good assassin.

A tall grandfather clock chimed with enchanting notes from the corner of the room, gently reminding everyone that it was now midnight.

'Good heavens,' said a fat water rat to their right, taking out his pocket watch and looking at it. 'Is that the time?'

'Admiral, why do you do that?' sighed Viporatti. 'Do you not trust my clocks? Listen, every clock in the house is chiming. Yet you whip out your watch as if that's the only true record of time in the whole world.'

'I do beg your pardon, Signor Viporatti,' replied the abashed guest. 'It was purely habit.' His voice fell to a hushed whisper. 'This is a chronometer, you know, accurate to a thousandth of a second. You will not find another like it until you reach the shores of Britannica. With this watch you may find your latitude and longitude. Please forgive me.'

'I forgive you. Or I will, if you will consider giving Herr Beck here a lift home in your sedan chair,' said Viporatti, smiling. 'One of my servants has said that it's raining out.'

'Oh, dirty weather, eh? I should be delighted. Herr Beck? I am Admiral Grossa Belli, at your service.' The admiral gave him a curt bow. 'I have the honour to be in charge of the Vequincian navy.'

The admiral was dressed in several shades of yellow, which tended to disguise his corpulence to a certain degree.

'I do believe I shall have to embark very soon, if that's convenient?'

'Most certainly,' answered Udolphus. 'I shall just get my hat and cloak.'

Before long they had both said their farewells to the composer and thanked him for a most educating and entertaining evening. Four very damp but burly jack tars lifted the sedan chair, casting wicked looks at Udolphus, who was aware that his extra weight had annoyed them. Inside the chair it was a little squashed, but was certainly drier than walking through the streets. It was a two-seater sedan it was true, for the admiral liked female company, being happily unmarried. But there was no doubting he was a big fellow. His hips, he had been told by one of his companions, had more blubber on them than a blue whale. Udolphus himself was as lean as a nomadic lurcher, but he found himself squeezed hard into the side of the box.

The sailors trotted through the rain-lashed streets and back alleys, thoroughly familiar with the city and its byways. When they reached Udolphus's lodgings, however, they stumbled, almost tipping out the admiral and his passenger.

'Clumsy lubbers!' roared the admiral in the penetrating voice that had terrorized sailors since he had been a captain. 'Have we hit a shoal?'

'Sorry, sir,' cried the carrier on the starboard bow. 'We'm tripped on some flotsam.'

Udolphus poked his head out of the small window. Rainwater was trickling off the sailor who spoke. This flowed down into Udolphus's tricorn hat and was funnelled by the curled brim onto a complaining yellow admiral behind him.

'Do you mind, signore? Bring your head back inside.'

'What sort of flotsam?' asked Udolphus, ignoring the complaints from his companion. He looked down and saw a body lying on the rain-soaked paving slabs outside Nelli's house. 'Good Lord! Someone's hurt.'

Udolphus opened the door to the sedan chair, but Admiral Grossa Belli put a claw on his forelimb. 'I would leave him alone, if I were you, signore,' he murmured, looking towards the shadows. 'We have no way of knowing if this was the work of buccaneers. They might still be around, waiting to pounce.'

'We can't abandon someone, just because we're afraid of who might be around,' cried Udolphus. 'In any case, we have four strapping mariners here to help protect us.'

'That's true,' said the admiral, looking dubiously at his sailors, as if he suspected they would run off at the first sign of violence. 'Off you go then, inspect the body. I think he's dead, whoever it is. He's certainly not moving. I'll wager my hat he's been beaten to a pulp.'

The figure on the ground had certainly been hit repeatedly with cudgels, for there were lumps on his head and shoulders. Udolphus turned him over gently, under the uninterested eyes of the admiral's crew. Then one of the sailors cried in an indignant tone of voice, 'Why, it's only a young 'un. Not much older than a cabin jack, by the look—'

Udolphus gasped. 'It's Lucci, my apprentice.' He looked back towards the alley and saw a thin trail of blood being washed away by the rain. 'He's been dragged here and dumped. How could anyone do this to a youngster? How could they?' Udolphus's anguish came straight from the heart as he cradled Lucci's head in his paws.

'Perhaps we should ask *why*?' said the admiral, looking over his shoulder.

Udolphus ground his sharp otter's teeth together. 'I know why, signore. This was done as a warning to me. If it had been robbers, they would have left him lying where he fell. But they dragged him here. They knew where he lived and they brought him here so that I should find him. This is the work of Rotzi di Coporoni's thieftakers.'

Lucci spluttered. The unraveller quickly reached into the mouth of the unconscious Lucci and made sure his tongue had not rolled back in his throat, where it might choke him. Then he felt for a pulse. Lucci's fur and the skin beneath were cold as death. Udolphus groaned. Yet, after a few seconds his claws detected a very faint beating. Yes, there was the pulse! Lucci was not dead! But the youngster was far from certain recovery.

'Is there an infirmary near here?' asked Udolphus of the admiral. 'Can we get him to a doctor quickly?'

'There'll be a physician on duty tonight in my flagship,' said the admiral, climbing out of the sedan. 'These tars know where he is. Lift him gently now, you rough salts, and place him carefully in the chair. Carry him quickly to my ship. We shall follow on foot at a lively pace. Go to it! Use all possible sail.'

The sailors did as they were told, setting off at a fast trot.

Udolphus and his companion came up behind, though the yellow admiral was of a slower nature than the unraveller, who tried not to be impatient with him. After all, he thought, Lucci was in good paws now. There was not a great deal he could do, if it were he at the young rat's side.

Eventually they passed through the dock gates and reached the moored vessel. A marine sentry at the gangplank hailed them, asking for the password, but a grimly silent admiral merely swept him and his musket aside. Udolphus, not quite so certain of not being shot in back, followed the admiral closely, down into the depths of the ship. There below they found Lucci in the sick bay with a physician hovering over him. Lucci's back was covered in wine glasses, drawing out the bad humours.

'Is he gravely hurt?' whispered Udolphus fearfully. 'Will he live?'

The physician looked up. He had a jar of leeches in his claws and one of the creatures was attempting escape over the lip. The physician flicked the squirming thing back in again to join its fellows. 'If he makes it through the night, he has a good chance,' he said. 'I've given him some strong medicine. He needs someone to stand watch, change his dressings and put salve on his wounds. Is there anyone who can do that?'

'I shall stand watch,' said Udolphus. 'Give me a short while and I can fetch someone else, in case I fall asleep. I'm sure our landlady, Signora Nelli, would be more than willing to assist me. She is quite fond of the youth. Ah, you are removing the glasses. That's good. Well, I'll be back in a short while.'

'No need for you to go, Herr Beck. I'll send a cabin jack for her,' said the admiral, leaving the sick bay.

He came back in a few moments. 'It's been done.'

Now that Lucci was in good paws Udolphus's anger spilled over. 'I'll never be able to prove that di Coporoni is responsible for this of course. He's as slippery and slimy as a Vequincian flatfish.' His voice rose. 'One these days though, I'll have his pelt for shoe leather, you see if I don't.'

As he shouted the words the other mammals present looked at each other, slightly embarrassed by the outburst, but full of understanding for the unraveller's rage. The thieftaker was universally disliked, but also feared, even by grand admirals. His cankered claws reached right into the heart of high society. There were always those in power who protected such creatures as di Coporoni for their own selfish reasons.

Udolphus's attention once more went to the plight of his poor apprentice.

The admiral reassured him. 'Our physicians are quite used to dealing with injuries, y'know. Sailors fall from the rigging, from the sparrow's nest, or get badly knocked about in sea battles. Or if they're thieves they might get a hundred lashes for stealing cheese. You know how it is. Rest assured, the physician knows what he's doing. If we'd come to him with a maiden and her female complaints, he'd have been all at sea of course, but batterings, cuts and bruisings he copes with on an everyday basis.'

'I'm not much good at delivering babies,' admitted the physician, lifting Lucci's head carefully to stitch up a huge gash above his eye, then replacing it on the pillow, 'but thumped-about bodies are my stock in trade.'

Nelli duly arrived, looking shocked. 'Oh, Lordy,' she cried, taking off her shawl and stroking Lucci's brow. 'Oh, the poor little darling. They've broken him to bits and you've sewed him back together again . . .'

Lucci's jaw was twisted and his head was as thick as hill country with lumps. One of his eyes was swollen and closed, puffed with blood; there were gashes and cuts on his forelimbs and shoulders; a front fang was missing, blood still seeping from the hole it had left, and part of his left ear had been bitten off.

The admiral felt his work had been done and retired for the night.

The physician had other patients to attend to – mostly drunken rats who had missed the gangplank and stepped out into the space between ship and harbour wall, thus ending up in the greasy waters below.

Udolphus and Nelli took turns to watch Lucci, who was now moaning a little in his delirious state.

'At least he's speakin',' said Nelli to herself. 'At least the poor waif's still got life enough for that.'

It was a fraught eight hours, but the following morning Lucci's eyes opened and he gave his watchers a faint smile. He still had a fever and was obviously in great pain. At about that time Udolphus dispatched a note. He told the runner, a sailor, to take it to the nearest apothecary. In it Udolphus explained what had happened. *It is not the injuries themselves, so*

127

*much*, he had written, *but the state of the patient's nerves and the shock to his system. I am afraid of infections and respiratory diseases setting in. Could you please provide us with a consumption draught or cough specific?*

At eight-thirty, however, Udolphus was a little taken aback when a compassionate Sophia arrived with powders and medicines.

'You? I had not realized,' he said suspiciously, 'that the closest apothecary was your grandmother, Signora Dropsi. I'm afraid if I had known I might have applied elsewhere.'

'And I had not realized,' said the young jill, 'that otters could be so ill-mannered as to reject help when it arrives.'

'I'm sorry. I'm afraid I trust no one at the moment. My dear apprentice is lying at death's door and someone put him there. For all I know your grandmother may be involved.'

'I am not interested in what you may or may not know, Herr Beck, I'm interested in getting a sick young jack back to health. Please, may I see him?'

Udolphus overcame his reservations and took the jill into the sick bay. Her large brown eyes beheld the battered Lucci and moistened. Lucci, ill though he was, deeply appreciated this personal visit from the apothecary's grandjill. In fact, he could not believe his luck. If anyone were to ask him at that moment, he might even have said that being attacked was worth it, to have at his sickbed the most beautiful water rat in the whole of Vequince. He even managed to raise his head off his pillow, to receive a spoon brimming with cough specific, his eyes never leaving her face.

Udolphus was now regretting his earlier suspicions regarding Sophia, though he still had his doubts about her grandmother.

'I apologize for my outburst, signorina. I must thank you for coming,' murmured Udolphus to Sophia. 'Your presence is probably the best medicine he could have.'

She looked a little worried at this, but Nelli said to her, 'Don't concern yourself, signorina – all you have to do is throw him a little smile now and then, and he will be as happy as a sand rat.'

At noon Udolphus felt he could return to his lodgings to bathe and change his clothes. Lucci was in good paws, since Sophia insisted on remaining at his bedside. When the apprentice attempted to get up, saying he wanted to go home with his master, Sophia took firm charge.

'You will remain where you are until you're told you're well enough to leave,' she said, her chin thrust forward. 'No arguments, now. I'm the nurse and you're the patient. You'll do as you're told.'

And this he did, with only a faint murmur of protest.

A succession of visitors came to see Udolphus at his lodgings that morning:

Admiral Grossa Belli in full dress uniform came by, to ask how the patient was faring.

A distraught, highly emotional Viporatti was upset that such a thing could happen to the apprentice of one of his guests. 'If things go on,' he whispered to Udolphus, 'we shall have to begin turning our violin strings into bowstrings.'

One or two of the other guests from the night before dropped by. In fact the roll call of visitors was very impressive, considering Udolphus was but a visitor to the island and the injured youth had recently been but a street urchin. Even Botcchio, he of the precious golden lungs, came with his two bodyguards in tow to express regret at the incident.

At three o'clock Lucci's uncle Septimi arrived, not because he had heard Lucci was sick, but to remonstrate with Udolphus. 'Di Coporoni's thugs called at my house!' he cried. 'They hammered on the door and demanded entrance. I only escaped injury because they thought I was not at home. Call off your cousin, otter. I have a bank draft here. It is the money Lucci's father left him. Tell the youth I wish never to see him again. Here is an end to the affair.'

Septimi placed an envelope on the table.

'I would like to hear that you are ashamed of yourself for trying to swindle your own nephew,' said Udolphus. 'The poor young jack has been on the streets since his parents passed away. You're a disgrace, signore. You would disgust anyone with any feelings of family duty and honour. However, I don't suppose I'll ever get you to admit it, so begone!'

Septimi scuttled away, his head bowed.

The final visitor was an expected one. Udolphus heard Rotzi di Coporoni's quiet, threatening voice, as he entered the house. Nelli had also returned from the ship. Her tentative replies told Udolphus that the thieftaker was in his usual intimidating mood. On hearing the footsteps on the stairs, Udolphus calmly took his pistol out of his cloak pocket and aimed it. When the rap came on the door he fired.

Udolphus was only really calm on the outside. His terrible simmering anger at di Coporoni for hurting his assistant was ready to boil over, or he would never have pulled the trigger. The shot went through the woodwork at about head height, but to the left of where the creature knocking would be standing. It left a neat hole in the door.

Udolphus opened the door now to reveal a shocked and furious Thieftaker General. There were yellow splinters of wood on di Coporoni's left shoulder. His clenched fist was still up, frozen in the motion of knocking. The other paw was on the hilt of a sword he was wearing. Udolphus had not seen the thieftaker carrying a rapier before now. He realized this dangerous rat was now feeling very threatened.

'Oh, I'm sorry,' said Udolphus, hardly able to keep the satisfaction out of his tone, brushing the splinters from the thieftaker's coat with a considerate paw. 'I was expecting someone else.'

'Who?' snarled di Coporoni.

'A burglar. I thought it was a burglar.'

'You were *expecting* a thief? You think I believe that?'

'There are robbers everywhere you look,' said Udolphus, mildly. 'One can never be too careful.'

Under the smouldering gaze of his visitor Udolphus

131

reloaded his pistol. 'Now, what was it you wished to see me about?' he asked, raising his brow. 'Actually, I was coming to see *you*. Someone tried to injure my apprentice last night. I understand you are responsible for law and order in the city. I would like you to find the perpetrators.'

'That's why I came. I heard about it too. I was going to suggest you get out of the city – take your apprentice with you if you like – it's becoming a little wild for Geranium shoemakers in Vequince.'

'Oh, I can't go now. Not when I'm so close to solving a mystery. Besides, there's no real harm done. Lucci was only a little hurt.'

It was di Coporoni's turn to raise his brow and frown. 'Only – a little? I heard he was almost killed.'

Udolphus laughed, not willing to give di Coporoni the satisfaction of knowing how horribly injured Lucci was. 'No, no. Nothing of the sort. Of course he faked being badly hurt, to mislead the footpads who attacked him. But once they had gone he got to his feet, brushed himself off and came home. He's not right as rain, of course. He has a scratch on his nose and his pelt was dirtied, but considering what could have happened—'

'A scratch on his nose?' muttered the thieftaker. 'A dirty pelt?'

'I'm afraid so. But still, the attack is a serious reflection of the lawlessness of your streets, thieftaker. Please do something about it, or I may have to send for you again.'

Di Coporoni growled, 'Send for me?'

Udolphus looked down the barrel of his pistol, as if making sure it was aligned correctly. 'Yes. You may go now.'

'I may go, may I? Listen, otter, get out of this city or you'll surely regret it. I can't be everywhere. I can't protect *everyone*. You may have made some friends while you've been here, but they can't help you when you're dead. Accidents happen all the time. The canals are dangerous.' He nodded darkly. 'And be careful with that firearm in future. If you'd been a better shot I'd be lying on my back and you'd be on your way to the gallows for murder. Leave the handling of weapons to experts.'

In the mirror by the door Udolphus could see a fly crawling up the wall above the velvet-padded chair behind him. He whirled round and, with one smooth movement, raised his forelimb, aimed and fired. He hit the fly so accurately it vanished into the bullet hole, driven there by the musketball itself. The ex-shoemaker then turned back and blew away the acrid smoke from the muzzle of his pistol. He stared di Coporoni in the face.

'I am a dead shot, signore. What they call in the army a *sharpshooter*. You may rest assured the pistol *is* in the claws of an expert.'

Di Coporoni's jaw had fallen open. Aware that he was again being mocked by the otter, uncontrollable rage finally overcame the thieftaker. In the next second a rapier had appeared in his claws. His intention was certainly to kill this upstart shoemaker: the silver blade flashed out at Udolphus's throat. But

133

the otter was quicker, sidestepping the thrust. Udolphus reversed the pistol in his paw so that he held it by the barrel like a hammer. There is nothing so deadly in the claws of an ex-shoemaker as a hammer. Udolphus had used one of these tools all his life. Its balance was so familiar, so easy in his claws, it was a terrible weapon.

He parried the rat's next thrust with the curved butt of the pistol, spun the rapier in his attacker's claws, and finally hooked it from his grasp. The sword flew across the room. Within a second the tall otter was on the rat's chest, driving him down to the floorboards. Udolphus's weight broke some of the glass daggers hidden in the lining of the thieftaker's coat. In another moment Udolphus's left claws were holding the thieftaker by the throat, the pistol-hammer raised high in the right. With one blow the ex-shoemaker could have brained di Coporoni, there and then.

'Beg my pardon!' snarled Udolphus, his rage finally spilling over. 'Beg my pardon or you die!'

The choking di Coporoni's eyes opened very wide.

'NOW!' threatened Udolphus. 'NOW!'

'I – I – I beg your pardon,' croaked the thieftaker.

Udolphus got off his adversary and calmed down.

Rotzi di Coporoni sat up, massaging his throat. Blood was seeping through his coat where the broken glass spikes had pierced his pelt. Finally he got to his feet.

'Do excuse me,' said Udolphus, genuinely appalled at his own behaviour. 'I lost my temper. I try never to lose my temper, for it is a terrible one with terrible consequences. Unforgivable.'

The thieftaker said nothing. He bent down, picked up his tricorn hat and jammed it on his head. Still coughing a little, he walked off along the landing and down the stairs. Udolphus heard the front door slam. The sword was still lying on the floor by the couch. He went and picked it up, propping it in the corner of the room.

Udolphus shook his head as he began to cool down. 'Unforgivable. I must watch that temper of mine. It'll get me into serious trouble one of these days. Now, I should go and apologize to Signora Nelli. Ah, there you are, Nelli,' he said, seeing her coming up the stairs. 'Do forgive me for those loud bangs. My pistol accidentally went off. I shall pay for any damage of course and ask your indulgence for inconveniencing you. The general has gone. He suddenly remembered an urgent appointment.'

Nelli stared at the hole in Udolphus's door. 'Did it hit him?' she asked.

'Missed, by a fraction.'

'Damn and blast those fractions,' she said. 'I never liked them since I had them at school. Never mind, better luck next time.'

She descended the stairs, leaving Udolphus staring after her with a grim smile on his features.

Udolphus felt he had won that round. There was no point in letting di Coporoni think he had hurt Lucci badly. Better to let him believe his ruffians failed. Better to let him go back to wherever he lurked during the hours when he was not bothering Udolphus to swear at his underlings. Of course, he would be back. That was even more certain now Udolphus had made a fool of the rat; now that he had been humiliated, the insecure di Coporoni was more dangerous than ever. Udolphus, and indeed anyone who called himself his friend, would have to watch his back even more closely now.

In a quiet moment Udolphus wrote in his notebook:

> These I believe to be involved in the plot: Pavolo, who uses Rotzi di Coporoni to do his dirty work. One or more of the following: Malacite, Dropsi, Botcchio. Some further creature or creatures actually within the government. More than likely the visitor from Jopon, who may or may not be aware that he is being used in a conspiracy to bring down the government of Vequince.

# Chapter Eight

It was Carnival and Udolphus was aware that a kind of quiet anarchy had settled on the city. During Carnival there was an unspoken rule that the law was not strictly enforced. It seemed to Udolphus that Vequince had become something more than its normal self. It was jolly, of course – carnivals usually are – but there was also an underlying note of wickedness. The streets were dangerous, with so many mammals who could not be recognized. Udolphus realized that once ordinary citizens put on masks, their personalities changed. They felt they could now do things which would normally worry them and horrify their neighbours. They lost their inhibitions. They were anonymous, and the darker side of their souls could emerge without fear of retribution. They lost all sense of propriety. Good manners went by the board. Social niceties were forgotten.

Of course, real criminals used this anonymous time to settle scores and rob the population where they could.

However, the good and normally staid Udolphus

enjoyed dressing up as much as anyone. His disguise consisted of the white Bauta mask made of lace, with attached veils that wrapped around his neck, a three-cornered black hat and a black cloak. He felt very sinister in this outfit. When he stepped out into the streets, he found that Vequince had become a place of gold, white, black and silver; haunted by ghosts of its own inhabitants who had lost their identities – perhaps even their very selves – in weird costumes.

'Ow! You startled me,' he cried, as he turned a corner and a clown figure all in white, with a painted white face, stepped away from a white building, seeming to emerge from the very stonework itself. 'I didn't see you there!'

The figure passed by him, silent and unsmiling.

'Manners!' called a prim Udolphus, after him. 'A "good morning, signore" would have been nice.'

'It's not usual to smile or to speak,' said another figure, suddenly at his side. 'It's part of the culture of the thing. One is a fantasy figure, divorced from the real world.'

Once again, Udolphus jumped. 'Who are you?'

'Today I am Mattaccino the jester,' said the masked mammal, a creature wearing a striped top with a ruff collar, red breeches and a white apron full of eggs. 'Today I play the eggs. Tomorrow I might be Scaramuccia, the day after, Cocalino or one of the other carnival characters. But rest assured, what I am not, *who* I am not, is myself.'

'And what, pray, is *playing the eggs*?'

'Watch!'

There were tall swaying figures in the campo: masked characters on high stilts. Every so often these stilted characters leaned artlessly against a wall and, since they were as high as the second-storey balconies, they poked their heads in through windows and chortled at those inhabitants still in their beds. One was doing it now, not far away from Udolphus and Mattaccino. Those in the house yelled at their tormentor to leave them alone, but this only encouraged the stilted character.

'Cock-a-doodle-doo!' he crowed. 'Time to get up! Off with those nightshirts. Cock-a-doodle-doo! Cock-a-doodle-doo!'

Mattaccino took a slingshot from his belt and put an egg in it. 'The shell has been blown and filled with dirty water,' he explained. 'No harm will be done.'

He swung the sling rapidly round his head and let fly. The water-filled eggshell flew through the air and struck the stilted character squarely on the back of the head. Dirty washing-up water ran down his neck. This caused him to spin round and almost topple over like a felled tree into the courtyard of the campo. He shook his fist at Mattaccino, who giggled and said excitedly, 'Quickly, we must run!' and grabbed Udolphus's sleeve, dragging him down a side alley.

Before long the unraveller found himself in the Piazza San Arvicola, outside the Café Flavorsum. Here were seated a great many jacks and jills in marvellous costumes. Some were dressed as giant birds, some as Harlequin and other such characters from the Commedia dell'Arte: Magnifico Pantalone and the hook-nosed Pulcinella. The costumes were rich and splendid, all with masks. Such gaiety and colour, such outrageous dress, heated the blood with excitement. Outside in the square more masked stilters raced about, eating their meals on high, bestriding canals and causing great havoc.

'Botcchio and his maskmakers must be coining in the money,' said Udolphus to his companion, whose voice he had now recognized. 'Everywhere one looks there are mammals in masks.'

His companion chuckled at this and nodded as if amused.

'So, do we drink hot chocolate?' asked Udolphus, sitting at one of the tables in the square. 'Will you join me?'

'Most certainly,' said the other. 'Yes, yes, hot chocolate.'

'You seem out of breath, signore.'

'It was our rapid escape from the stilted one. Ha! I hit him right on the bean, didn't I? Always was a good shot, even as a young jack.'

'Then I take it you are now an *old* jack,' said Udolphus.

A sturdy figure passed by their table. It took only a cursory appraisal to guess that this was none other than the maskmaker Botcchio himself, taking advantage of anonymity to roam the streets without his bodyguards. Even though he was wearing a golden mask Udolphus recognized the wheezing and the lumbering walk of a rat almost too heavy for his own bones to support. How those bones must press into each other! thought Udolphus. What constant pain he must have to bear.

Botcchio sat down at the end of a row of tables.

Udolphus was suddenly aware he was being spoken to by his companion.

'Older, anyway,' Mattaccino said, laughing and trying to attract one of the harassed waiters. 'Not ancient, though. How do you like our carnival, signore? Forgive me, you are surely a visitor, for you seem all at sea! You must be looking forward to the Feast of the Mardi Gras, here on the piazzetta, and you must not miss the Flight of the Angel. That is performed by an acrobat, who zooms from the top of the campanile to the Duce's Palace on a rope stretched between the two, carrying a bunch of flowers for the Duce himself.'

'Sounds exciting.'

Mattaccino leaned forward and whispered, 'As a visitor to our beautiful but dangerous city, you must be careful, signore, during Carnival. Murders may be more easily committed. Our enemies go under disguise, do they not? You must beware of any who approach you. You are too naïve, too trusting. For instance, what if I were an assassin?'

'I know who you are, signore, even though you are attempting to put inflexions in your voice in order to try to sound like Signor Viporatti. You say you know who I am. How is that? Did you follow me from my house this morning, for this cannot be a chance meeting.'

'I did, but there are other signs. For instance, you

are too tall for a mouse, too lean for an elephant.'

Udolphus could have kicked himself. There *were* polecats and pine martens and others of his height in the city, but very few. Here he was, walking around like a masked flagpole in the mistaken belief that he could not be recognized. Of course anyone wishing to do him harm could make an intelligent guess that he was Udolphus Beck, the otter from Geranium, the sworn foe of Rotzi di Coporoni, Septimi and those plotters who wished to bring down the government of Vequince.

'I am rather foolish, am I not?'

His companion shrugged and did not disabuse him of the fact, saying, 'You are entitled to be foolish at Carnival. It ferments a little madness in the minds of many. Look at me! A highly respected member of society, a judge and politician, throwing eggs at other citizens!'

The characters of Brighella and the Captain walked past the table, arrogant, haughty, sneering at everyone in the room.

'I will be very careful,' said Udolphus.

'You must treat *everyone* with suspicion,' warned Roma Volecci – for it was he – placing his precious eggs in a bowl for safekeeping. 'There are many Mattaccinos around. You could easily make a mistake and walk right up to a Mattaccino with acid-filled eggs and murderous intent.'

A character in a dark-red costume drifted across the square like a demon escaped from Hell. The Red Slayer?

'I suppose you wish to know where we are, with regards to unravelling the plot?'

'Since we are incognito we must take advantage of the situation.'

Udolphus quietly brought his companion up to date with his findings. Roma kept nodding as Udolphus passed on the information in a soft voice. When Udolphus had finished, Roma thanked him but made no further comment on the discoveries. They then both turned to more mundane subjects, knowing that they might be under scrutiny from hostile eyes.

As their chocolate finally arrived, a wheelbarrow race was going on in the square. Udolphus thought how much Lucci would have enjoyed it. The otter had left him that morning, now restored to his little room in Nelli's house, bemoaning the fact that he could not get up and join in the fun. He was still in a poorly condition.

'So,' said Roma, 'you guessed who I was from my voice, yet I tried to disguise it. I tried to pretend I was Viporatti. I believe I copied his tone and mannerisms quite accurately. How did you guess I was not he?'

'Because – and I hope you won't take this as an insult – you do not have his grand style. Let's be honest, Signor Viporatti is a dandy, a beau of the first order. He is flamboyant and extravagant in his gestures; his fur and tail styles are copied, even in such faraway places as Geranium. Viporatti sets the tone for fashion: whatever style he wears the twittering macaronis – those empty-headed water rats with more money than sense – soon adopt. He is quick-witted, sharp and sometimes even vicious in his retorts. He's able to carry all this off, not because he's a genius, but because of his effervescent personality. Anyone else would be shunned for it. You, signore, could not be a Viporatti, not in a thousand years. It's not your present garment which makes this announcement, of course, but your air of good sense. Your steady demeanour.'

The other laughed, then said, 'What about di Coporoni? What if I were really di Coporoni pretending to be Viporatti?'

Udolphus reached out and squeezed one of Roma's biceps. 'Not enough meat on you, signore, I'm afraid.'

'Surely then it was not just my voice? There must have been other clues.'

'You were too familiar with me when we met in the street this morning. You also have a gesture of which you may or may not be aware – you have a habit of flicking three claws out to emphasize a point. I noticed it the other evening and you have used it several times today. You also click your tongue when you ask a question, as if adding a punctuation mark to your sentence. Finally' – Udolphus lifted the tablecloth and pointed down at Roma's feet – 'you are wearing the same shoes.'

Two creatures in green costumes passed by them, and just as they sat at their table Roma Volecci let out a wild laugh. The two figures turned and glared from behind their emerald masks, no doubt thinking they were the object of his fun. They were not, of course, for he was laughing at Udolphus's powers of detection.

'Ha! It was just the shoes, was it not?'

'No,' replied Udolphus, 'it was all the other things I mentioned too – after all, someone could have borrowed your shoes.'

'True. True. Amazing. You, signore, are as much a genius as is Viporatti, in your own field.'

At that moment the pair were distracted by a commotion in the far corner of the square, under the gaze of the basilica. Two gangs of masked youths had swaggered into the piazza and had immediately begun a fight, using swords, claws and teeth. Both groups were disguised as grotesque birds: one gang were clearly thrushes, the other, stonechats. The brawl, witnessed by a thousand carnival-goers, but interrupted by none, spilled over towards the Café Flavorsum. One young water rat went down and others, from the rival gang, began beating him with the flats of their swords. Even when he squealed for mercy, they did not let up. Then his own supporters rushed in and rescued him from further harm.

Finally, one of the gangs started to retreat. It was the thrushes who ran off towards the harbour, followed by howling stonechats waving weapons. God help it, thought Udolphus, if one of the thrushes trips and falls. Their pursuers were in a mad, wild, bloodthirsty frame of mind, and they might kill their victim without stopping to think of the consequences.

'What,' he said, 'was all that about?'

'The apprentices,' sighed Roma Volecci. 'The guild apprentices. Those stonechats are maskmakers. The thrushes are apothecaries. There are others: the alchemists are owls and the glassblowers, cuckoos. When they meet during Carnival they do battle. It's traditional that every new apprentice must join with his fellows – a sort of initiation rite to secret cults within the guilds. The Council of Ten – well, we've tried to stamp it out, but the tradition runs deep. You must be very careful not to intervene. Those apprentices will throw you into the canal along with their captured rivals, rather than brook any interference in their wild brawls. It's the usual way of dealing with their prisoners, to tie them up and toss them into the nearest canal. Best to stay out of it and leave them to it. They don't bother ordinary citizens, not usually, unless they step in and try to stop them.'

'But surely some of them are seriously hurt?'

'There's always a death. Always. One year we had four. It leaves bitter parents, but the guilds encourage it – don't ask me why. And by the way, if you hear a knock on your door at night, make sure you know who it is before opening. These apprentices go round slitting noses with their daggers. You open the door, innocently push out your nose to see who it is, and you get it slit from top to tip with a razor-sharp knife.'

After this grisly description Udolphus decided it was time they were leaving. It was getting rather crowded in the café and they might be overheard. 'Walk with me on the promenade?'

'Certainly.'

Roma Volecci rose. Udolphus followed.

As they passed the maskmaker Botcchio's table, Udolphus leaned down and whispered, 'Batiloro.'

Botcchio jerked upright. A *batiloro* was a beater of gold leaf for masks or picture frames. The maskmaker knew he had been recognized. Botcchio quickly got up from his table and made his way out of the square.

Soon the pair were strolling along a cool, windy promenade. Udolphus kept his eyes about him for any signs of danger. He did not for one second think that just because he was masked and out with another citizen that animosity towards him had relaxed. He felt sure the conspirators were just waiting their chance to either cut him down, or perhaps implicate him in something illegal, in order to have him deported.

Out on the lagoon citizens were flying kites from boats. Kite-flying was a popular pastime in the city parks and over stretches of water. Some of the elaborately fashioned kites were stringless, launched from crossbows. The flyers were very accurate with these kites and could shoot them from boats and land them at a companion's feet on the quay. One such kite, a model of a gull, came flying over the surface of the green lagoon and Udolphus had to duck to avoid being struck on the head.

He waved to the kite-flyer, to show he was not injured, then spoke to his companion. 'You called yourself the Silver Claw. I know what the silver claw is, and who wears it, but I should be interested to learn why you signed yourself such.'

Roma Volecci nodded his head slowly. 'Several reasons. The least important is that I'm a Vequincian and we Vequincians love secrets, intrigues and rumours. So I chose a false name which appealed to me. The *reason* it appealed to me was that I was once the Chosen One myself.'

'But,' protested Udolphus, 'you are a Volecci. The Voleccis are not a new family. They have been rich merchants for a long time. The Chosen Ones come from the streets, from amongst the waifs and strays.'

'I am a Volecci by adoption. After I wore the silver claw I of course became page to the Duce at the time. During that period I was able to do a great service to a Volecci I now call Father. I saved him from assassination. A Florion killer crept into his bed-chamber. It was my habit to sleep in the doorway to the Duce's chambers and I saw the shadow lurking, followed, and raised the alarm. The assassin was not caught, but a life was saved. For this service, and others, I was taken into the house of Cato Volecci.'

Udolphus turned to face his companion, looking through the eyeholes of his Bauta mask. 'That is an extraordinary story.'

The other laughed. 'Not here in Vequince. Here anything is possible. Rags to riches is a common tale.' His tone became serious again. 'Yet, there is another reason I chose the name. I put a young creature in prison, one such foundling, a female—' A paw went up as Udolphus opened his mouth. 'Please, do not interrupt me. It is for her own good. For her own protection, nothing more. Once you have unravelled the plot we shall be able to allow her to leave the prison and join society.'

'This jill, I take it she was also a Chosen One, and wore the silver claw?'

'She was chosen, yes, but she refused the silver claw, having seen the glint of a poisoned needle inside.'

'Ah,' said Udolphus, 'I remember Lucci telling me of this.'

Roma continued, 'It was Lucasta, for that is her name, who first told me of the plot. We needed to find out more, so I took the opportunity of having her picked as the Chosen One. She was to be my little spy in the court and around politicians – this would have been an easy task as page to the Duce. Unfortunately our enemies discovered what we were about and tried to kill her with the device in the silver claw. I was the judge at her trial and managed to have her secretly transported to a cell in the prison. I am the only one who knows where she is. There she will remain until such time as we can safely release her.'

'May I speak with her?' asked Udolphus.

'Of course, but I would suggest not until you feel you are close to exposing the conspirators and will put her in no danger. She is in there under an assumed name' – Roma whispered a name in Udolphus's ear – 'and has been there for several weeks. It's not a pleasant place to be. Prison reform is a slow process. Many of my colleagues do not want change, thinking that foul conditions in the jails will deter criminals. But I intend to chip away at their resistance and improve things eventually. You must realize that as an adopted member of the Volecci family, my influence is limited.'

'Of course. I will be most cautious when it comes to this youngling, Lucasta. Already I have some strong ideas concerning those who are involved in the conspiracy.'

'Then why not expose them immediately?'

Udolphus sighed. 'I have no real proof. They will laugh at my accusations, walk away and make a new plan for the future. What I do not yet know is *when* and *where* and precisely *how* they intend to carry out their foul deed. Then there is the involvement of the guilds. Is it just one, or two, or all of them? As soon as these unknowns are unravelled I shall come to you.'

Roma nodded. 'As I have told you, we are planning on bringing tighter controls on three of the guilds – the alchemists, the maskmakers and the apothecaries. The others – the gondola-makers, glass-blowers, the swordsmiths, arrowsmiths and marbled paper-makers – we believe are conducting themselves in a proper manner. However, for too long those first three guilds have benefited from a privileged freedom to do very much as they wish. When controls were threatened in the past, bribes to council members halted the proposals in their tracks. But we Voleccis are already a very wealthy family. We scorn corruption and will bring the guilds to heel.'

'Well then, I shall leave you and continue with my work.'

'Herr Beck, I have every faith in you, and of course I will stand by you when the time comes.'

Udolphus paused before saying, 'Thank you, and

you will remember I asked you to provide me with a permit to visit the prison?'

'Oh yes – I shall send it round in the morning.'

They shook claws, their expressions grim.

'Now,' said Roma Volecci gravely, 'I shall go and sling some more eggs at unsuspecting citizens.' His tone changed to one of gleeful fun. 'You probably think it highly inappropriate, a member of the government playing the eggs? But why not? I can do it without being recognized – that's the whole point of Carnival. All year I sit in dusty rulers' chambers and in the dry courts, making judgements over life or death, and a horrible responsibility it is too. During Carnival I can let myself go. It's a release I look forward to every year. I can be foolish for a time.'

'Oh, I understand,' said Udolphus. 'It's something I've been enjoying too. Geraniums are a bit too quick to judge their fellow citizens. We could do with a masquerade so that the more timid mammals could let themselves go a bit. They would appreciate being anonymous.'

The pair parted. Both mammals kept their eyes and ears open as they walked away from each other, wondering if they were being observed. But Roma, at least, was not recognizable by anyone with lesser powers of observation than Udolphus.

After the politician had left him, Udolphus found himself walking alone alongside a narrow canal. He was reflecting on recent events. He reminded himself that he still had to visit Malacite, the leader of the Guild of Alchemists. Carnival was not quite the appropriate time for such a visit and it was doubtful if the alchemist was at his workplace, but Udolphus decided to walk through the district where the alchemists had their premises on his way back to his lodgings.

The canal beside which he walked was one of those quiet backwaters which saw only the occasional barge or rowing boat, since it served no large warehouses and had no access to the fronts of houses. On his right was a long building which he recognized as the infirmary, the sight of which made most mammals shudder. Even in these enlightened times hospitals were dreaded places where so-called surgeons were let loose with sharp knives and other instruments of torture. Patients were dragged into such places kicking and screaming, to be operated on, usually against their will.

Udolphus kept to the main thoroughfare where there were comforting crowds around him, but he had the eerie feeling that he was being watched, perhaps even followed. Every so often he glanced down adjoining alleys and contemplated the attractive stillness of the waters there. Evening was now coming on and had settled into that old-gold mellowness which a mature sun throws down at that time of day. It was warm on his fur, even through his carnival clothes.

Then all of a sudden a noisy group of alchemist owls appeared at the end of a deserted alley. They seemed to have a captive: an unfortunate glassblowing apprentice in the costume of a cuckoo. The cuckoo was struggling madly, sobbing and whining, while his captors hooted and jeered at him.

'We're going to do something different for once,' they cried. 'No canal ducking for you, my friend. You're going to hospital.'

'You've got a crushed paw,' explained another of the owls. 'We'll get the doctor to remove it, before gangrene sets in.'

'I haven't got a bad paw,' cried the distressed cuckoo. 'You leave me alone! You let me go!'

The glass-blowing apprentice, from the sound of his voice, was clearly very young and very frightened. There was a catch in his voice which only encouraged his tormentors to sneer at him. Udolphus considered how cruel young mammals could be. He himself was not a great deal older than the biggest of these apprentices, but he realized how mob mentality could turn a mild and normally law-abiding youth into a vicious thug.

'My paw's all right,' shouted the cuckoo again. 'My paw's fine.'

'It won't be in a minute,' cried one of the owls, a big fellow with a rough voice. 'Not once we've stamped on it.'

They began to force the poor creature to the ground and Udolphus realized they were actually going to carry out their threat – the big owl was making ready while the others held down their prisoner. A cold anger came over the otter. He had always hated street gangs. They were mindless monsters made up of individuals who, on their own, would run a mile from violence.

Leaving the busy street behind, Udolphus ran down the narrow alley to the deserted canal. He wrenched the leader of the owls off the trapped youth, rolling him onto his back.

'Leave him alone,' growled the unraveller. 'Go home to your mothers.'

The alchemist apprentices stared at him. The three holding down the hostage relaxed enough for him to struggle free. Within a second the prisoner was on his feet and running, his cuckoo mask slipping from his head, revealing a very young water rat's features. After a very short while he was gone, over a bridge and round a corner, leaving Udolphus to face the wrath of the owl-masked enemy.

The owl leader climbed back to his feet and drew his rapier. 'It worked. We've got the one we want,' he snarled. 'Grab him, quick,' he ordered the others.

Udolphus was surrounded by strong youths, who gripped his forelimbs and other parts of his body. They held him so fast he could not draw his pistol. Though he was quite a strong otter, he was no match for a dozen young, burly water rats. Their leader drew back his sword, ready to thrust his blade into Udolphus's stomach. One of his followers seemed disappointed at this.

'Wait a minute, Rocco! That's not the way we do it. Let's drown him like we always do. It's traditional.'

The leader hesitated, then sheathed his rapier. 'Well,' he said in a gleeful tone, 'we don't want to break with tradition, do we? We have to respect our cultural heritage. Take off his mask.'

154

One of the owls pushed down Udolphus's mask. His face was caught in the dying light of the sun, striped by the long thin shadows of tall buildings and campaniles. He was also still wrapped in the veils and high collar of the Bauta costume. The unraveller's features were unclear in the darkening gloom of the fading light, but the owl leader thought he was scared.

'Look at him. Look at the otter. Shaking like a leaf.'

Clearly, from the smell of Rocco's breath and that of those around him, a lot of mead-drinking had been going on. These apprentices were in their cups. They had imbibed too much sweet wine, which had confused their brains. This over-indulgence was to Udolphus's advantage. The apprentices were not as alert and clear-thinking as they would be if sober.

'Whatever you think of otters, in your prejudiced way,' said Udolphus calmly, 'is not relevant here. You're about to commit murder. You – most of you – will go to prison for the rest of your lives. One or two of you, the murderer almost certainly, will be executed.'

'Who's going to know?' jeered one of the smaller owls. 'In any case, *his* father will soon be one of the rulers of Vequince—'

'Shut up!' snarled the leader of this motley crew of water rats. 'Keep your tongue still, you idiot!' He seemed to come to a decision. 'All right, we'll do it the usual way. It's expected of us. Not our fault, is it, if he drowns? Tie his front paws together. That's it. Now his back paws. Quickly now. Someone might come along. That's it, nice and tight. We don't want him getting free of his bonds. That wouldn't be right.'

Within a few moments Udolphus's front and back paws were lashed firmly to each other. He was going to be dealt with in the traditional way, by being thrown into the freezing waters of the canal. They swung him back and forth with yells of delight, then with 'One, two, three . . .' Udolphus was tossed into the canal.

When he hit the surface the shock of the coldness took his breath away and he sank slowly in the murky waters to the mud below.

# Chapter Nine

It was not long, a minute or two only, before Udolphus was back on the surface again. His mask had been forced from his face, but it remained around his neck, held by its cord. The thick protective waistcoat he wore all the time weighed him down only a little. Looking around, he tried not to swallow any of the water. The infirmary nearby pumped all its waste into this canal. There would be a hundred diseases here, not to mention the blood and gore from as many operations. Even now he could see shapeless fleshy bits of body organs floating by his nose.

'Keep head up,' he mumbled. 'Breathe through nose!'

The gang had underestimated the swimming powers of Udolphus Beck, thinking that bonds were sufficient to immobilize him. Although otters – and water rats – had long since ceased spending all their time in water, some – and Udolphus was one of those – still retained their native skills. He regularly dipped and swam in his local river. His muscles were toned, the otter's inherent love of the water had been nurtured, and he was an extremely skilful swimmer.

The gang of ignorant alchemist thugs might have been able to drown an otter who worked as a bank clerk and ate stodgy foods, or an otter who owned estates in Geranium and hunted sparrows for sport, but Udolphus was as much at home in the water as he was on land. With his front and back paws bound, he swam like a seal, using his hind legs and forelimbs as flippers. Indeed, he was able to spread his webbed claws like fans and drive himself through the water. Then, of course, there was his marvellous tail, which helped to steer and propel his body.

'Drown Udolphus Beck!' he muttered, his thick, oily coat keeping the cold from his bones. 'They must have straw for brains.'

He reached the steps which served the hospital boats further down the canal. There he sat for several minutes, untying the cords which bound his lower limbs. When he was free he trudged back through the streets, sodden to the very skin beneath his fur. He finally stopped a passer-by and asked him to untie his forelimbs. He did so with a puzzled expression, but Udolphus simply laughed and said, 'Carnival,' and the passer-by laughed too, knowing that during this holiday stranger things occurred than bound wet otters asking to be released from their bonds.

At one point Udolphus came across a familiar circle of card players and his paw automatically went to his purse, only to find his money must have fallen out in the canal. Still, despite the fact that he was soaked, he stood and watched the game of chance for a while, the yearning in his breast very strong. In fact at one point he asked if there was any chance of playing on credit, but the contemptuous looks of the card players very soon put paid to any hope there.

Udolphus finally wrenched himself away from the oak-leaves and the sycamore-seeds, convinced that he would have made a killing had he money in his pocket. He made his way back to his lodgings, avoiding any cul-de-sacs. Now that he had studied the maps in the library and Lucci had taken him all over the city, Udolphus was aware of the hazards of being trapped in blind alleys. If anyone thought they could get him that way, they were not taking account of his superb memory.

'Master?' cried Lucci, when Udolphus slopped past his apprentice's room on the way to his own. 'What happened?'

Lucci was now well on the mend. His right paw was still in a sling, but he could walk and was gathering strength by the day. Sophia's ministrations had a lot to do with his recovery. She was a relentless nurse, urging him to his feet every day, making him exercise when he felt like giving up. Her strong will and sense of purpose would not allow him to fail in his efforts to regain his former self.

'I fell in.'

'You never did, master. Not you.'

'All right, I was thrown in by a bunch of alchemists' brats.'

'The owls! Of course, it's Carnival.'

Udolphus was aware he was dripping all over

159

Signora Nelli's landing, but he asked, '*How* long does Carnival last?'

'At least three weeks, master. Maybe more. It depends.'

'On what?'

'If the citizens want it to . . .'

In Geranium holidays were programmed exactly to the second, no more or less. Udolphus, used to order and discipline in the streets, threw up his forelimbs in a gesture of disbelief. He continued to his room, where he stripped off his clothes and towelled himself down. Then he climbed into a bed with crisp sheets and starched pillow case, consigning the day's events to the past. Tomorrow, he thought, is another day. And at least he now knew that the alchemists wanted him dead – and their reason for that would be that they were involved in the conspiracy.

The next morning there were even more maskers in the streets than there had been the day before. There was talk of miracles, though Udolphus did not actually witness any. He heard the story of a blind foundling being able to see again. It seemed a mother had given birth to a litter of twenty-four young. A giant catfish was caught, weighing more than a porpoise. Vines in a courtyard off the Beach of Coal had suddenly produced opals instead of fruit. A wooden statue smiled and a stone statue shed tears of quartz. Every year, during Carnival, there were miracles. The citizens expected them and they were never disappointed – at least by the reports of them.

160

Udolphus – wearing his mask once again – decided to try the workshops of Malacite, to see if the alchemist was working. Even though the apprentices were roaming the streets causing mayhem, their masters might still be at the forge, melting and melding metals. And he was right. Malacite was indeed in his workshop, his furnace at white-hot heat.

'Signor Malacite,' he said, 'I understand your profession seeks the three great secrets of the universe.'

A burly water rat turned from the hissing heat of the furnace. Udolphus could see that his whole body was pitted with burn marks. Sparks and drips of molten material had taken their toll on this alchemist during his experiments. In some places the white-hot metal had splashed him and had burned right through: his ears were like lacework, his paws were sieves. He was a dictionary of patches and missing parts, his over-bright, flecked eyes staring at Udolphus as if he could see right through him. When one looked closer, as Udolphus did, one could see that Malacite's nose had disappeared and had been replaced by a bronze one. His whiskers were also gone: copper wires were there in their stead.

'The three great secrets,' murmured Malacite. 'Yes. How to turn base metals into gold. The search for the universal solvent, which will turn even the granite mountains into liquid. And the elixir of life. Wealth, power and immortality, in that order. Yes, we search for the answers. We have been somewhat successful with the first but, as yet, not with the other two.'

'I have heard that Dropsi the apothecary has found the elixir.'

Malacite stared. 'So it is reported.'

There was silence between them for a while, finally broken by Udolphus.

'So, you managed to make gold from lead?'

The answer was cagey. 'Sometimes. Not just from lead, but other base metals too. But I say too much. It is, after all, a secret. Say, who are you, under that Bauta mask? A visitor from Geranium?'

'So, when they say you dilute the gold you sell to the monks to illuminate their books with, that isn't true?'

The barrel-chested water rat stepped forward, an iron poker in his right paw. 'Who says these things?'

Udolphus held up his paws, as if to ward off any accusations directed at him. 'Rumours, tittle-tattle, you know.'

'Well it's not true,' growled Malacite. 'They lie. What *may* happen is that when we turn copper into gold, some of the copper remains. It's not possible to get pure gold from a transmutation – not yet.' He smiled. 'It's hardly the fault of the alchemist, is it, if the science of alchemy has not yet advanced to its ultimate goal of perfection.'

'Then you don't import gold from the Orient and add copper to it?'

'No. That would be against the law. I always say to my son Rocco that alchemists are law-abiding citizens ... Look, who are you? Take off that mask if you want to talk to me about such things. Do you wish to

162

use my services, or sell me something? What do you want, stranger? Tell me your name.'

Udolphus kept his mask on but said, 'I am Beck, the unraveller.'

Malacite at first looked shocked and Udolphus thought, No, I'm not dead, as you thought I was.

The alchemist's face soon settled back into a surly expression, however, as he got over his surprise. 'If you say so, though I can't see behind that mask. You have the height, it's true. I've heard of you, Beck. You've been to see Dropsi and Botcchio. What do you want?'

'I wondered if you were aware that the government is planning to bring you to heel.'

'Oh, that doesn't bother me,' said Malacite airily. 'I have nothing to hide, after all. I'm an honest citizen. Let the maskmakers and the apothecaries squirm. The alchemists are free of sin.'

'Well, I certainly hope you're right. I sincerely do. I've heard some nasty tales about gulls and other birds. I'm glad to hear they're not true.'

'If they searched these premises now,' cried Malacite, 'they would find nothing. I know what you've heard. You've heard that alchemists believe the sun is made of molten gold, the moon and stars of solid silver. You've heard that we believe birds flying to these celestial bodies bring back precious metals and cache them somewhere on the Earth? It's true, I do believe that about the sun, moon and stars – and the birds. But I have never captured and tortured any living creature, gull, thrush or sparrow. That part is a lie. I swear it on my poor beleaguered body, my much maligned soul.'

'I may have heard these accusations, but again, it is all just gossip. Thank you for your time, Signor Malacite. Have a prosperous day.'

Udolphus left the premises. He had now visited all three of the most powerful guilds in Vequince, having purposely left this one until last. He was uncertain whether the apothecaries and the maskmakers were in on the plot to bring down the government, but he was sure about the alchemists.

He recalled the words of one of the owls, before they had thrown him into the canal: *His father will soon rule Vequince . . .* The speaker had been talking about Rocco. Rocco was Malacite's son. Clearly the leader of the Guild of Alchemists was in on the conspiracy up to his tattered ears.

Udolphus had no doubt that Rotzi di Coporoni was part of the plot too, along with Signor Pavolo. Who else? None of these were actually *in* the government. Udolphus did not feel that any of these three conspirators had the vision or the brain to foment a worthwhile plot. There had to be someone else – probably someone who already held great authority. Someone who wanted to rule as sole dictator, who would reward the other three. Someone who would make them rich and powerful, once he was in control.

'Back to the lodgings,' murmured Udolphus. 'Time to have a talk with young Lucci.'

On his way home the otter – despite being alert for trouble, as he had to be at all times – was able to appreciate the hundreds, perhaps thousands, of different masked characters in the streets. As he was from a country which liked its citizens to conform, it was naturally the traditional costumes he approved of the most. There was Zanni, the villain; the female Moreta, in her roguish dress and round, demure mask; the long-nosed and bespectacled Doctor During-the-Pestilence, white mask, black flowing gowns and professor's cap; Gnaga the maid with her cat-like face and voice, sometimes cradling a swaddled shrew in her forelimbs. These, and the characters Udolphus had already seen, filled the streets with their rumbustious gambolling, playing tricks on those who did not wear any costume. Finally, and there were only one or two of these, there was the sharp-faced, red-masked character of Violent Death, or the Red Slayer, who stalked the alleys and passageways, lurking in the shadows.

Those on stilts were still racing around causing havoc. Two of the stilters were even now brawling high above the streets, punching noses over something or other. The riotous apprentices were still a roaming menace. These had now lost all interest and charm for the foreign visitors, who simply found them a nuisance. Udolphus avoided contact with such groups and made it home without being accosted.

On a silver plate by the door he discovered an envelope addressed to him. On opening it Udolphus found the permit he had requested from Roma Volecci. There was nothing else: simply the permit itself.

Udolphus rooted out Lucci, who was so enthralled by Sophia it was difficult to get any sense out of him. The young jill was there, changing his sling for a clean one, her glossy fur smelling faintly of a perfume designed to turn young jacks mad with longing. Udolphus, youthful though he was, did not entirely approve of jacks and jills as young as Lucci and Sophia wearing fragrant scents. He felt perfume was more for mammals of his own age and that these two should smell of nothing more than good clean soap.

'Sophia, I'm glad you're here,' he said as he entered Lucci's room, his loud voice making them both jump guiltily. 'You can help us do some unravelling.'

'Yes, signore?' she said, looking a little uncertain.

'Now, Lucci,' said Udolphus, sitting in his assistant's only chair, 'you know I told you that your uncle has finally relinquished your inheritance? Well, the bequest left by your parents is now yours. I have banked the money. You may use it any time you wish to draw on it, but Lucci – my advice is to use it wisely, young water rat. You have been on the streets once, you don't want to end up there again, for this time it will be your own fault.'

'Yes, master – but I wish to remain in your service until I am a fully qualified unraveller and can earn my living that way.'

Udolphus smiled, his whiskers twitching. 'Good. Good. Now, you will remember I said we might have to visit the prison at some time? That time has now come. We are close to knowing all who are in this plot, though of course we don't know where they will

strike, or when. That will be the most difficult unravelling of all to do: the where and when.'

'Master,' said Lucci, trembling a little, 'I'd rather
not go to the prison, if it please you.'

'Oh, Lucci,' said Sophia primly, 'you must obey
Herr Beck, or you'll never become a journeymammal
and be master of your trade.'

Udolphus smiled at her earnestness. 'We're getting
close to the conspirators, Lucci. We must find our
source. We should have done it before now, but events
have tumbled over themselves. It's time for us to pay
a visit to the prison. I have a permit here' – he waved
it at them – 'which will get us over the Bridge of Lost
Souls and behind the grim walls.'

Lucci looked troubled. All the vim and verve had
gone out of him for the moment. He was back to
being a street urchin. When you were homeless you
avoided the authorities – the Thieftaker General's
watchmen; officials in the civil service and politicians;
and especially the prison. Who knew if you would
ever come out again? Lucci had visions of some officer
looking at him and saying, 'You know, I could swear
that's the jack who robbed the . . .' and Lucci's
imagination was quite capable of filling in the blank
with anything, anything at all.

'We will go together,' said Udolphus firmly. 'Come,
stir yourself, Lucci. You too, Sophia, if you're coming
with us. It does no harm to see misery once in a while,
if only to remind us how fortunate we are. It stirs our
social conscience and makes us strive to improve that
hidden, squalid, murky world which most would

prefer to forget exists. Come, you two, on with your cloaks!'

After Udolphus Beck had left the workshop, Malacite fumed. How dare this upstart otter come in and attempt to ruin his plans! Both he and Rotzi di Coporoni had tried to get rid of the Geranium and so far both had failed badly. It was time to make sure. Malacite was so close to his goal now he could not afford to allow anything to go wrong. Of course, Beck could not possibly know their whole scheme, but clearly his suspicions were leading him in the right direction, and that had to be stopped.

'Rocco!' he called, swishing his tail. 'I have an errand for you.'

His son came out of the depths of the workshop, where he had been listening to all that passed between his father and Udolphus. Rocco had recognized the stranger's voice and was now aware that the meddle-some otter had escaped death. He realized now that he should have used the rapier, but he and his apprentice friends had been drinking heavily, and had not been quick-witted enough. Obviously the canal was no place to throw an otter, bound or not.

'Yes, Father?'

'You're an idiot. It is unfortunate I have an idiot for a son. Now, go to the Black Sail Inn and fetch Scoratchi.'

Rocco did as he was told, keeping his own secrets.

When he returned with Scoratchi, his father was waiting impatiently. Scoratchi was one of those

168

demons who sometimes slip out of Hell and into the body of a mortal. There is no other way to explain why such wickedness exists amongst mammalkind. He was originally a Florion, but his nationality meant nothing to him. He would kill a fellow citizen, even one he quite liked, as easily as a despised enemy. So long as he was paid. Scoratchi was an assassin with no conscience, no soul, no ethics or morals. Beside Scoratchi, di Coporoni was an infant when it came to evil. Scoratchi was lean and hollow-cheeked, with a tail like a whip. His eyes were of so light a hue they worried you. When you stared into them you felt you were looking into a bottomless void. There was nothing behind them but the coldness of death. It was like looking into the eyes of a cobra.

'You wanted to see me?' asked Scoratchi, his voice like two pieces of sandpaper being rubbed together. 'What do you have for me?'

'I want you to kill the otter, Beck,' replied Malacite, trying not to stare into those horrible eyes. 'You will be paid well.'

'Consider it done,' said the other, running his small red tongue over his two front fangs. 'What costume does he wear?'

'Bauta, but get the right one.'

'Of course, there're dozens, nay hundreds, of Bauta wearers at Carnival. I will make sure *my* victim is the Geranium otter, Beck. I'm not a fool, alchemist. But how would you like it carried out? The garrotte? It's not easy to throttle an otter – you have to reach up, they're so tall. A pistol is loud and attracts attention.

169

A knife, under the ribs. Will that be to your way of thinking?'

'Yes, yes,' murmured the alchemist, certain the assassin carried the scent of Hell's brimstone and roasting souls in his clothes, in the way that smokers have the smell of tobacco. 'Just so long as he's dead.'

The crossed the Bridge of Lost Souls and climbed into the prison, above the chambers where the Council of Ten held their parliament. Lucci just caught a glimpse of the blue sky through one of the small latticework windows. If he were a convict, that passing flash of freedom would have to last him until his release (which might be never) for there were no windows in the dungeons themselves. After that, there were candles and lamps, but no natural light.

What struck Sophia was the stench of filthy straw, unwashed bodies, diseased and rotting flesh, and – worst of all – the overpowering stink of utter hopelessness and despair.

Udolphus, who also hated the smell, was doing his best not to gag. Although the other two did not know it, this was the first time he had been in such a place. He was old enough to anticipate the dread, yet still young enough to be shaken. He was curious, yet at the same time he did not want to look. They passed cells where the only opening was a narrow grille at the bottom of an iron door, so that visitors had to lie down in the muck to speak with the prisoners on the other side. There was no hope in those cells. Hope was something that had flown through the last window, as the condemned mammals had crossed the bridge.

The jailer walked on ahead, jangling a ring of iron keys.

'You understand who I want to see?' said Udolphus. 'The one who is called La Malattia?' This was the false name under which Lucasta had been sent to prison by Roma Volecci. It meant *the diseased one* in the old language. Roma had called her that so that she would be put in a cell on her own. It also kept away inquisitive visitors and turnkeys.

The jailer shuddered then answered, his throat rattling with the sound of phlegm, for even officers of the law did not escape the unwholesome atmosphere of this hellish place. 'I know the one. It's believed she has the mange and that she will die within the year. She's at the end of the row.' He hawked and spat out the offending bodily fluid. Sophia was careful not to tread in it, as she passed the spot where it lay. 'You've only got ten minutes, mind. It's more than my job's worth.'

'I understand,' replied Udolphus. 'Just leave us to speak.'

'No talk of escape. I can't have that. This is an oubliette. Prisoners come here and are forgotten, even by their families. If one ever got out, why, that would give the others hope. We can't have that. Think of the unrest it would cause. Think of the problems it would give the likes of me.'

'No, no. Nothing like that.'

They came to the last cell in the row. Udolphus had

to lie down on the ground with his furry cheek to the grimy, cold stone floor. It stank down there, of a kind of dirt he preferred not to name, pressed between the cracks of the flags. The jailer had now moved away. He stood in a corner some distance away, his fore-limbs folded over his chest.

'You in there,' Udolphus called softly through the grille, a candle by his head, 'come to the doorway.'

There was a scurrying sound in the cell and almost immediately a young ratty face, pockmarked by flea bites, appeared on the other side of the grille.

'What? What is it?' The voice was of a young female water rat. 'No one has spoken to me for six weeks.'

Udolphus's voice dropped to a whisper. 'My name is Udolphus Beck. Your master sent me.'

'Oh – oh. Am I to be released?'

'Soon, youngling, soon. I want you to tell me your story.'

The young rat on the far side now pressed her mouth to the metal grille. 'He said you would come. I will tell you. I was on the waterfront, fishing in the dark one night, when I overheard two mammals. They didn't see me at first – I was hidden behind a bollard. They were plotting to murder the Council of Ten. Then the moon came out from behind a cloud—'

'Those deadly moonshadows,' muttered Udolphus. 'Yes, yes, go on.'

'Finally they saw me. One of them chased me all over the city, but I escaped. I went and waited outside the Council chambers and stopped the first of the Ten who emerged. It was the water rat who is now my master. I told him the story. It just so happened that within a few days the new Duce was to be crowned. He told me to stand at the front of the foundlings and he would choose me to wear the silver claw . . .'

'Go on.'

Lucasta hung her head. 'I was excited. I know it was wrong of me but I told some of my friends I was going to be the Chosen One. There was a jealous jack who did not like me. He went to the Thieftaker General and told him what was arranged. Although I had not mentioned the name of my master, di Coporoni knew that I was to be a spy in the corridors of power.'

'Did you recognize any of the conspirators, that night you overheard their plans?'

'One fled into the night and I never saw him properly, leaving the other to chase me. Shall I describe the one who ran after me?'

'If you will, but quickly, we have not much time.'

Lucasta said, 'The main thing about him was that his whole head was white. It was as if he'd dipped it in a barrel of flour.'

'Hmmm,' said Udolphus, 'Pavolo.'

Lucasta continued, 'He was at the ceremony. When I stepped up to do the choosing, I noticed him change the silver claw. As they went to put it on me I saw something glinting inside. A needle. I guessed then the tip of that needle was poisoned and I refused to put on the glove. I protested that it was a booby-trap, but the Thieftaker General stepped forward and scoffed at me. They *all* laughed. No one would listen to me and before anyone inspected the booby-trapped claw it had been changed back again for the real one.'

Udolphus continued the story for her. 'You were then very lucky that your master managed to have himself appointed as the judge at your trial, and so you ended up in here for your own protection. What about the young jack, the one who betrayed you to the Thieftaker General?'

'He was found with his throat cut the day after the coronation.'

'Ah, di Coporoni leaves no witnesses.'

The jailer jangled his keys and walked over. 'You've had long enough, otter. Time to go.'

'Another gold bezant, for two more minutes?'

The jailer retired again, clutching his coin, but clearly nervous about this secret meeting between the otter and the young convict.

To the prisoner, Udolphus said quietly, 'Lucasta, I'm going to have to leave you in here. This is the safest place at the moment. Can you tell me anything, anything at all which would help me discover the identity of the other conspirator? Was he or she perhaps an alchemist? Did he smell of forge smoke? Or medicine? Was he wheezy and chesty?'

Lucasta's eyes opened wide. 'Smell? Scent – yes, the scent. I'd forgotten it until now. I just didn't think of it again, but I got a faint whiff of – what's that stuff you put on rashes? You know, that stuff to make you better.'

From behind Udolphus came the soft voice of Sophie. 'Iodine.'

'Yes, that's it. That stuff.'

'Good. Excellent. You've done very well, Lucasta. You have no idea how they are going to murder the government, I suppose? That would be useful knowledge. I have my ideas but yours could confirm them.'

'I'm sorry.'

'Never mind. Even if you had heard them talk about the method that night, they'd have changed it by now. Keep well, young Lucasta. We will return for you, once we have foiled this plot.'

On the way out of the prison, Sophia spoke. 'Herr Beck, this Signor Pavolo – I think I know who he is – a distant cousin of the Voleccis.'

'Ah, the jealous cousin. It all begins to fit together now. Now, if I can just manage to stay alive for a little longer—'

'Why, signore, whatever do you mean?' asked Sophia, clutching at Lucci's paw. 'Are you unwell? Can I get you a potion?'

'No, no, nothing like that. What it is, is this – I expect to be attacked and killed very shortly. It will happen, I'm sure. Very soon, I believe.'

# Chapter Ten

Udolphus's prophecy, his fears about his own safety, were to be fulfilled sooner than he expected. The blood-red figure of Violent Death was waiting in the wings. The trio of unravellers had just crossed over the Bridge of Lost Souls and had walked along the passageway to the street. Udolphus remembered looking through one of the small latticed windows on the bridge and seeing a fleet of galleons gaily sailing out of port, the sun dancing amongst their colours and picking out the cross spars. A few moments later an assassin leaped forward out of the shadows, a frightening figure in a flapping scarlet gown. The demonic mask on his face seemed to become animated as the dagger was raised and plunged several times into the chest of the startled otter. Then Udolphus fell, a name upon his lips, to the cobbles below.

'Murderer!' shouted Lucci in anguish, taking his forelimb out of its sling and waving it painfully. 'Help! He has murdered my master!'

The assassin let out a horrible triumphant yell of

glee and ran off down a narrow alley, his red gown streaming out behind him. A distressed Lucci ran after him, shouting for him to stop, calling for assistance from bewildered passers-by. Sophia was torn between staying to see if there was anything she could do for Udolphus and chasing the rash Lucci. Her fears were that Lucci too would become a victim, for the assassin clearly had no conscience. The dagger might soon be plunged into her young jack's breast.

She chose life and her heart over blood that had already been spilled and ran after Lucci. 'Lucci! Desist! He'll kill you too!'

She raced after the pair, weaving between maskers revelling in the streets who were obviously unaware of the drama that was taking place. Turning a corner, she struck the stilts of a tall masker who was leaning against a wall. If he had gone down like a felled tree, he might have been seriously injured. As luck would have it he only slid down, his back against the bricks, his stilts skittering over the flagstones. Sophia glanced back quickly to see that he was sitting with splayed stilts, back against the wall. He appeared indignant but unhurt. She continued with her chase.

Sophia was faster than the recently injured Lucci. She had always been a good runner and she employed all her talent now. Her tail went up, she went down on all fours, and she fairly flew through the city streets. She caught up with Lucci as he passed the campanile of Rodenti di Doretni, bringing him down with a flying tackle. When they both regained their feet, the flustered Lucci glared at his attacker in disbelief.

'What did you do that for?' he cried, dusting himself off. 'Now you've let him go.'

They were in a campo full of revellers. Lucci could now see at least half a dozen figures wearing the Violent Death costume and mask. None of these seemed anxious to evade him. Lucci was quite capable of ripping off the masks of every one of them, but he realized with a creeping despair that even if he did he would not recognize his quarry. Now that there were several, how would he know which was *his* Violent Death? The assassin had escaped.

'I could have caught him,' he grumbled at Sophia. 'I almost had him.'

'And what would he have done then?' she retorted. 'Allowed you to place him under arrest. He would have killed you too, Lucci.'

Lucci stared into her big brown eyes and saw the logic in her argument but, true to his masculine pride, said, 'I wouldn't have cared.'

'Well, *I* would,' she replied, a softness entering her tone. 'One mammal killed is enough for one day.'

Lucci suddenly let out a cry of anguish. 'Oh! The master! He lies bleeding on the ground.'

The pair took to their heels again, running back to the entrance to the prison. But where was Udolphus? His body had gone. Whether a corpse or simply a wounded otter, he was no longer lying in a crumpled heap on the cobbles. Someone had either tended to his wounds and taken him off to hospital – or had stolen his broken body. The latter would not have been out of the question, for assassins often had accomplices, who would run up after the deed had been done and kick the remains into the lagoon or a canal. Udolphus could now be floating away on the tide.

'Come, dear Lucci,' said Sophia, taking his paw in her own, 'we must go and look in the hospitals, to see if he has been taken care of.'

In any other circumstances Lucci would have been utterly thrilled to be called 'dear' by this jill for whom he had a great fondness, but he could not even take pleasure in the feel of her soft paw in his own. His beloved master Udolphus had been attacked and perhaps killed, and it was all Lucci could do to stop the tears tumbling down his furry cheeks. But time enough later for weeping. Now he had to find Udolphus.

The feeling of elation that Scoratchi always experienced after killing a victim never lasted long. Even before he reported back to Malacite he had sunk into a deep depression. He had no conscience, it was true, so it was not remorse that was responsible for his low feelings. It was simply that the act did not deliver what he always expected it to. Scoratchi wanted that feeling of being all-powerful to last much longer. He wanted to bask in the glow of triumph. But such feelings were fleeting. And there were always the nightmares that followed his dreadful crimes. These had yet to be borne in the dark and grey hours. His conscious mind might not be concerned with murder, but his subconscious would torture him mercilessly, causing him to wake in great sweats of terror for many nights to come.

'It is done,' he said morosely, entering Malacite's workshop. 'The otter is dead. Where is my gold?'

Rocco, who had been standing by his father's forge, shrank back into the shadows, a look of horror on his young features. It was not the murder that concerned Rocco, but the consequences of their conspiracy. Now there really was no turning back. They had stepped over the mark and would either become rulers of a great city, or abject prisoners in a dungeon. There was now no ordinary path where he and his father could continue their profession as alchemists. Either they would become puppet despots of the Mudditchis of Florion, or they would be cast into some black pit to rot away, forgotten by sunlight and the world.

His father Malacite had no such dark thoughts. 'Good,' he said. 'Now we can get on with the real business. So, the Council of Ten – those damn Voleccis think they can take away my livelihood, do they? Alchemists have been diluting gold ever since the first water rat emerged from the lakes! It's our right. It's our given *trade*. It's what we do.' He threw up his paws. 'And where's the harm? Gold and silver are all in the mind, anyway. It's just metal from the earth, like tin or copper. Just because mammalkind has decided gold is *precious*. Why, if you can't tell pure gold from diluted gold, what's the difference? If everyone believes it to be precious, then so it is, diluted or not.'

Scoratchi had thrown off his mask and gown. He opened the leather bag and inspected his coins. 'These had better be pure,' he muttered. 'Otherwise I'll be back.'

'You see?' cried Malacite, scratching one of his holed ears with a pitted claw. 'Everyone is suspicious. It's all in the mind, Scoratchi.'

'It'll be a dagger in your heart if these coins are fake!'

Malacite hardened under these words. 'Yes, well – we have to get you out of the city now,' he said, becoming brisk and businesslike. 'A red gondola will take you over to the mainland. After that you'll be on your own. You'll need to affect a disguise of course.'

Scoratchi looked up from counting his forty pieces of gold. 'Why? Why would I?'

'Because you may have been recognized.'

'No one knows I'm here, except you.'

Malacite sighed, placing a persuasive paw on the bony shoulder of the assassin. 'Yes, but you have the *look*, my friend. You have that air of being the most dangerous water rat in the known world. Mammals are beginning to regard you with awe and respect. There is that aura of the killer about you which is impossible to hide. Whether you like it or not, you are *special*, a genius with the blade and bullet. Now that someone has been so successfully assassinated, they will be looking for you. Your trademark is your utter efficiency, the brilliance of your attacks, and they will know it is you.'

Scoratchi was impressed by the flattery, but still unsure. 'Are you certain?'

'Absolutely. Rocco, what do you think? Do you not see the terrible glare of death in this handsome face? Is that not the glint of deadly danger in those eyes? Is this not the visage of the Prince of Terror we have before us? Speak, Rocco, give us your opinion.'

Rocco's voice was hoarse, but he replied, 'Oh, indeed, Father. The very picture of the King of Shadows.'

'There, I told you so, Scoratchi. Now, I have the very uniform you need in which to escape. Here, the white mask of Pierrot the clown, and his pure white loose-fitting pants and blouse. See the large black buttons? Are they not pretty? Who would suspect that a bloody killer would lie behind such an innocent-looking mask and costume. Why, you will look like an entertainer of kittens. I will even give you a lute to carry, to complete the gay figure of Pierrot.'

'I shall feel a fool in that guise.'

'No, you shall *look* the fool, but underneath, we all know, will lie the cunning and artful assassin.'

Scoratchi gave in. 'All right then. Is the boat ready?'

'Waiting at the quay. Here, quickly, into this garb.'

They helped him dress. Rocco's feverish claws trembled as he put the loose top on Scoratchi. His father's paws had no such tremors in them though, as they helped the killer on with his pants.

'Now,' Malacite said. 'On with the mask.'

Scoratchi's features became the universal face of Pierrot.

'Good, good,' murmured the alchemist. 'Now, take him to the quay, Rocco. Show him where the gondola awaits.'

Rocco nervously led the assassin out of the

182

workshop and through a passage to a backwater canal. There was indeed a red gondola waiting. Scoratchi boarded the vessel, saying, 'Where is the gondolier?'

'Why, it's better you row yourself,' said the jack. 'The fewer citizens know about this, the better.'

'True, true.' Scoratchi took up the oar.

Assassins need to be familiar with all forms of transport in order to effect an escape. He had learned how to row various vessels, gondolas amongst them. He knew that they yaw naturally to starboard, being broader on one side than the other. The gondolier stands on the stern of the vessel, on the broader side, and corrects this tendency with his beechwood oar. Soon Scoratchi was floating down the scummy inner canal, then out onto a main canal, and finally he was in the lagoon itself. He began to cross the lagoon, breathing heavily with the exertion. His lower vision began to mist over, but he thought that was because he was wearing a mask while doing physical work. Then the mist increased, became tinged with redness, and finally crept up and over his whole sight.

He let go of his oar and tore off the mask. 'Why, there is no smoke out here,' he coughed, 'yet my chest feels as if there is. I burn inside. I am surely sucking in bad humours. What must I do to breathe? I can't breathe. It feels as if I am in that damned Malacite's forge, sucking in the smoke and sparks from his fire. Is this magic? Have I been bewitched by my enemies? Oh God' – somehow they all cry for His assistance at the end – 'please send me help!'

Now there was a tight feeling in his breast as his

throat closed. A zero coldness began to steal into his bones and the light began to drain from the sky. Scoratchi sat down, his thin rodent head in his crooked claws. Would no one come to his aid? Was there anyone within hailing distance? Or was he all alone on that part of the lagoon? He had no way of knowing, since his vision had gone.

'I'm blind,' he croaked, far out on the azure waters, with not a soul to witness his distress. 'Someone tell me what's happening to me.'

His blindness became complete, his breathing gone, his lungs collapsed. Before long the light in his mind went out. Literally dead on his feet, he slipped into the bottom of the gondola. Pierrot the clown was dead and at the mercy of the currents. His boat would be taken by the swift, turbulent waters around the lagoon and carried to one of the sea-borne city's gathering points for flotsam – one of those headland beaches on which were deposited the ocean's rubbish.

It was not *magic* of course, for there is no such thing. Only science. Science had killed him. Malacite had given Scoratchi one of Botcchio's masks soaked in a poisonous fluid obtained from an apothecary. The heat from Scoratchi's breathing had triggered a release and the liquid in the pores of the mask turned to a lethal gas. The gas had filled the mask and the assassin had breathed it in. In a very short time his brain had been snuffed out like a blown flame, never again to ignite.

Malacite could not afford to have Scoratchi, a creature with no morals or integrity, running loose in the world. Why, the assassin could have sold what he knew to the authorities from a safe place, could he not? Therefore he too had to die. With such a terrible conspiracy in progress, there must be no witnesses left alive, just in case something went wrong.

The red gondola floated away, out into the open sea.

In the alchemist's workshop there was great satisfaction. Things were going exactly to plan. The outsider was dead and so was his assassin. The scape-goats, Dropsi and Botcchio, would soon be implicated in Scoratchi's murder, exonerating Malacite and the alchemists. The way was open for the annihilation of the Council of Ten, along with the Duce himself, thus creating a vacuum of power in the city.

The Florion army of the Mudditchis would cross the lagoon in their ships and invade the city. Once the Florions had subdued the populace of Vequince, the way would be open for the traitorous councillor – whoever he was – to become sole dictator. Malacite, di Coporoni and Pavolo would all be given high positions. Great wealth and power would follow.

First, they had to kill nine members of the Council of Ten, and the Duce, this being the signal for the Florions to attack.

'Our first job, my son,' said the greedy and ruthless Malacite to Rocco, 'will be to take over the other guilds. Pavolo and his friend the councillor – you do not know his name, but I do – will tax the merchants' galleons for their share of the bounty. Di Coporoni will have control of all the residences and businesses such as restaurants and also the Palace Guard. You and I will take control of the Guild of Maskmakers, the Apothecaries' Guild, and that of the glass-blowers and marbled paper-makers.'

'The last two will be easy, Father, but the maskmakers and apothecaries will fight. They have their gangs of apprentices in great numbers, as you know. Blood will run in the streets. Shall we be able to beat them in open civil warfare? I don't know, I'm sure.'

'You were always a worrier. Once they are leaderless, they'll be like headless sparrows – all flutter but no direction. If Botcchio and Dropsi are not executed before that date for the murder of Scoratchi, we will make certain of it. The first will need but a push into a canal. I have it all in here' – the chief alchemist tapped his ravaged head – 'and will leave nothing to chance. We shall be as rich as emperors, son.'

'Will I have my own army, Father? May I raise my own legions?'

'Of course.' Malacite placed a tattered paw on his son's head. 'You shall be commander-in-chief of all the soldiers of Vequince and responsible for all foreign wars. Di Coporoni will be in charge of internal security and will raise a force of secret rats to root out insurrection and tyranny, but you may take care of any fighting abroad. There will be the spoils of campaigns in other lands, as well as the wealth to be had here. You may loot and plunder as you please, for we shall be the law, we shall be the masters of not only our own destinies, but those of others as well. Burn down cities, slaughter populations if you like. No one will raise a whisker.' There was a pause before, 'Of course, we shall have to pay tribute to the Florions for a while, and pass over some of our trade to them, but there will still be plenty for us. In time we'll break the Florion connection, once our citizens have accepted us completely, and then we'll be in clover.'

'But the thieftaker will let me massacre the other apprentices – the maskmakers and the apothecaries? I have waited so long.'

Malacite smiled. 'Better than that, my son. You will conscript them into your army and put them in the vanguard of any attack. Better to use them as cannon fodder than to execute them.' He stared into the middle distance with some satisfaction. 'Their leaders will be in prison or, better still, dead before then of course. By this time tomorrow in fact, if things go according to our plan. Di Coporoni is dealing with that. We have the evidence – a body, poison, a mask. We just need the tides and currents to do their work. I've never known them to fail.' He rubbed his claws together.

'Of course.' The water rat youth's mind was still on the revenge he would take on the other apprentices. 'I hadn't thought of conscripting them. They'll have to obey my orders. I'll march them until they're nearly dead and then send them into battle at the head of the line. That'll teach them to taunt me. That'll pay them back for their jibes. Let them be stuck on the lances and swords of our enemies.'

'Exactly. Now, let's go and taste some of that wonderful pasta your mother cooks. She has dinner ready on the table . . .'

A boat was washed up onto a promontory beach by the natural motion of the currents and tides. There was a body in the bottom. The boat was discovered by the Thieftaker General's men amongst the driftwood, seaweed and rubbish that had been cast into the sea. Rotzi di Coporoni was summoned and he in turn asked for a judge to be present.

A judge duly arrived on the scene, an elder of the city named Goeg Ruttio.

'This citizen,' said the thieftaker to the judge, pointing down at the stiff corpse of Scoratchi, 'has been murdered.'

'How do you know this?' asked Ruttio. 'He looks as if he has had some sort of seizure.'

'You see the darkness in the eyes, the greenness around the fangs? I've witnessed similar deaths. Those discolorations are caused by a poisonous gas, which also comes in liquid form. That mask' – di Coporoni poked the item in question with a stick – 'has been soaked in the poison. When the victim first put on the mask, there would have been no reaction. However, when his breath warmed it, the gas would have been released, and so the deadly fumes went down his throat and into his lungs.'

'You seem to have deduced a great deal in a short time,' said the judge, who was suddenly unsure of who was for and who was against the government.

'You appear to be an expert in these things.'

'Oh, signore,' replied the thieftaker, 'if you were here with me on the streets, you would see such things all the time. Wouldn't he, jacks?' A murmur of agreement went up from the thieftaker's minions. 'All the time. I have witnessed a similar murder carried out with a warrior's leather helmet. The circumstances were almost the same, except the victim was not thrown into the sea, but died on guard duty at the palace. That's how I knew what to look for in this case. That's why the signs leaped out at me.'

'I don't remember that case.'

'It was not common knowledge, signore. The victim was a maskmaker's son who had got himself engaged to an apothecary's daughter. It was said the families got together to murder him, since neither side wanted the alliance to take place. We tried to prosecute, but there was no hard evidence. In this case, however' – he prodded the corpse with his toe – 'we are fairly certain the victim was killed because he knew too much. He was coming to tell me about a conspiracy or something, which involved the guilds.'

'I see.' Di Coporoni was very convincing. 'So who do you suspect in this instance.'

'Why, Dropsi the apothecary, who would have mixed the poison, and Botcchio the maskmaker, who provided the mask. It's well known they have been preaching sedition of late amongst the citizens. They are traitors, signore, who should be under lock and key before they commit even more heinous crimes.'

'Arrest them and bring them to me,' said the judge.

'I will visit justice upon them, should they be proved guilty. In the meantime I shall report your good work to the Council, who will no doubt be very grateful. There have been rumours of a plot against the government recently. You feel these two villains might be implicated?'

'Almost certainly, Judge,' replied the crafty thieftaker.

After Ruttio had gone, di Coporoni was quietly satisfied. He had diverted suspicion away from Malacite and onto two innocent creatures, Dropsi and Botcchio. He grinned and, turning to his minions, said, 'Well, you heard the judge. Arrest the two conspirators.'

'B-b-but the apothecary,' stammered one. 'Her touch is fatal!'

'And,' said another, 'the maskmaker has minders.'

'Use a long pole with a loop that you can slip around the neck of the witch, then throw a fishing net over her. And if Botcchio's bodyguards give you any trouble, you have my permission to kill them. Take the two prisoners in the same gondola and when you are in deep water, capsize it – accidentally, of course – then save yourselves by swimming to shore. No one can blame you for responding to natural survival instincts.'

One of the minions chuckled. 'Golden lungs will sink like a stone, down into the mud. Once all this is over, we can go and fetch him up. Cut the treasure from his chest. Why leave good gold lying on the lagoon floor?'

Another said, 'And the witch is but a breath away

from death already – the cold water will kill her within minutes.'

Di Coporoni grinned again. 'Which will be very convenient for us. And so die all conspirators!'

The thieftakers laughed out loud at the irony.

Lucci and Sophia had to admit defeat. The pair had covered the city in an attempt to find Udolphus. Not a trace could be found, not in the hospitals or clinics, or any other place. Lucci was as upset as a water rat could be that his new master had been murdered. But who would be interested in such a crime? Certainly not the Thieftaker General. Rotzi di Coporoni would be only too pleased to learn that Udolphus was dead. So what was Lucci going to do with this great fury in his breast?

'You heard what the master said, as he lay there full of stab wounds,' muttered Lucci. 'He whispered the name *Malacite*.'

'Yes, I heard,' replied Sophia, 'but what are we to do? Malacite is a powerful creature in Vequince. Who would go against him?'

'The Voleccis,' replied Lucci grimly. His very whiskers quivered with rage. 'And I shall give them the evidence they need to throw him in the dungeons.'

'But we don't know the master was right. We have no proof, Lucci. You might get yourself into more trouble this way.'

'I don't care about trouble. I care about the master. One thing the master taught me was to think for myself. I have a plan.'

Just at that moment Rotzi di Coporoni came round the corner accompanied by two of his burly thief-takers. On seeing Lucci his eyes widened in triumph. 'There's the stinking little shrew – grab him quick!'

The thieftaker's minions moved forward, but Sophia stepped in their way to block them, while Lucci made his retreat down a side street. Once out of their sight, he ran straight for a Byzantine church. He entered through the large doorway. As in most Vequincian churches, there was a magnificent rood screen called an iconostasis, which was there to separate the congregation from the high altar. The massive screen was of carved wood and formed of many oak statues. Lucci, having been on the run from the law from an early age, had often used the iconostasis as a hiding place. In the gloomy reaches of the church he fitted himself between two of the many statues of water rats just his size, so that when he stiffened, he became part of them. With so many figures there, in the dimness it was extremely difficult to separate him from the rest of the screen. When his two pursuers entered the church they immediately began looking under pews and in the more obvious places: behind the organ, in the Jill Chapel, in the vestry, up the bell ropes and in the belfry.

Two or three times they passed right by him, as he locked himself in a fixed position within the great rood screen. But once again Lucci found they looked everywhere but directly at him. He was right under their noses, but they did not see him. He kept his eyelids and mouth tightly shut, so that his teeth and eyes would not glisten and give him away.

Eventually the two thieftakers gave up in disgust and tramped from the church, convinced he had evaded them by escaping out of some other door.

The alchemist was halfway through his dinner when there was a rap on the door. Malacite called to his wife, now in the kitchen, to answer, but she complained she could not leave the pie in the oven or it would spoil. His son had gone out to find some of his friends. Thus Malacite answered it himself.

A sergeant-at-arms stood there, with a dozen of the Palace Guard – a small force of about a hundred mammals whose sole duty it was to protect the Duce. Malacite could see that behind the sergeant was the street urchin, Lucci, apprentice of the unraveller, Herr Beck.

'Malacite the alchemist? You are under arrest for sedition,' said the sergeant-at-arms. 'You will accompany me to a holding cell, where you will be questioned by my Lord Wigg.'

Malacite staggered back, aghast. Had his plot been ruptured by a mere stripling? A guttersnipe? Surely not. Recovering quickly, he began to protest.

'I've done nothing. Where's the Thieftaker General? Why isn't he making the arrest?'

'This is a ducal matter,' said the guardsjack. 'This involves the king himself.'

Malacite was now both frightened and incensed. 'What's that miserable scruff – what's his name?

Lucci? What's he been telling you? It's all lies, whatever it is. I have no involvement in any treachery – if that's what it's about. I know nothing of any plots or intrigues. Would you believe a foundling off the streets rather than an upright citizen? He would bring about my fall from grace because of his jealousy. Urchins like him are a menace to decent society.'

'The youth is not an urchin,' stated the sergeant, grasping Malacite by the collar, 'having a private income and wealth of his own.'

Malacite spluttered, 'Where would such a creature get money and estates?'

Lucci stepped forward now and, to his consternation, the alchemist could see that the youth was dressed in fine clothes – a velvet cap and velvet breeches with a silken doublet – and was wearing a sword at his hip. His black leather shoes had a silver buckle on the bridge. Lucci looked clean and smart, the very picture of a gentlejack.

'Why, hadn't you heard, Malacite? I'm the beneficiary of my father's will, which my uncle kept from me all these years. I have bought property and am a full citizen, with rights. I'm entitled to the full protection of the law and everything. You're not very well informed.'

Lucci had been smiling a little, but now his expression changed. He addressed the sergeant-at-arms seriously. 'When I was living on the streets this creature tried to corrupt me by offering me and my friends money to stay away from the ceremony of the Silver Claw, so that his own son would be chosen.

Rocco is not a foundling, but if no orphans were available, they would have to choose a youth from a good family. I have jacks and jills who'll swear that every word I say is true. This water rat told me – and others,' cried the youngster, 'that he wished to influence the Duce's decisions, and thus those of the Council of Ten. If his apprentices were the only younglings at the ceremony, it was certain he could get his son Rocco into the position of the Duce's page and work his evil ways!'

Malacite hissed, 'You lying little—'

'All right, enough of that,' said the sergeant. 'You can make your protests to my lord the judge. This is his decision now.' He paused before adding in a lower voice, 'But it seems to me a serious crime has been committed here and I think it's prison for you, laddie.'

At that moment Malacite's wife came out of the kitchen and saw her husband had been arrested. She began wailing and tearing at her ears, which poked through her mob cap. Then Rocco came home and tried to kick one of the soldiers, but was knocked down. He too was arrested, along with his father.

It was, from Lucci's point of view, all very satisfactory.

# Chapter Eleven

When Lucci went to bed that evening, he tried not to feel sad. He tried to feel victorious. After all, he had won the affections of a beautiful jill and had avenged his master's death. Malacite was now in a dungeon, probably regretting all his terrible sins. Lucci's accusation was a lie, of course. He had brought false witness against the alchemist. Malacite had never tried to bribe him or any of the street urchins. Yet the apprentice of the missing Udolphus did not care.

'I shall see him in fetters and chains,' muttered Lucci, after saying his prayers and asking God for his forgiveness. 'I shall see him rot in a cell, like Lucasta has done these past months. I hope they torture him.'

Lucci had accomplished all this, but really, deep down, he felt no great triumph. The fact was, Udolphus was dead, murdered by that fiend in the red costume of Violent Death. He would be floating somewhere out in the ocean, for the sea carried away many Vequincian crimes. No vengeance could bring the unraveller back.

Lucci stared out of his window before laying his head on the pillow. How peaceful it all looked. Galleons moored offshore were rocking on the gentle waves, their lanterns swaying to and fro. A cradle moon did much the same amongst the night clouds. The many-coloured gondolas were now at rest too, bobbing amongst their mooring posts. Such a beautiful world, really, yet empty of reason or true justice.

Lucci snuffed the candle by his bed and fell asleep.

He awoke shortly afterwards with a start.

Someone had come in through the window.

Someone was in his room.

Someone who smelled strongly of a mixture of nutmeg, cinnamon, saffron, rosemary and cardamoms.

What kind of murderer was this? A cook with a meat chopper?

He lay there, his heart beating fast, waiting for the strike of a weapon or the grip of a strangler's claws about his throat.

'Who's there?' he croaked. 'Who is it?'

The moonshadows – those terrible moonshadows – picked up a movement by the wardrobe. A figure came swiftly out of the corner, black and menacing, towards the bed. Lucci let out a cry of terror, but a paw clamped itself on his mouth, stifling the sound.

'Quiet!' hissed his attacker. 'You'll wake Nelli.'

The paw was removed and Lucci said, 'Master?'

A match was struck and the candle lit.

There in the soft glow of the flame stood Udolphus.

His features were craggy and awful to the frightened Lucci. If he was no longer menacing, he was indeed still terrible to behold. Any creature back from the dead is bound to be a grim and dreadful sight. Indeed, this could not be the Udolphus that Lucci had loved, but some cipher, some cold thing without a soul, wandering the earth looking for a peace it would never find.

'Go back to the sea,' ordered Lucci, pointing through the window. 'Go back to your eternal home, you poor lost creature.'

'Go back yourself,' said Udolphus, sitting on the end of his apprentice's bed. 'It's a bit too wet in there for me.'

Lucci stared. He saw that this walking-dead otter was not in the least bit damp. If he had come from the ocean he would be soaking and hung with weed, festooned with seashells. But he smelled like a spice cupboard. Could it be true? Was he indeed alive after all?'

'Udolphus?' cried Lucci, unable to contain his joy, 'is that you? Are you really alive?'

'Well, I certainly hope so,' replied the unraveller as all the clocks in the town struck midnight, 'or the laws of science are very much awry.'

'What happened? You were stabbed to death.'

'Stabbed, yes, but hardly to death. Oh, I did sustain a few pinpricks.' He rubbed his chest. 'Actually it hurt quite a bit. The blade pierced my hide by about an inch each time he struck me, but for the most part my padded armoured jacket took the brunt of the blow.'

'Your protective jacket!' cried Lucci. 'Of course!'

At that moment the pale figure of Nelli appeared in the doorway in a voluminous nightgown, carrying a candle. Her tail was swishing back and forth behind her: a clear indication of her agitation. She let out a little gasp and her paw went to her mouth.

'They said you was dead,' she whimpered. 'Murdered to bits near the basilica.'

'Go back to bed, Nelli. I'm fine. It's all been a mistake. But you must not tell anyone I'm alive, or they'll try again. Being dead, I can wander around in a costume and mask without hindrance. It has great advantages. Of course, I'm still just as tall as I was, but I've been using stilts and a long coat. They're leaning against your wall outside. That's how I reached Lucci's bedroom window.' He cleared his throat, then added, 'It's a brilliant disguise. It's almost impossible to judge someone's height when they're at the top of a pair of stilts. It's great fun, by the way. You should try it – Lucci, I mean, not you, Nelli. It'd be most undignified for a signora to stilt. Can it be a verb? To stilt? Well, it is now. I've just made it so.'

Lucci tried to imagine his rather stiff and formal young master wobbling about on stilts and could not.

'I don't know what to say,' replied the trembling Nelli, trying to straighten her nightcap. 'I'm ever so pleased you're alive, signore, even if you are smellin' of herbs and spices and whatnot.'

'Well so am I,' Udolphus said, looking down at himself. 'While I was practising with the stilts I toppled over several times. Once I fell through the canopy of a market stall and into the basins beneath. They were full of spices, fresh from the Orient, as you have gathered.'

Udolphus sniffed hard before continuing. 'It's rather fragrant, isn't it? But do go back to bed, you'll catch your death yourself. Don't worry, Signora Nelli, everything is going according to plan. Or it was,' he added sternly, looking at Lucci, 'until my apprentice here put Malacite in jail. Now we've placed the conspirators on the alert. One of their number is in prison and likely to be tortured and that will put them on edge, sharpen their wits.'

Lucci hung his rodent head, his whiskers drooping. 'I'm sorry, master. I thought it was for the best.' His head came up. 'I'll withdraw the charges tomorrow and they'll let him out.'

'No, no, they'll smell a 'roach if you do that. Best leave him there now, for we hope to have them all behind bars soon. The trouble is we still don't know where they're going to strike. I still have no real proof that there is a conspiracy. We have only Lucasta's word, and she will not be regarded as reliable by the authorities. To accuse someone of treachery is a very serious business – treason is probably the worst of all crimes in the eyes of the Council of Ten – and I don't want to end up in prison myself, for bringing false charges against prominent citizens of this fair city. We must bide our time and keep our senses primed.'

Nelli drifted away like a ghost, back towards her own room, still sniffing loudly.

Lucci said, 'All right, Udolphus.'

'I have to tell you, young Lucci, that the plot thickens. Di Coporoni has publicly accused Dropsi and Botcchio of being conspirators, probably to divert attention from himself. He had them arrested at night, bound and hooded, and taken to a gondola. Since I have been stalking di Coporoni these last few hours I was there close by – well back in the shadows – when his minions arrived with their hooded victims, one of whom I recognized as Botcchio, the maskmaker.

'I followed the boat as it took one of the narrow canals towards the lagoon. Jumping on board, I pushed the two thugs into the canal and carried on with the craft to a suitable spot where I could release the prisoners.'

'But signore, how did you know it was Botcchio and Dropsi on board?' asked the mystified Lucci. 'Can otters see through hoods?'

Udolphus smiled 'Of course not, youngling. I was surprised to see that the bows of the gondola were high out of the water, and the stern very low, indicating that one of the two hooded passengers in the stern was extremely heavy. So heavy in fact, the two gondoliers were having trouble steering the craft. I deduced that such a displacement could only occur if the passenger in question were an elephant, which of course I could see he was not. Therefore the weight had to be from unnatural causes.'

'Botcchio,' cried Lucci, 'with his lungs of gold.'

'Quite so. I borrowed some mariner's gloves in order to release the unsavoury grandmother of your sweetheart, untied Botcchio, and told them both to lay low for a while. They have gone into hiding.'

'Master, you are brilliant!'

'Oh,' replied the modest otter, 'only a little.'

'And what's next?' asked Lucci keenly.

'I think I know all the conspirators now. You remember that faint whiff of iodine smelled by Lucasta? When I went to the party at Viporatti's house there was a councillor there by the name of Chapaquida. He had one of those ringworm sores on his neck which some of us get from time to time, very difficult to get rid of. It had been treated with iodine, which I thought was a silly mistake, for ringworm is a fungus and needs a different sort of treatment altogether to normal sores. No wonder the sore had remained all that while from the night Lucasta had smelled him.'

'Ah!' cried Lucci.

'Thus Signor Chapaquida is, I believe, the fourth conspirator. The most important one. He is a member of the Council of Ten and enquiries have led me believe he has ingenuity and insight. He is definitely intelligent enough to have formulated this plot. How and when still eludes me, but I think the art of origami, or paper folding, has a lot to do with it. You will remember those paper cuts on the paws of Signor Pavolo?'

'Master, you are a genius!'

'Modesty forbids me to agree with you. But now, young Lucci, we still have work to do. I'm trying to find one of those visitors on my list. You will remember there was a master of origami from Jopon, a water rat named Yumi Horishma. I have scoured the noodle parlours without success, but just before dark tonight I found that a Y. Horishma had applied for a professorship at the university. He's been refused, of course, for the clerics and professors in Vequince are very jealous of their posts and positions, and fear competition from outsiders. Joponese scholars are very knowledgeable, very clever, and are envied.'

'So, what is it you're going to do now, master?'

'I still wish to find this creature and interview him. He has not left for Jopon, of that I'm certain. Which means he's remaining here because he still thinks he can get into the university. Someone has promised him a reward for his services. He's helped someone who expects to be in power shortly – in a position to over-rule the Vequincian clerics and allow him entry to the university.'

'Malacite!' cried Lucci. 'He's the promiser.'

'Perhaps. Or Rotzi di Coporoni. Or indeed, possibly Signor Pavolo? I shall sleep on your floor tonight, Lucci. Di Coporoni *might* just check my room to see if I survived the attack. He's a wily creature, that thieftaker, and not as easily satisfied as Malacite.'

Lucci leaped from his bed. 'No, master,' he said firmly. 'You shall sleep in my bed, while I stand guard.'

'I shall do no such thing. *You* will do no such thing. When I was an apprentice I slept under my father's workbench, so as to be up at the crack of dawn and tapping in nails as he entered the shop. He was a hard taskmaster, my father – though indeed, a loving one.' Udolphus sighed. 'I miss him.'

'Please use my bed, signore.'

'No. I will sleep over there, in the corner. The night is balmy. If I could borrow one of your blankets . . . ?'

'Certainly, master,' said Lucci, giving up. 'But I don't know how I'll sleep, with you on the hard floor.'

However, the little rat went out like a snuffed candle the moment his head hit the pillow, and left Udolphus on his back staring upwards, wishing he had his old starry ceiling above him.

The following morning Udolphus tucked into some sprats at the breakfast table.

'Lucci,' he said, 'would you go out this morning and do some investigating? It's rather difficult for me when I have to go everywhere on stilts. Be very careful. Now that you have put Malacite in jail the other conspirators will be very wary. However, I'm certain they believe you did it out of revenge for my murder, rather than because you know of the plot and who is involved. They'll be watching you closely – I wonder if you have any friends who might help you?'

'What do you wish to know, master?'

'The address of the Joponese cleric.'

'I know what I'll do,' cried Lucci. 'I'll get the other street orphans to help me. They can't follow us all!'

'What a brilliant suggestion, young Lucci. I wish I had thought of it. But one can't be clever all the time.

You will make a great unraveller some day, of that I'm sure.'

Lucci beamed, his furry ears twitching with pleasure. He shovelled down his breakfast and then complimented Nelli on her cooking, which sent the landjill into a flutter. However, something was still bothering Lucci and the astute Udolphus asked what it was.

'I don't understand, really,' said Lucci. 'Why we don't just go straight to the authorities now and have the Thieftaker General and Signor Pavolo arrested? I mean, we might not know how they're going to carry out their plot, but if they're in jail, or being watched, they won't be able to do anything, will they?'

Udolphus said gently, 'This would be a good idea if we were absolutely certain that we knew *all* the conspirators. However, as I told you, Lucci, one of the Council of Ten is, I believe, the mastermind behind the plot. I think the traitor is Signor Chapaquida, but I'm still not absolutely certain about his guilt – and I certainly can't prove it.'

'So, even if we get di Coporoni and Pavolo arrested as well as Malacite, there's still someone else to carry out the plot?'

'Precisely! Probably the most important member of the group. There, I told you that you would make a wonderful unraveller, Lucci. Now, off you go – and remember, watch your back.'

Lucci went back up to his room and changed into very plain clothes. He did not want to go back to his old street friends wearing finery. Not that they would be jealous, but it did not seem fair. Once all this unravelling was over, Lucci intended to buy a big house with a lot of beds. He was not wealthy enough to take care of the young street rats completely, but he could at least provide them with somewhere warm to sleep at night. In a city as rich as Vequince the street rats could feed themselves by hanging around the docks and waiting for a cargo of edible goods to be unloaded. There were always spillages of some kind and the younglings would leap in and gather these up. But on the other side of the coin rich cities are short on accommodation: everyone wants to live there in order to share in the wealth. So having a night roof over their heads would make a great deal of difference to his friends.

It was a sparkling day, the sunlight on the waters of the lagoon blinding as it picked out the peaks of the waves. Lucci hurried along the busy waterfront to the docks, where the ships would be berthed. Here he found the lighters already ploughing back and forth from ship to shore, ferrying cargoes to the warehouses. His friends were there, watching boxes of sugar being hoisted and swung from deck to shore using winches. The group of ragged waifs were licking their lips in anticipation of a rope breaking or a hook failing and a case of sugar bursting on the dockside.

'Huppa!' he cried, coming up to them and using the usual urchin greeting. 'Sugar, eh?'

'*Brown* sugar,' said Puccio Pucci. 'The best kind. Is your forelimb better? Any bruises still?'

'Nearly new,' smiled Lucci.

'Huppa, Lucci!' cried Poggio, Ricci Spini, Carlo and Broccoli, almost with one voice.

Broccoli then quipped, 'Back on the streets again, eh, Lucci.'

Lucci smiled at their warm jibing. 'No, as you see I'm now a fine gentlejack, with proper clothes and everything. Even a long furry muff for my tail, when the weather turns cold. No holes in these breeches, eh? No threadbare cuffs to this jacket. But listen, my master has sent me to find out if you want a silver coin each. You'll have to earn it, of course.'

'Of course,' agreed Ricci Spini, but then in a lower tone of voice, said, 'There's someone watching you from the shadows of that warehouse, Lucci. He followed you along the quays.'

'Never mind him, my friend. I shall lead him a merry dance all around the city today. But you, my raggle-taggle orphan friends, you must be about my master's business. We need to find a Joponic cleric, a water rat by the name of Horishma. You scruffy tykes know the buildings and streets of this city as well as you do the hairs on the backs of your paws. Go forth and seek him out. I'll meet you during the course of the day, here and there, but when you see me just clap me on the shoulder and say, "Huppa!" then whisper what you've found as you walk away. Understood?'

'Understood,' muttered Carlo. 'And the coins?'

'Later, but you know you're sure to get them.'

At that moment a rope snapped and a crate fell onto the dockside, bursting open, spilling beautiful brown sugar like sticky grains of gold over the flagstones. A tattered cheer went up from the foundlings and there was a free-for-all as they dived in and scooped up pawfuls of the sweet raw sugar. Lucci, finding old habits hard to break, was in there with the best and worst of them. They stuffed it into their mouths, crunched and swallowed at least half a dozen pawfuls before they were chased away by the dockers. With full bellies, they set off in various directions to scour the city. If this cleric was out there, they would find him, for they knew every follicle on the backs of their paws.

Later, by the yellow house in the Campo San Termite, Lucci happened upon Broccoli. 'Huppa, Lucci!' cried Broccoli, and whispered as he passed, '*Nothing yet.*'

A short time afterwards Lucci bumped into Carlo by the bookshop of Medici Caroni. 'Huppa! *Not a thing.*'

Two hours passed before Lucci saw Ricci Spini in the distance; they waved, and Lucci caught a slight shake of Ricci Spini's head.

In the mid-afternoon, just as the hot sun was starting to wane, Lucci felt a paw on his shoulder and turned to find Poggio there.

'Huppa! Huppa!' cried Poggio, in a voice which promised things, but then hissed, '*Not a sausage.*'

Evening came around. The big red ball that was the sun was touching the wavetops with its fiery bottom. Lucci was watching it, wondering why he could not hear the sizzling, when Puccio Pucci almost ran into him. The young rat was breathless, but he managed to croak out a weak 'Huppa!' then added in a tiny voice, '*Calle del Traghetto. Big red house with tall chimneys.*'

They passed on, Puccio winking. A sudden flush of joy went through Lucci. He and his friends had succeeded. How pleased Udolphus would be. Instead of scurrying back to Nelli's lodgings, Lucci walked idly along in the dying light of the day, kicking at loose stones and whistling through his two prominent front fangs. He had no desire to communicate his good fortune to the watcher who had been tailing him all day. How bored that mammal must be, Lucci thought, for he had done nothing but wander around and visit Sophia at her grandmother's apothecary.

While he had been at the apothecary he had got himself into dreadful trouble. He had insulted Dropsi. Sophia was now angry with him and had said she would never speak to him again.

Sophia's grandmother had always frightened Lucci to death. The ancient rat with her matted-fur skin hanging from her bones was a ghastly sight. She smelled as if she were already in the grave. Her prominent eyes stared and the smirk on her face was awful to behold. How could such rotten green teeth stay in someone's jaws? Lucci had wondered. They should surely have dropped out ages ago. And those black crooked claws! He was glad she wasn't around today.

'Your granny,' he had whispered in Sophia's ear, 'is ugly enough to scare a barbarian cobra, let alone a civilized water rat.'

He had giggled. Sophia had stared at him in horror. Then the indignant jill let him have a mouthful, ending with those dreadful words, '. . . and don't ever speak to me again.'

On he walked, through the angled narrow alleys and over the many bridges, past houses that put every other city in the world to shame. Prugae might boast its wonderful town hall and Vianna its palaces, but almost every building in Vequince was a work of architectural splendour. Lucci, lost in dark regrets and passionate longings, noticed none of this.

Eventually he reached the lodgings, feeling both elated and miserable at the same time. He had done his work for Udolphus, surreptitiously handing over a purse of silver coins as promised when passing Spini in an alleyway, but his private life was in tatters. Sophia had shown him the door and he had no idea how to get her to open it again.

His stalker remained on the far side of the street, seemingly interested in the chimney pots.

'Hello, anyone home?' he called, as he entered. 'Nelli?'

'*Signora* Nelli, if you please, young whippersnapper,' said that stern landjill, coming out of her living room. 'Don't shout so. I was just enjoying a nap. Herr Beck is upstairs, in your room.'

Lucci took the stairs two at a time. Just as he reached the top the Devil came out of his bedroom. Rotzi di Coporoni, in his thick long coat, grinned evilly at Lucci.

'Ah, the informer.' He took Lucci by the nose and

twisted it. 'You're the one who put my friend Malacite in prison, eh?'

Lucci's eyes were watering but he was more concerned about what had happened to his master. 'How – how did you get in here? This is private property . . .'

The thieftaker gave the nose a final twist, then said, 'Nowhere is off-limits to the law. I came in through the window, of course – do you think I announce my entrances to the world? So, what have you to say for yourself, you squealer? Should I run you through here and now with my blade? Who would know? Malacite would thank me very handsomely.'

'Malacite is a murderer!' cried Lucci. 'He killed my master. He deserves to be in prison.' The young water rat did not want the thieftaker to know that he was aware of the plot, so he made up another untruth. 'My poor master never hurt him, yet Malacite hired an assassin to kill him. Why? What did Udolphus ever do to Malacite? I hate him, that alchemist. I'd do the same tomorrow and the next day. I'm sure he murdered my master out of sheer spite, nothing else, just because Udolphus insulted him.'

'Insulted Malacite? How?'

'He made fun of his pelt – the fact that it was full of burn holes.'

'Go on.'

'He called Malacite a living colander. Asked if his parents were cheese-graters. Suggested he might worm his head. Asked him if he was a weevil colony. He must be religious, he said, as he was certainly quite

211

*holy*. Asked him if had he been *bored* lately. Called him a spaghetti sieve. Said he could walk in the rain and not get wet; that the wind could play tunes through him. Asked if the army had *drilled* him or if someone had *poked* fun at him. Fisherjacks could use him as a sardine net; a tennis racket had more guts and less holes. Suggested he might hire himself out as a wire fence – and if Malacite was ever executed they'd have to hang him, because a firing squad's bullets would go right through. Things like that . . .'

Di Coporoni laughed out loud. 'Beck made all those witticisms? He's very inventive – *was* very inventive, that blasted shoemaker. I always thought Geraniums had no sense of humour. Well, well. So that's why you think Beck was killed, eh? Well, you could be right. You *are* right. I think I'll let you live for a little while longer. You amuse me, infant. But keep this in mind. One of these days you'll open your eyes in the middle of the night, thinking you've heard something in the darkness – and you'll be right. Someone will be there. Someone with a sharp knife, or a knotted garrotte. When they find your remains in the morning they'll be sick to their stomachs by the sight. It will not be a pleasant death.'

With that the thieftaker went to the landing window, opened it, and exited, sliding on his back down the roof to drop onto the kitchen garden below. Lucci rushed to the window, his heart still beating with fear, and watched the big rat's boots crushing radishes and cabbages as he trod thoughtlessly on the vegetables that Nelli had so lovingly grown.

Lucci saw the thieftaker walk across the street and speak with the rat who had shadowed him all day long. The pair had a brief exchange, then both went their separate ways, the stalker at last leaving Lucci in peace. He rushed into his room, looking this way and that, calling, 'Udolphus? Master? Where are you? Did he kill you again?'

The wardrobe door swung slowly open.

# Chapter Twelve

Udolphus stood in the wardrobe, a pistol in his paw.

'If he had tried to use his sword,' said the otter, who had hidden the moment he had heard di Coporoni's voice, 'I would have shot him dead through the slats.'

Lucci was badly shocked. He shuddered and pulled his coat tighter round his body. He was, after all, just a young water rat and not used to the violence of the cloak-and-dagger world. Udolphus had become hardened to it all over the last couple of years, but poor Lucci – threatened as he walked the streets, menaced in his own bed while sleeping – was beginning to think he was in a nightmare.

Udolphus understood, for he said in a sympathetic voice, 'It's been a long day – there've been many long days.'

'Yes, master, there have,' agreed Lucci. 'And I think this has been the longest.'

'You should get to bed.'

First Lucci told his master all he had learned

about the Joponic cleric's accommodations.

Udolphus reached back into the wardrobe and took out his black cloak and tricorn hat, putting them on.

Lucci asked, 'Where are you going, master?'

'To pay some visits.'

'Not on stilts – in the dark?'

Udolphus had the bad grace to laugh at his assistant's concern. 'No, no. The night will disguise my height somewhat. I shall shrink down into myself a little and keep to the deep shadows. I shall bend my tall otter's body into a crooked S shape inside my cloak and slink through the blackness.'

Lucci smiled in spite of his fatigue and low spirits.

'Well,' said Udolphus, 'I aim to be just like that fellow – sneaking through the murk. Now, off you go to sleep. I shall see you in the morning, bright and early.'

'Can't I come with you?'

'No – and Lucci, promise me you won't try to follow me. I don't want you out at night. Promise me you won't go wandering the streets once I've left.'

Lucci scowled. 'I promise.'

'Good.'

Udolphus then crept down the stairs. Once outside, he breathed in the sea air gratefully. All day he had been confined to Lucci's bedroom. He had slept some of the time of course, but a great deal of it had been spent thinking. Too much thinking can make one's mind feel as dusty as an attic and so he was glad to shake out the cobwebs.

He glided along the canal paths, keeping close to the buildings and out of the direct glare of the moon. After several days of Carnival the revellers were getting a little ragged at the edges. Instead of cavorting about the streets and campos all night, they had started drifting off to bed early. You could have too much of a good time. Like thinking, enjoying oneself can be exhausting after a while and one starts to long for the softness of one's bed. The hunched Udolphus encountered few passers-by and those he did were not interested in a crooked old mammal in black scurrying through the shadows.

Once he came across some watchmammals, thief-takers of Rotzi di Coporoni, but they were swinging their lanterns wildly as if they had been imbibing in merry-wine, which they probably had. Udolphus locked himself to the moonshadow of a statue in the portal of an old church and remained frozen until the group of water rats had passed by. Then he thanked the shadow and moved on, along the water-ways where the gondolas bobbed and clattered against each other. Finally, after crossing a humped bridge, he reached the Calle del Traghetto. There he found the red house with the tall chimneys.

He rang the bell.

There was a scuffling and a grumbling from within. In the stained-glass panel above the door Udolphus could see the light of a lamp coming along the hall-way. Then a voice called, 'Who is it, at this time of the evening?'

'Excise officers!' snapped Udolphus, standing up

straight. 'We believe you to be harbouring a smuggler.'

The light wavered and there was a whispering: male and female voices.

'You must open up,' said Udolphus briskly. 'This is the law.'

The female voice ordered the male to open the door. Bolts were slid back and locks were unlocked. Eventually the door swung open and a timid-looking male water rat wearing nightclothes stood before Udolphus. Behind this creature was a po-faced female water rat with forelimbs folded.

'It's that foreigner, in't it?' she said, nodding towards the back stairs. 'It's 'im up there.'

'I'm afraid it is,' replied Udolphus sternly, aware that the male rat was looking round him for the other excise officers. He turned and called in a gravelly voice, 'You stay there, Jack, and send someone to the other end of the street to block that off. He won't escape this time.' In a softer voice, 'Now, signora, if you would be so kind as to show me the room.'

'You'll need your truncheon,' she said, 'to knock 'im on the 'ead if 'e tries to get away.'

Udolphus stepped into the hallway. 'I am trained in unarmed combat,' he said. 'My paws are terrible weapons.'

'Oh,' she murmured, impressed. 'An otter thing, is it?'

'Precisely.'

The male water rat remained below, his mouth wide open. The female led Udolphus up the creaking stairs and along the landing, to a door.

'In there,' she said. 'I'd chump 'im one, soon as 'e shows 'is face, if I was you. Take no chances.'

'I'll bear your advice in mind, signora, but I don't wish you to get hurt in the mêlée. Please, would you mind withdrawing? I believe your husband is as concerned about your safety as I am.'

'My brother,' she said. 'Silly old fool. 'e's the one what give 'im the lodgings. If it was up to me . . .' She remained looking doubtful for a few moments, but when Udolphus kept staring at her, she melted away down the stairs.

Udolphus rapped on the door.

Sounds came from within and for a moment the unraveller thought the Joponic cleric might indeed be making a run for it, but then the door opened and a middle-aged fellow with long silken whiskers stood there, blinking.

'Good evening, Horishma san.' Udolphus bowed politely, knowing it was bad manners to stare into the face of a Joponic mammal. 'My name is Udolphus Beck. Excuse me, it is very rude to visit you without an invitation, but I would like you to answer some questions.'

He received an even lower bow in return. Then for a moment their eyes met, before good manners returned. The water rat cleric was dressed in a long white robe with large sleeves. The robe was covered in black and gold symbols from the rat's own country. It was a robe to admire. Udolphus would have given a good pair of boots for such a robe.

218

'On what authority,' replied the cleric, 'do you come here?'

'I must beg you to forgive my rudeness. I have heard that clerics from your islands are adept at bare-claw fighting, so I would appreciate it if you would remain on the far side of the bed, while I question you from here.'

'You are a very wise otter, Beck san. I have heard your name. You are the one they call *the Unraveller*.'

'At last,' murmured Udolphus. 'Someone has got it right.'

'You are famous amongst crickets and nightingales.' Another deep bow. 'I am honoured to meet you, Beck san. But I am but a peaceful wandering priest. Our religion permits no violence.'

'I have no time to go into details, Horishma san, but I must know who asked you to come here. This is a matter of life and death for the island of Vequince. Who was it who sent for you? And why?'

'Alas, I know not the mammal's name. His letter was signed *The Golden Rat*. When I arrived I was met by a Signor Pavolo, who promised to use his influence to obtain me a post at the university, if I taught him the fine art of paper folding. I asked to be introduced to the Golden Rat, but my request was denied.' The cleric shrugged. 'So, wishing to remain here for a position at the university, I did as I was asked. I have no shame in that. Origami is a harmless occupation, after all.'

'On the surface, I would agree with you, but I believe Signor Pavolo is involved in a conspiracy to bring down the government.'

There was genuine surprise on the features of the Joponic water rat. 'In that case, please ask your questions.'

'Before I came here tonight I had already deduced that you were here to teach one of the conspirators your skills at paper folding. I noticed that Signor Pavolo had paper cuts on his paws when I met him, and of course it followed that he was the one you taught. What I would like to know from you now is, what object, what animal, what *thing* you were asked to concentrate on.'

Horishma shrugged. 'There were many. A fish. A bird. A boat. A fabulous beast: a dragon. A frog. First I had to show him the rudimentary techniques which cover all origami. Then, once he became more adept at folding the paper, he asked me to teach him to make those objects I have just mentioned. The marbled paper they sell here is particularly good for origami. It is stiff, but not too stiff. It is slightly shiny, but not over-shiny. We used several sheets, I remember. Signor Pavolo is not a patient mammal, but eventually, under my guidance, he was passing good at it.'

'Damn!' muttered Udolphus. 'They're either very clever or they haven't yet made up their minds which one to use. Frog? Fish? Boat? All connected with water. Bird? Could be, but not necessarily so. A dragon? Also a flying creature. Well, I must be vigilant. At least you have given me some clues to sharpen my focus. I thank you, Horishma san.'

A deep, deep bow. 'I thank you for your advice. I am so honoured to have met the great Udolphus Beck. I wonder if you would be so kind, before you leave, to sign my boots. They were made by your father.'

Udolphus was amazed. 'Indeed?'

'Certainly. I sent all the way from Jopon for them, providing only the measurements. When they arrived they were a perfect fit.'

'That's astonishing. Not only that they fit perfectly even though ordered by post – though of course his shoes and boots were always precisely made – and extremely durable I might add. But also I never knew my father's shoemaking skills had reached as far as the Orient.'

Udolphus, ever suspicious, watched carefully as the cleric went to his wardrobe and took out a pair of brown leather boots. Indeed, the ex-shoemaker recognized the hallmarks of his father's work immediately. A tear came to his eye. Horishma produced a writing kit such as only Orientals carry with them, comprising a shaped block of solid ink in a carved wooden box and several paint brushes. Udolphus selected a brush, wet it in a small green bottle of water, and inked it. With one eye on the cleric and the other on his task, he signed the heels of both boots. Horishma was delighted.

'Before I go,' said Udolphus, taking out the small square of marbled paper he had purchased at the shop, 'is this the paper you purchased in order to teach Signor Pavolo?'

221

Horishma studied the square and said, 'Not quite, but very like.'

'You do not have any of the original?'

'Signor Pavolo kept every scrap.'

'I see. Thank you again, and good night.'

Udolphus made his way towards yet another great house, almost a palazzo. He had been to this dwelling before and had left it in the rain with the yellow admiral, Grossa Belli. It was indeed the residence of probably the greatest living composer, Viporatti. This was not a call Udolphus wanted to make, but one of the assumptions of an unraveller is that no one is above suspicion. Once or twice before, Udolphus had made the mistake of allowing someone the benefit of the doubt; and once or twice before he had regretted it.

As he approached the house, this time on a fine night with the heavens shot with stars, he could hear a spinet playing. He paused for a moment on the top step, listening to the notes, and imagined Viporatti sitting at the wing-shaped instrument with its oblique keyboard. The sound was not only delightful, it was fantastical. The claws that touched the keys that plucked those strings that made those notes were perfect in their execution. The music entered Udolphus's heart, swelled it, and forced tears from his eyes. How daintily now came each single note and how splendidly they were strung together into a melody. What genius, thought Udolphus, sighing. How he hoped he was here on a fool's errand and that Viporatti was innocent.

He rang the bell.

After the third attempt a fierce-looking butler wrenched open the door and stared with a visage of thunder into Udolphus's face. 'Can you not hear?' he hissed, his tail whipping back and forth behind him. 'Viporatti is playing!'

'I hear,' said Udolphus, 'but unfortunately I must interrupt. Is the recital a special one, or simply practice?'

'*All* Viporatti's recitals are special. This one more special than others, for he is entertaining the Fabulous Beast.'

'Really?' Udolphus said, stepping forward eagerly. 'What, a performance just for the Beast?'

'You cannot go in. Please come back tomorrow.'

'Impossible,' muttered Udolphus, trying to look over the butler's shoulder. 'I must see the composer tonight. I'll wait until the recital is over and speak with him then. Where may I wait? Ah! I have it! Is it possible to go and sit somewhere quietly in a corner of the recital chamber? I promise to be as silent as a wraith. I shall slide sylph-like into the room and not breathe a single breath until this profound performance reaches its finale.'

The grim-featured butler led Udolphus down the hall and into a room full of books. 'You will be so kind as to wait here in the library,' he said. 'When the performance is over I shall tell the composer you are here.'

With that the creature left. Udolphus could hear the music even better in the library than he could on the street. He settled back into a padded chair and soared as if on the back of a bird. Once or twice he swore he could hear a strange, high hissing, which sounded as if it stemmed from great pleasure, rather than dissatisfaction. This was followed by a loud rustling. It was an uncommon sound which made the hairs on the otter's spine stand on end. It was not ugly or menacing, but it was so eerie it could have come from beyond the grave. That rustling. How chilling, yet how fascinating! Only a wall between him and what was once thought to be a mythical creature. It was a situation never before imagined by the shoemaker's son.

Udolphus drifted away; when he came to he realized the music had stopped and there was a chinking sound in the doorway. He looked up to see Viporatti standing there with a cup of hot chocolate in his paw, rattling his saucer politely to wake up his visitor.

'So,' said the composer cheerily, 'my music sends you to sleep. Fie! It has kept kings on the edges of their seats, otter.'

Embarrassed, Udolphus sat bolt upright in the great leather chair and tried to gather his wits. Viporatti was in one of his usual outrageous waistcoats: a cornflower blue with silver buttons. His velada coat was a deep, dark red, the same shade as the pelt-tight breeches that ran down to his knees. There was a spume-white cravat at his chin, but his wig was also the deep-red colour of an uncut garnet. His shoes were black with red bows. He looked superb, every inch the beau. Udolphus could not dress like that in a million years: he had not the confidence.

Viporatti saw his visitor staring at his waistcoat and advanced with the cup of drinking chocolate in one claw, but pointing with the other to the buttons. 'Representations of the heavenly bodies,' he explained. 'Starting from the top – Mercury, Venus, Earth, Mars, Jupiter, Saturn and Uranus. All the planets of our solar system. Aren't they splendid? One of our Vequincian philosophers did the templates.'

'Which would make your face the sun, of course. How extraordinary. Yet my studies have led me to believe that there may be other planetary bodies out there, beyond Uranus,' said Udolphus. 'Have you read the works of the otter Schindherst? He has a mathematical formula which predicts further orbs beyond those we can yet see with a spyglass.'

'How interesting! New planets? I shall have to have some new buttons made to accommodate them. And new buttonholes!' Viporatti now wagged a claw. 'But now that I think of it, your apprentice, my dear unraveller, has put my friend Malacite in jail.' He sat down opposite Udolphus. 'It was he who fashioned the buttons for me. But I suppose he deserves to be there, if he has been exploiting the young for the furtherance of his own ambitions. How sad these animals are, to give in to their feral instincts and attempt to gain power and riches by foul means.'

'Well, signore, you are the lucky one, with your talent. And I too, I suppose, am fortunate. But I am here on a grave mission. I would be grateful if you could answer a few questions.'

'Fire away!' laughed the composer, settling back in his chair. 'It's wonderful to witness an unraveller unravelling.'

'There was a Vequincian at the concert party to which you kindly invited me, by the name of Pavolo. Can you tell me why you invited him?'

Viporatti stroked his hairy chin with his left claw. 'Pavolo. Pavolo. I don't think I know him. Can you describe the creature?'

Udolphus did so with great economy. 'He has the head of a corpse.'

'Aha! Yes, the cousin of the Voleccis. But, my dear Beck, I'm sure I didn't invite this tragic fellow. He must have come with one of the other guests. Yes, I'm sure of it. I always write all my invitations with my own paw. I do not know this creature and certainly didn't invite him myself. If he was there, then some other guest brought him along. They do take these liberties, you know. I can anticipate your next question. Who was the guest who brought this Pavolo? Ah . . . Pavolo was masked, was he not? I do believe the creature came with Signor Chapaquida.'

Udolphus reached forward and grasped the paw of the composer. 'I think you're right. Signor Chapaquida. Yes, that fits in with my theories.'

Udolphus was happy, on two counts, with Viporatti's answer. Firstly he was satisfied that Chapaquida was most likely the fourth plotter. He was also relieved that there had been no duplicity on Viporatti's part. The composer's openness was to

Udolphus a confirmation of his innocence in this matter.

'I'm afraid I had to test you, signore, to find out if you were involved with these mammals. Forgive me, but if you were my own brother . . . but what a shame you're not. I should love to have a brother whose music soars. There you are then. I'm sorry to have bothered you. I must go . . .'

Viporatti helped his new friend on with his cloak and plonked his tricorn hat on his head. 'You must come again,' he said. 'I shall look forward to it.'

Udolphus stopped in the doorway and said, 'I – I suppose you won't be entertaining the Fabulous Beast again, will you?'

'My dear Udolphus,' murmured Viporatti, 'I would love to invite you to join us next time, but I doubt there'll be one. Between you and me, the Fabulous Beast doesn't appreciate good music. Oh, it likes the ditties sung by washer rats at the public scrubtroughs. Songs like, *My Sweetheart Was a Dilly, But She Dallied with Another*. But real music, *proper* music such as mine, just sends it to sleep. All it wants to do is play with a ball.'

'Play with a ball?' repeated the fascinated otter.

'Yes, you know – an inflated spherical object. It seems it gives it unfailing delight to knock the thing mindlessly here, there and anywhere.'

'What a waste,' said Udolphus, still trying to picture a two-legged creature prodding a ball. How did it balance on one leg while it was kicking something with the other? Did it not fall over? Perhaps it had wings which helped it keep upright on one leg? It was true there were no wings visible in the pictures of the Beast, but perhaps it folded them down its back, or its side? Half-stork, half-flamingo? How radical.

'I should have listened with great admiration and delight,' he added. 'I *did* so for most of the recital.'

'Yet even you fell asleep in the end,' sighed Viporatti, teasing the otter. 'My music is before its time.'

'Oh, definitely. Most definitely. *Well* before its time.'

Udolphus went out into the night, where lurked all the dangers of a city gripped in the vice of a conspiracy.

# Chapter Thirteen

Lucci lay awake for a long while. His injured fore-limb was still bothering him a little: the ache in the bone was not agony but it was persistent. He was beginning to miss Sophia's friendship dreadfully. Young love might be dismissed lightly by adult water rats, but in a youthful breast it burned like fire.

'Idiot!' he snarled at himself for the umpteenth time, knocking his skull with his knuckles. 'You should be hung from the Bridge of Braggarts by your tail. You should be tossed onto the Beach of Seven Martyrs and left for the sea to wash away like so much driftwood. You should be sent to the Alley of Arrowsmiths and your pelt shot full of wooden shafts.'

Suddenly he decided. 'I must try to speak with her.'

But there was a problem. He had promised Udolphus he would not wander the streets. He looked out of the window. There in the moonlight he saw something which made his heart race. 'That's it,' he muttered. 'I'll wander the canals instead. I made no promise about the canals.'

He put some pillows in the bed and pulled the bed-clothes up over them, in case Udolphus came back. Lucci wanted Udolphus to think he was still in bed asleep. The unraveller, though youthful himself, would not approve of a love-sick Lucci wandering around without protection, especially at night. Once the hump in the bed was good enough to pass a cursory inspection, Lucci got dressed and descended the stairs into the narrow street below.

The moonlight was shining on the canal which ran by Nelli's house. There was a yellow gondola like a big banana moored under the archway. I won't be walking the streets, he thought, I'll borrow this craft. As he clambered into the gondola, it rocked dangerously. He took up a position at the stern of the vessel and, with the oar in its rowlock, pushed himself out into the canal.

It was, like most things, not as easy at it looked. The gondola veered all over the place as Lucci fought with the oar to straighten its course. Twice he crashed into the wall of the canal.

But he was bright and clever, and after a while he got the hang of it. If you wanted to turn left you put in extra effort when pushing the oar forward. To turn right you pulled the oar back with great force. There was an innate rhythm and skill which was awakened within him.

The canals were called *rii* and the one which ran by Nelli's house was the Rio di San Paolo. Lucci followed this into the Rio di Margette, which in turn led into the Grand Canal itself. From then on he knew that if he turned right and stayed on that side, he would eventually come to Dropsi's shop, which was next to the Scuola San Giovanni.

There were few other craft on the canal. A lacquered funeral barge passed by but the black-garbed rowers paid him no attention, their eyes straight ahead, their minds on their job. Lucci heard one say to the other, 'You would wrangle over an ass's shadow . . .' The rest was lost to his ears.

Finally Lucci came to the shop and managed to moor his gondola to a post on the water's edge without falling in. Then he went round to the back and looked up at the window of Sophia's room.

'Sophia,' he called softly, 'I'm sorry.'

Of course, she did not hear him.

'Sophia? Sophia?'

No reply.

A bat swooped low by his head and mocked him.

Like many other youths in the same situation before him, he threw a handful of gravel at a windowpane. It rattled like hail on the glass. He waited for a few minutes, then tried again. Eventually the window opened and there was the face of his lovely Sophia.

'Sophia,' he hissed eagerly, forgetting she was still angry with him, 'it's your friend, Lucci.'

'Lucci? I know him not,' she cried softly. Then coldly, 'Go away, water rat.'

'Sophia, please give me another chance.'

'Why should I?'

'Because – because I'm so very very sorry. Your

grandmother is not ugly ... she's – she's just *interesting*.'

Sophia said, 'Please go away, Lucci. It's the middle of the night. All decent mammals are in their beds, asleep. Have you no decorum? Have you no sense of etiquette?'

'No,' he grumbled now, becoming annoyed with her, 'I was brought up on the streets. The middle of the night was when I went looking for stale crusts in the gutters, so that I wouldn't starve. I had no bed that wasn't cold stone, perhaps with a little straw from the dockside boxes. Decent mammals? They used to kick me as they passed by during the day, when I was trying to catch up on my sleep, calling me a lazy tyke and telling me I should get up.'

Sophia had no answer to this obviously, for she continued to look down on the wretched Lucci without speaking. Finally she said, 'I'm coming down. Wait a minute.'

In a few moments she was standing in front of him, a shawl about her shoulders. Her whiskers were twitching in a most alarming manner, but Lucci was lost in those soft, dark eyes.

'I just came to say I was sorry,' he said. 'I know it was a bad joke, but I'm not much good at – what did you say the other day? – *social graces*. I haven't got any of those yet. But I'm learning,' he added fiercely. 'I'm learning a few of them social graces. Udolphus is teaching me. He just hasn't got to the bit where you learn you're not supposed to make up nasty jokes about mammals. When I was on the streets it was how we got our own back on those who treated us badly – rich and pompous water rats who knocked us out of the way with their silver-knobbed canes. We made fun of their big noses, or short tails. It was a way of getting even.' He held up his paw. 'It was wrong, I know that, but you get into the habit. I'm sorry I insulted your grandmother. She's probably a nice old biddy – and I wish I hadn't likened her to a cobra.'

'Well,' admitted Sophia, 'she can have a sting in her tongue.'

'Do you forgive me, Sophia?'

The jill lifted her vole face. 'I – I will, but you must never insult my family again.'

He felt so light-hearted he was tempted to say, *Even the ugly ones?* The habits of the streets die hard. But instead he said, 'I promise. I truly promise.'

'Well then, go home, Lucci. I'll see you in the morning. It's the ceremony of the Duce's Marriage to the Sea tomorrow. You may take me to see it.'

Lucci jerked upright. 'The *marriage* ceremony! I'd forgotten that.'

He saw Sophia through her back door, then went down to the gondola. As he passed a sewer hole at the end of the street, the lid flew off and Dropsi's head appeared. Her face was like that of some hideously starved gargoyle: pinched and hatchet-like, wrinkled as a dried prune, eyes like painted eggs protruding above her pointed cheeks. Her lips were like two garden slugs left out to dry in the sun. This sewer was obviously her hiding place from di Coporoni.

'If you break her heart,' she rasped at Lucci, 'I'll

give you such a poisoning. Your eyes will boil in your face, your ears will shrivel to dead molluscs and green gas will hiss from your nostrils like steam from a kettle.' Dropsi then gave him a dreadful smile, before adding, 'I'll give you a deadly long-goodbye kiss with these two lips of mine.'

The sewer hole cover closed on the monstrous visage.

Lucci was left trembling at the thought of being kissed by those hideous lips.

He returned to his gondola with mixed feelings. He had won back Sophia's affection, but clearly if his friendship with her was to last, he had to suffer the indignities of contact with Dropsi. Sophia would not hear a word against her. So Lucci was left with no choice but to accept Sophia's grandmother into his life, if he wanted Sophia there too.

Once in the gondola he made his way slowly back down the Grand Canal towards the Rio di Margette. It was getting very late and he wanted to be back before Udolphus. He knew the otter would have a fit if he realized Lucci was boating around the canals in the early hours, visiting young females and exchanging social chit-chat with apothecary poisoners.

Back on the Rio di San Paolo, he had the archway to Nelli's house in sight when he saw two of Rotzi di Coporoni's thieftakers sitting on mooring bollards, smoking pipes and talking in low voices.

Lucci quickly drew the yellow gondola to the side of the canal and lashed it to an iron ring. He climbed out and slipped along the bank by a row of houses opposite the two thieftakers. He moved like a phantom, parallel to them, keeping to the deep moon-shadows thrown down by the buildings. Suddenly, one of them looked across the water. He then took the clay pipe out of his mouth and tapped it against the side of the bollard. Red-hot ash spilled from the bowl of the pipe and was scattered into bright sparks by the breeze. The thieftaker was still talking. He had not seen Lucci. His voice floated over the canal, clear and audible in the quiet of the night.

'. . . what're you goin' to do, when you get your share?'

'Wot?' said the other. 'You mean afterwards, when we're rich?'

'Yeah.'

The second thieftaker folded his forelimbs, his pipe stuck in his mouth. 'I'm gonna buy a big boat. A sanpierota, wiv one of them tri-anchorated sails.'

The other one laughed. '*Triangulated*, you mean.'

'If I said wot I said,' the second thieftaker growled in a menacing tone, 'it's wot I mean.'

'If you like,' replied the first. 'Wanna know what I'm gettin'?' He was not inclined to wait to be asked, for he continued without a pause, 'A whacking great house, wiv about ten rooms.'

'Will there be enough loot for that?' The second thieftaker was clearly excited by the prospect of a big house. 'I mean, a boat's a boat, but a big house is somefink else.'

'Why, rat, they'll be pots of the stuff. If our boss is one of the govermint, then we can 'ave wot we like, can't we? What 'e says, goes, dunnit? Stands to reason if you're the govermint. There won't be no Council of Ten to tell 'im wot to do. 'E'll do wot 'e likes, no mistake. We've been blaggin' wiv 'im, wot? Five years now? 'E'll see we're all right. No more sewer grub for us. No more sleepin' in doss 'ouses. We'll be golden rats, you an' me. No mistake.'

The pair were silent for a while, the one who had emptied his pipe filling it again and lighting up. The flare of the match threatened to expose Lucci, crouched against the wall, but the two thieftakers were too lost in their contemplations of the plunder they would get, once their 'boss' was in charge of the city, to notice him.

Just as Lucci was about to move on into the safety of Nelli's archway, the first thieftaker cackled loudly.

'Wot?' asked the second one.

'I was just thinkin' wot a nasty turn the Council of Ten's goin' to get at the ceremony. A nasty turn. Get it?'

'No,' replied the other dully. 'Can't say I do.'

'You know, *a nasty turn*.'

There was another moment of silence, then the second thieftaker suddenly roared with laughter. 'Oh, bloody 'ell, that's a good one, that is. I'll tell it to the boss tomorrer. 'E'll laugh 'is socks off, 'e will.'

''S my joke,' snarled the first. 'I should get to tell it.'

'Jokes can't be private property, that's a fact under law, that is. They're universal, they are. I heard that once, from a monk. Un-iver-sal. Big word for you, brother – but it's true. It means jokes belong to everybody and you can't own 'em. If I see 'im first, I'll tell 'im, so there! You got to 'ave respect for the law, eh?'

The other thieftaker grumbled, 'Wot are you spoutin' the *law* for, brother? The law? Why, we've just done for a mammal's life, we 'ave. Murder, that's wot they call it. Law? You'll be tellin' jokes from the scaffold before you're much older, if you're not careful. Me too. Come on, it's time we were on our way.'

The pair then got up and went down an alley.

Lucci rose, cramped, from his hiding place. Murder! He wondered who those foul rats had killed now. They had no regard for any kind of life, those creatures. But what was he, Lucci, to do? He could not tackle two strong adult thieftakers. They would likely kill him too without any compunction or remorse.

'They'll get theirs one day,' he muttered, as he climbed Nelli's staircase. Lucci was a strong believer in divine retribution. When you lived on the streets, you had to be. You had to believe that bad mammals would get their come-uppance and good mammals would eventually triumph. Otherwise there was nothing to keep hope burning.

There was a snuffling noise coming from Lucci's bedroom.

'Oh heck, I hope Udolphus is not back yet.'

But if he was, he was, and Lucci would have to explain why he had gone out in the middle of the night. Udolphus would understand.

When he crept into his room, however, there was the tall lean figure of Udolphus, standing over Lucci's bed. He was sobbing quietly. Clearly something had happened to upset him, and Lucci went and quietly stood by his master, ready to offer consolation.

The otter was staring down at Lucci's bed.

Lucci's gaze followed that of his master.

Two large knives were planted in the hump in the bed.

'My poor Lucci,' wept Udolphus, stumbling forward. 'I should have stayed to protect you – but they came – and they murdered . . .'

He stumbled forward, tears streaming down his furry cheeks, and pulled back the bedcovers. After a second's silence he let out a shocked cry. Feathers were spilling out of the savaged pillows beneath the blankets and sheets. Large holes had been ripped in all the bedding, where the killers had struck with their blades, before leaving them stuck in what they had thought was Lucci's body.

Udolphus stepped back, treading on Lucci's foot, and Lucci let out a yell which made his master jump.

'What, Lucci? Is this your idea of a trick?'

Lucci hopped around, rubbing his paw. 'No – no, master. I went out. Before I went I left the bed looking as if I were still in it. They – they came to murder me. They think they've done for me. I heard them say so.'

'You heard them? You mean, di Coporoni's thugs? They were here? And they think you're dead? That's both of us they think are gone, then. But did you see them?'

'Yes, master. Two big thieftakers. I heard them talking about a murder. I didn't know I was the corpse. They were laughing.'

'Well, they would, wouldn't they? They're the dregs of the sewers, those thieftakers.'

'No, no, they were laughing at a joke one of them made.'

'A joke?'

'Yes, but I didn't understand it. It didn't sound funny to me. They said the Council of Ten were going to have a nasty turn. One of them didn't get it at first, but then he did and burst out laughing.'

Udolphus seemed just as puzzled as Lucci about the joke. 'Perhaps it wasn't a joke at all. Perhaps it was just their way of looking at the results of the plot? Well, so long as you're safe, young jack.' Udolphus's expression changed slightly. Through the window a florid dawn was shyly entering the sky. 'Just what were you doing, roaming the city in the early hours of the morning? You promised me you wouldn't wander the streets. Do you break your promises so easily, Lucci?'

'No, master, for I didn't wander the streets. I took a gondola and rowed around the canals.'

This silenced Udolphus for a moment, but then the otter said, 'And you think that play on words makes a difference?'

'It's not a play on words, it's true.'

'Whatever. And your excuses for boating around the midnight canals, when you should have been in your bed getting murdered?'

Lucci had to smile at his master's flippancy. 'I'm sorry, Udolphus – I had to see Sophia. I was so very miserable. The music in my heart was broken and I had to get it mended.'

'Broken music, eh? Ah, young love. It gets us into all sorts of trouble, that does. Well,' Udolphus sighed, 'I'm so glad you did what you had to do. Now, the pair of us better get some rest, but we'll lock and bolt the doors and windows. I doubt they'll be back, thinking us both corpses, but nevertheless, better safe than sorry. You'll have to sleep on those torn pillows. And may the feathers tickle your nose.'

'Master,' asked Lucci, as he remade his bed, 'have you ever been in love?'

'Me? No, Lucci. Not me. A ridiculous state of emotion, if you ask me. In Geranium we don't hold with love. Practical creatures, the otters of Geranium. Oh, we get married for the sake of procreation, to keep the streets full of otters, but love is such a silly thing. Not for sensible creatures like us. You Latin types wallow in it, I know, but we northerners scorn it.'

'So you *have* been in love?'

Udolphus threw down a pillow. 'Yes.'

'Who was she?'

'We need not go into that.'

'When was all this, Udolphus?'

The pillow was pummelled again with savage paws. 'I have no wish to talk about it.'

'Master, you're destroying that pillow!'

Udolphus looked down in surprise. 'Oh, am I?'

They prepared to go to sleep, Lucci in his bed, Udolphus in the corner of the room.

Then Lucci remembered something. 'Oh, master – I forgot to tell you. There's a ceremony tomorrow – sorry, today. I know how you like ceremonies.'

'Is there?' Udolphus sounded a little uninterested, possibly because he was so tired. Lucci almost dropped the matter, but since he had started he decided to finish. 'Yes. It's the Duce's wedding.'

The fur on Udolphus's brow wrinkled. 'The Duce is getting *married*? I thought he already had a wife.'

Lucci giggled. 'Yes, of course he does. Not married to another water rat. Married to the sea. It's sort of' – he searched for the kind of word that Udolphus would use – 'symbolic.'

'A symbolic marriage to the sea. Oh hum – well, if I wake up in time, I'll potter along and have a look.'

'You should do, master. Everyone will be there. The Duce will be dressed in ermine and gold, and wearing his *corno* hat. And he'll use the golden barque – you know, the *Bucintoro*? You saw it when he was coronated.'

'Crowned. Crowned, Lucci, not *coronated*.'

'Oh yes, crowned. Everyone will be there.'

'So you said.' Udolphus lay down and closed his eyes. 'They'll all be watching from the shore, I suppose.'

'Well, yes, but the Council of Ten will be on board the *Bucintoro*, with the Duce.'

Udolphus shot bolt upright on his blanket on the floor. 'The Council of Ten will be with the Duce?

They'll all be on the same vessel, out in the lagoon?'

'Yes.'

'That's it,' said Udolphus. 'Lucci, my young rat, the conspirators will strike tomorrow – no, it's today, isn't it? Today they'll attempt to assassinate the whole governing body of Vequince, the Duce included. Once they're dead the Florions will come with their mercenaries and attack. The city will be leaderless. Helpless. There will be confusion and chaos. Citizens will run through the streets crying havoc, as the shrews of war are unleashed. Pavolo, di Coporoni and Signor Chapaquida, we think, will step in and offer to negotiate with the invaders. In fact, as we know, they are in league with the Florions, and will become their puppets when this is all over.'

Udolphus paused to let this information sink in, then continued, 'However, the citizens of Vequince will not know that the very rats who step forward to save them are the conspirators themselves. They will look to this evil trio to rescue them, and when di Coporoni, Pavolo and Chapaquida form their interim government, which as we know will be a permanent one, they'll be unopposed. They'll be regarded as saviours, not assassins. Then they'll trump up false charges of treason against certain innocent citizens – leading figures who might get in the way of their schemes – and accuse them of the assassinations. Viporatti, for instance, and Admiral Belli, and other citizens with influence. It's a very good plan.' He looked at the clock on the mantle. 'What time is the ceremony?'

'Three o'clock.'

'We must get a little sleep. I shall be ragged else. Then we will go to the ceremony.'

Lucci was left wide-eyed, staring at the ceiling, knowing that everything was coming to a head.

# Chapter Fourteen

Lucci and Udolphus rose at noon, after they had been called three times by Signora Nelli. Both otter and water rat were grave. These, as oriental mammals would say, were interesting times. Today would see the culmination of all that Udolphus had worked for in Vequince. As with most of his unravelling, he was not one hundred per cent sure of all his facts. In the unravelling world one never is. In the final confrontation, one has to work with what one has, and trust the rest to providence. Udolphus began to dress in his Bauta mask and costume, but Lucci shook his head.

'No, master. The Duce's marriage is a solemn ceremony. There'll be no Carnival today. Everyone will be in their best clothes and on their best behaviour. And they won't be wearing masks.'

'Oh? So no stilts either?'

'Definitely no stilts. You will be arrested, master.'

'So, we will need to walk the streets as ourselves and risk further injury and death. So be it. After today it will not matter. Today all will come to a head. Pass me my hose – sorry, my stockings, young Lucci. A thousand thanks. And the shoes? Now finally, very carefully, my pistol – you have loaded it, have you not? Good. Now we are ready to partake of some of Nelli's sweetmeats. Just politely ease a pawful from the tray as we leave through the door, for we are out of time.'

Once in the street, Udolphus hunched down into the deep collar of his cloak, but he could not hide his height. What remained in his favour were the crowded streets and the incredible maze that formed this wonderful and spectacular city. The General's thieftakers were about, of course, but in such a mob they could not move quickly. Even if they saw and recognized him they would have trouble catching him.

'Where are we going?' asked Lucci, as they threaded their way through the masses. 'This isn't the way to the San Merci di Lido, where the ceremony takes place.'

'We're visiting Admiral Grossa Belli first. I should have done this first thing this morning but I was too exhausted with the night's events.'

Udolphus said no more, preferring to save his breath for hurrying through the streets and campos. Eventually they were outside the house of the admiral. Udolphus rang the bell and when a jackservant answered he asked for the admiral. Grossa Belli granted them audience in his study, the walls of which were covered in glass boxes full of Brimstone butterflies, which have yellow wings. The admiral was frowning deeply and looking at his pocket watch when they entered.

'Make it quick, Herr Beck,' said the fat admiral, who was wearing a bright yellow uniform with Geranium lace cuffs and collar, 'I am due at the port in five minutes, to make final preparations for the ceremony.'

'I will be brief,' said Udolphus. 'Admiral, I would ask you to put the navy on full alert – and also to prepare the army generals – discreetly, of course. We don't want to cause alarm and we don't want to warn those who are against us that we're on to them. It's my belief that an attempt will be made today on the lives of the Council of Ten and the Duce. It's my understanding that the Florion army, transported by Florion ships, will attack immediately afterwards.'

'What?' The admiral's furry jowls quivered. 'Are you serious, Beck?'

'Never more so, Admiral.'

'Then we must stop the ceremony.'

'If you do that, the assassins will only bide their time and strike again. I have no proof against them: only personal knowledge, which no judge would accept. Also one of them is a traitor and I have no proof to support my suspicions. It could even be Roma Volecci playing a double-game with me. Admiral, if we warn the conspirators now, and they postpone their plans, the next time we might not be so lucky as to discover where they are going to strike. I agree this is a terrible decision to make.'

The admiral's eyes grew round. 'But think of the

consequences! We're sure an attack will be made, but we do nothing to warn the Council?'

'Warn the Council by all means, but do you think this will prevent them from carrying out the ceremony? It's my experience that politicians and monarchs simply dig in their heels when something of this nature threatens. They're not easily influenced by threats. I expect they get them all the time, from crazy rats, from pranksters. Do you think my warning would stop the ceremony?'

The admiral thought about this for a few moments, then said, 'Honestly? No. I think they would still go ahead with the ceremony, if under tighter security.'

'Then don't tell them, for in doing so you'll send signals to the conspirators, and that would have the same effect as stopping the ceremony altogether. By all means tighten security, but as I said before, do it discreetly. We don't want to frighten them back into hiding, only to have them emerge on another occasion, when I am not here to unravel their evil.'

Grossa Belli saw the sense in this, but it was a brave mammal who could carry this plan in secret. If anything were to go wrong he would almost certainly be accused of that heinous crime, procrastination. A water rat with less courage than the admiral would have run straight to the Council of Ten and warned them they were about to die. It was partly due to the admiral's character that he did not do this, and partly due to the respect and admiration in which he held Udolphus Beck.

'I will gather my captains together,' he said. 'And

we will form a plan to defeat the enemy, should they attack.'

'Thank you, Admiral,' said Udolphus, giving the water rat a civil bow. 'I am your servant, signore.'

The admiral outlined his plan. The navy's ships would normally all be out on the water for the ceremony, though not prepared for war. Today, once the ships were on the lagoon, each captain could inform his sailors to load the cannons and make ready the arms. This could all be done quietly and out of the public eye. Also, once they were under way, no sailor could leave the ship and warn the plotters, either by accident or design. Should nothing come of the conspiracy, the crews could then – just as quietly – revert to peacetime operations, and the captains simply call it an exercise.'

'Excellent!' Udolphus said, and Lucci murmured something similar, being a little overawed in such high society. 'What about the army?'

'Here there is more difficulty,' replied the admiral, frowning and swishing his tail. 'Vequince has no standing army. We see no need for such an expense with water between us and the mainland. Any invader will need ships to reach us. Instead, Vequince has a militia. That is to say, ordinary citizens – shopkeepers, glass-blowers, street cleaners – all pick up arms and make ready to defend the city themselves. They get a little training of course, but for the most part they are amateurs. This is no bad thing. If you remember your history the Athananians beat the Pershans with such a militia, even though they were outnumbered a hundred to one.'

'Um, the Battle of Megathon.'

'Precisely. But you see what a problem it poses here?'

'Let's leave the army out of it then and rely on your navy to stop the fleet, should they decide to attack anyway.'

'Good.' The admiral paused for a moment, staring at the floor. Then he looked up and said, 'I hope we're doing the right thing here, Beck. Of course, if you're wrong, and there's no conspiracy—'

'There is, I am certain of it.'

'– or something should go wrong and we lose the Council and the Duce—'

'Well, there I am not quite as confident, but I think I have enough to go on to prevent a disaster. There is an inevitability about these matters.'

'Then we have to leave it in your paws, Beck.'

Udolphus added, 'One small piece of information still evades me, but I hope it will fall into place at the time of the attack. If it doesn't—'

'We're all doomed,' finished Lucci, in a sombre voice.

'Well, perhaps that's being overly pessimistic, young water rat, but certainly things will not be rosy.'

'I must go,' said the yellow admiral. 'I shall see you later, Beck, in what I hope will be a celebration.'

The three left the house together. The admiral was whisked away in a sedan chair, while Lucci and Udolphus walked towards the waterfront, from where they would have a good view of the ceremony. Udolphus wanted to get there early so as to find the most advantageous point. Then he could bed down a little, hide his height, and wait with alert eyes.

The place was heaving with colourful rodent bodies. Everyone was in their finery – flocked waist-coats, fairytale lace, gossamer, pearl buckles, silver buttons, brightly hued ribbons, marvellous bonnets, dazzling rapiers. Cloth with dyes that took their names from popular imports – coffee, tobacco, tea – were predominant amongst the males, while the females preferred pastel tones. Skirts billowed and bulged like sails over wildly hooped petticoats. At every turn one could hear the swish of frock coats and the rustle of silk dresses.

Sweeping gestures were the order of the day, as water rats bent their silk-stockinged knees to neighbour and friend, doffing their tricorn hats with great aplomb. The air itself was full of scented wig powder and ochre snuff from flick-lidded jewelled boxes. The Marriage of the Duce to the Sea was a popular ceremony. All the luck, fortunes and trade of Vequince was tied up with the sea. The population was a superstitious one and attended these gatherings religiously. No one wanted to upset the city's brilliant commercial record. All their livelihoods were bound up in their merchant fleet and in the ocean that carried it on its back.

Even Dropsi and Botcchio had come out of hiding and were standing together on the quay. There to protect them from wrongful arrest were two hawk-eyed lawyers in wigs and robes. The pair had decided between them that after the ceremony they would throw themselves on the mercy of the courts. They had done nothing wrong and they were prepared to defend themselves. Di Coporoni's rats would not be able to abduct and murder them while there were crowds around them, especially with the two lawyers there to witness any subversive action.

Out on the water itself there was a motley flotilla of craft, from stately galleons to gondolas, getting a seaside view. Every boat on the island was there, crammed with watchers, jostling each other. Gaily coloured sails – lateens, lugsails, spankers, leg-o'-muttons, jibs, spinnakers – all were weaving and fluttering on the water. Small boats were battling fiercely with larger craft for the best viewing space, the little ones forever in danger of being blocked completely by the high wooden walls of big ships. It was a struggle out there, between Goliaths and Davids, for the best spots.

'Up there,' said Udolphus, pointing to a bell tower. 'Let's go to the top of that campanile, Lucci. We can see everything from there.'

At that moment one of di Coporoni's thieftakers spotted Udolphus. The rat's eyes opened wide with disbelief, especially when Lucci turned round and he saw him too. This rough thieftaker then signalled Rotzi di Coporoni, who was equally surprised to see two mammals he thought were dead and gone and feeding the flies. The Thieftaker General soon recovered, however, and hissed an order to his minions. Several thieftakers began to move through the crowd towards Udolphus and Lucci. This hapless pair had no lawyers to prevent them being arrested and dragged away.

'Into the tower, quickly,' said Udolphus.

Lucci said, 'But, master, the Devil's rats will just come in and get us.'

'No they won't,' cried Botcchio, overhearing. 'Signora Dropsi, will you take the other entrance?'

Lucci and Udolphus slipped inside the west entrance to the bell tower. Botcchio planted himself right in the doorway, his burly arms folded, his sturdy legs apart, his great barrel chest filling the gap. Several thieftakers rushed forward and tried to pull him out of the way, but he was a dead weight with all that gold inside him. None could move him, no matter how hard they tried. It was like trying to shift a bag of lead. They heaved and shoved, straining and groaning, but it was a hopeless task with so heavy a figure. It would take a crane to get the maskmaker out of that doorway.

'Ha! Not easy, is it, you runts?' cried Botcchio triumphantly. 'Not when you can't threaten me with guns and knives.'

One of the di Coporoni's rats drew a sword on hearing this, but Botcchio's lawyer, standing in the watching crowd, cried, 'I am watching, thieftaker. This is not the middle of the night. You can't get away with murder here.' There were mutterings of 'Quite right' and 'Shameful' from the spectators. The thieftaker was forced to sheathe his sword again.

They gave up on Botcchio and went round to the

east entrance, only to find Dropsi sitting in this door-way, smiling evilly.

'Get out of the way, witch!' shrieked a thieftaker. 'Let the law go through.'

'Any rat who tries to pass me will be lovingly caressed,' she said simply. 'I will stroke him into his grave.'

Di Coporoni himself now arrived. He looked up at the bell tower and shrugged. 'The otter can't get up to much from right up there,' he said to his minions. 'Leave him. We'll deal with him later. Let's watch the ceremony and enjoy the fun.'

His rats laughed. Yes, they cried. Later would be soon enough.

Inside the bell tower Udolphus and Lucci climbed the hundreds of steps to the top, where they found a crowd of water rats. On each corner of the campanile's square platform high above the streets was a soldier of the Palace Guard,. each armed with a large musket as they stared with a stony expression over the scene below.

While they waited for the ceremony to start, some water rats began a game of cards in the corner of the campanile. Udolphus's eyes flicked back and forth from this group to the mass of mammals below. He shuffled and shifted on his feet. Finally he succumbed to temptation.

'Just a few hands,' he murmured, 'while we're waiting.'

Lucci grabbed his master's sleeve. 'No, you can't – not today.'

The gambling fever was upon Udolphus, but he fought hard to get it under control. 'Lucci, all I'm asking for is a quick game—'

'No quick games today,' snapped Lucci. 'No card games at all. Today we have to keep our wits sharp.'

At that moment there came the boom of a cannon over the bay, signalling the start of the ceremony. Udolphus looked out over the lagoon and saw the ships of the Vequincian navy forming a semicircle on the seaward side of the aquamarine waters. The royal barque, the golden *Bucintoro*, was being rowed slowly away from a packed quay with flags flying from two dozen masts.

Udolphus looked around. It seemed he had been jerked back to reality at last. He stared at Lucci while the card players looked on. The gamblers were no doubt expecting him to strike his assistant for being so impertinent. A wave of intense shame washed through him. Udolphus knew he was in the wrong. Although he was a great brain when it came to unravelling mysteries, he was still a feckless and weak young otter when it came to cards. What had he been thinking of?

'Lucci,' he said, taking the youngling by the shoulders, 'I am truly sorry. Forgive me. I am a terrible otter.'

'Eh?' cried a gambler, seeing his victim wriggling off the hook. 'Ain't you going to play then?'

A guard intervened here. 'You shouldn't be playing cards in the first place. This is a ceremonial day, not a holiday for gamblers. You should be watching the ceremony, not betting on the turn of a card. Go to, or I'll arrest you all.'

There were murmurs of disapproval from the rest of the viewers as well as they glared at the card players with dark looks. The card players shuffled their feet, looked a little shame-facedly at their critics, then melted away into the rest of the watchers. Udolphus turned and stood by a guard, staring out into the lagoon.

His senses were highly tuned. He had turned from card playing into a mode of high alertness. His eyes were everywhere. Lucci was a little lost. He did not know what he should be looking for or why. So he simply stood by his master, ready to assist him should it be required.

Forty-four rowers with maroon oars moved the golden *Bucintoro* out into the lagoon in stately fashion. The vessel was not just beautiful; it took one's breath away with its splendour. It was magnificent. It glittered and glistened from stem to stern in the afternoon sun. Indeed, one would be forgiven for thinking that its cargo *was* the sun; that it shone from within and sent its bright rays forth over its chosen city. The royal barque represented all the wealth and prestige of the Vequincian nation, lined with red velvet, with a lid-like roof that could be raised so that the watchers could see the statesmen and royalty inside. It was an unparalleled work of art.

'Lord, those citizens must be bursting with pride,' said Udolphus. 'What a glorious sight.'

On the front deck of the *Bucintoro* was a golden

throne on which sat the purple-robed Duce, a gold-leafed parasol to protect his royal rodentness. On the side decks the Council of Ten perched on gilt stools. They sat bolt upright in their scarlet robes, staring straight ahead, ten water rats taking part in a solemn and stately ceremony.

*Except there were nine!*

'One of them is missing,' muttered Udolphus to Lucci. 'Is it Signor Chapaquida? Can you see? Called in sick, no doubt, to avoid the ensuing carnage. Do you know the missing rat, Lucci? Who is it? I must know if I was right . . .'

'I wouldn't know any of the Council if you sat me on their laps one by one,' replied Lucci with a little spirit in his voice. 'I'm not usually invited to dinner with the great and good.'

'Now, Lucci,' admonished Udolphus, 'you've seen them at other ceremonies. You must know them by sight. It really doesn't matter. We'll find out soon enough. Ah, look, the Duce is standing now. What's he going to do? You *can* tell me that?'

'He's going to remove his ring and throw it into the sea.'

'Quiet!' hissed someone near Udolphus. 'Hear the words. Hear him speak.'

Indeed, the whole of the shoreline and all those in the boats and ships had fallen into a deep silence. The Duce moved to the bows of the golden barque, right up to the prow, and stood for a moment staring out over the azure waters. Then he removed a ring from one of his right claws, held it aloft for a few moments while a single young rat played a drum roll, then he tossed it high into the air. It sparkled as it rose and fell in an almost perfect arc, disappearing as it hit the surface of the lagoon.

The Duce's voice boomed like a cannon over the waters. 'We marry you, O Sea, in token of our true and perpetual possession. We invoke divine protection for all those who sail on you and for all those who toil on you. You have been our salvation from poverty and may we continue to serve you as well as you serve our citizens.'

With those words over, pandemonium broke loose. A mighty cheer went up. Water rats began to throw coloured paper streamers out onto the water. Fireworks went off on the shore and from the ships, filling the air with bright baubles of burning light. The world was suddenly alive with music: flutes, drums, trumpets, horns. Silver-paper fish were tossed into the waves, as rats and other mammals chanted fishing songs. Stringless kites were launched from crossbows on the shore and went flying out over the lagoon, towards the golden *Bucintoro* with its important passengers. These were in the shapes of mammals, birds and fish of all kinds.

Then suddenly all eyes were on single kite, of huge proportions, a kite in the shape of a bird, which was launched from the roof of a basilica.

'Ooooohhh!' went the crowd excitedly. 'Aaaahhhhhh!'

This wonderful kite soared over the heads of the multitude and out towards the *Bucintoro*. Even the grave politicians on board were smiling and pointing. Someone had gone to enormous trouble to build this beautiful kite and everyone who saw it, the Duce included, was suddenly clapping. The crowds caught on and soon the whole of Vequince was united in their appreciation of a work of art. Out towards the royal barque went this fabulous paper bird with unerring accuracy, for Vequincian fliers were experts at this game and could land a kite on a golden bezant.

Udolphus peered through narrowed eyes at the pattern of the marbled paper from which the kite was made and recognized it instantly. 'Lucci,' he said sharply, 'what bird is that?'

'Bird, master? It's supposed to be a tern, I think. Yes – yes, it is. A royal tern.'

'A royal tern. How apt! Yet I think it's our *nasty turn*. We had the wrong spelling, Lucci. This is our petard. This is our bomb.'

The kite moved in slow and stately fashion through the air, gliding on a warm current with unerring accuracy towards the golden *Bucintoro*.

Udolphus glanced across at the roof of the basilica. There, amongst his cronies, with a face as dark with wrath, was Rotzi di Coporoni. They stared at each other, unraveller and conspirator. The thieftaker was smiling as he mouthed the words across the void between the two buildings.

'*Too late, otter!*'

'No it's not,' growled Udolphus.

With astonishing swiftness the otter snatched a loaded musket from the nearest guard.

'Hey!' yelled the soldier. 'What—?'

But Udolphus was already aiming at the kite. It was a shot that only the best of sharpshooters could make. There were probably only a dozen creatures in the known world who could hit that kite from the bell tower. Happily, Udolphus was one of them.

In aiming, he adjusted for wind. He allowed for trajectory. He took into account drift and spin caused by thermals rising from the warm water. He made the last tiny concessions to the kick of the musket and the trueness of the smooth-bored barrel. Finally, he squeezed the trigger and permitted the weapon to do its work.

The giant paper tern was but a score of metres from the golden *Bucintoro* when Udolphus fired. The muzzle of the weapon flared, the bullet on its way to its target. The red-hot ball from the musket struck the tern kite's belly.

Immediately there was an enormous explosion which thundered over the waters and rocked the whole lagoon and shoreline. It appeared to punch a hole in the very sky itself. Bits of flaming marbled paper fell from the blue, showering those on the decks of the golden barque. Stunned politicians simply stood there, watching them fall. Sailors, more alert, began to stamp the lighted bits out as they touched the decks.

The explosion seemed to have knocked the wind out of the whole audience. Citizens and visitors just stood there for a minute, shocked and dazed by the terrible noise which had left their ears ringing and their heads numb. Then, once again, pandemonium ensued. Screams rent the air and rats began running in all directions.

Those in the campanile hopped and skipped down the stone steps to the ground below, with the Palace Guard yelling for calm, telling everyone not to panic.

Out on the waters, the *Bucintoro* was racing for the shore, its rowers plunging oars in at the double, the time-drum no longer beating its slow rhythm, but pounding out a rapid *bang, bang, bang, bang, bang*.

Udolphus gave the astonished soldier his musket. 'I'm sorry to have startled you,' he said to the guard. 'It was a necessary action.'

The rat merely gaped at him as he took back his weapon.

'The plot is foiled, Lucci,' cried Udolphus, not without some satisfaction in his tone. 'We have beaten the conspirators. We shall soon be absolutely certain of the fourth member, for he will be the missing councillor.'

'Hurrah!' yelled Lucci. 'Hurrah for Udolphus Beck!'

One of the bemused soldiers asked, 'What's happened here? What's going on, otter?'

'A plot against the government – look! Look out there, on the far shore! An invading army. The barbarians are on the beach.'

The soldiers and Lucci followed Udolphus's pointing claw and were horrified and amazed to see the glittering ranks of a massive rodent army poised to cross the lagoon. The banners and standards of this army, with their bronze spear points and brass cannons gleaming in the evening sun, proclaimed them to be Florions. There were squadrons of cavalry as well as row on row of infantry, all clad in bright armour. Musketeers stood with their weapons shouldered. Pikejacks clustered amid a tall forest of pikes. Grenadiers with paw bombs, artillery gunners with rammers and sponges, officers with sabres drawn: all stood in silent but threatening pose, ready to board the expected vessels which were to carry them over the water.

'They'll need us at the garrison,' cried one of the guards. 'Come on, lads, let's get there quickly.'

The four soldiers flew down the stairs with their muskets, their tails taut with tension and excitement.

'Lucci,' murmured Udolphus, still studying the scene, 'look now, out on the water.'

Lucci looked. A fleet of Florion ships!

Leading the Florion vessels were Jerboan pirate ships with red sails, coming up the straits at full sail. Their decks were crowded with buccaneers brandishing cutlasses and pistols, thick leather belts around their waists and red kerchiefs on their heads. Mean-looking motley crews they were, with not a drop of mercy between them.

Udolphus knew that such pirates were renowned for their ruthlessness. They would swarm over a vessel or a small island and kill everything that walked or breathed. If you took the lowest criminal elements, the sludge of normal society, and removed the worst of these scum, the utter dregs, these would be your Jerboan pirates.

'Jerboan pirates,' muttered Udolphus in disgust, and looking back towards the Florion army he added, 'And Zugspitz mercenaries. These Florions don't care who they consort with, do they?'

'See over there,' cried Lucci. 'Admiral Belli's fleet.'

# Chapter Fifteen

Lucci's cry was not one of further alarm, but of high excitement.

'Our jacks-o'-war are going to fight them!'

The ships of the Vequincian navy had split into two formations. One moved swiftly towards the pirates. This brave line blocked the pirates' passage up the straits, thus halting their progress. The other ships, a smaller fleet, turned towards the mainland shore.

Thanks to Udolphus's warning, Admiral Belli's fleet was ready for the enemy. Instantly their carronades and mortars were booming, and round shot was falling like hail amongst the troops waiting to invade. The larger fleet now engaged the pirates, intent on driving them back from whence they came.

Great splashes indicated where the cannonballs fell short or long of their mark, but soon the Vequincian gunners got their range. Balls fell onto the decks of the foe, causing huge splinters to fly and holes to appear. Grapeshot flew in a blizzard of iron and ripped the sails to pieces, tore down the masts, peppered the pirate crews. Rockets whizzed through the air to set light to canvas and blow up magazines on the enemy vessels.

It was a glorious if bloody battle out there on the lagoon.

Admiral Belli's sailors and marines were grim-jawed and determined. How dare the Florions invade their beautiful city! This was their homeland, to be defended to the last. Black powder and smoke – the smoke of war – wafted in clouds over the waves. The air was full of the stink of gunpowder. There was a storm of wood and metal everywhere. Timbers shrieked and timbers fell, to crash like trees on the decks.

Thanks to Udolphus the Vequincian navy had not been caught on the hop. Their warships had been totally prepared. Grossa Belli's captains had primed their sailors and their vessels had been sharp and ready – nay, *eager* – for action.

The air remained thick with pungent gunsmoke, which drifted like sea fog over the water. A fireship came out of the line of pirate vessels and was sent towards the home fleet, hoping to break Admiral Belli's line. There was no panic. The yellow admiral's seajacks were used to such tactics and they blew the blazing hulk out of the water before it reached them. Then they turned their fury on the pirates themselves, showering them with cannonballs, and relentlessly pursuing them out towards open sea.

Some of the buccaneers' ships were sunk, others limped away, sails in tatters, hulls full of holes. The pirates were no match for a fleet of warships that was fully armed and ready for action. The scum of the seas had lost the advantage of surprise.

And behind the pirates the Florions turned tail and sailed away. They had no stomach to face a furious Vequincian navy. The Vequincians were the best sailors in the world. Only surprise could have turned the day, and surprise had been lost.

On the far shore the Florion army, with its Zugspitz mercenaries, was already marching away towards the distant hills, knowing their cause was lost. Without ships to assist them they had no hope of crossing the lagoon and entering the city of Vequince. They were also being continually pounded by the navy's guns and large gaps were appearing in their ranks.

A small contingent of Florion infantry, commanded by a loud and flamboyant colonel, attempted to retaliate and fired muskets at the Vequincian ships. This rodent colonel called on his rats to stand firm; entreated them to stay and fight for their honour. But many invading soldiers fight only for money: they see no profit in dying for glory. They were not defending their homeland; they were the aggressors. Soon even the fiery Colonel Mudditchi and his Florion troops had to leave the field, or be caught in a hail of musket balls from the Vequincian marines.

'The enemy retreats!' cried Lucci from the top of the tower. 'The foe is vanquished!'

Udolphus placed a paw on his apprentice's shoulder. 'You've done well, Lucci. I could not have unravelled this mystery without you. I am very very grateful to you.'

Lucci shrugged, uncomfortable under such praise. 'Oh, you know . . .'

'Yes, I do know, and I believe you have become a very good unraveller in your own right.'

Lucci glowed.

'Now,' said Udolphus, his voice taking on a stern note, 'we must go and explain ourselves to the Council of Ten,' he said, quietly. 'Or rather, the Council of Nine, the missing one being a traitor.'

They descended the stairs from the top of the campanile, down to the square below. However, as Udolphus stepped through the doorway into the square itself, he saw a semicircle of enraged, rough-jawed thieftakers waiting for him with thick cudgels in their paws.

'There 'e is!' one of them cried. 'Get 'im.'

Here was the otter who had snatched riches from their paws just a few minutes ago.

Udolphus quickly shut the door on Lucci behind him and stood waiting on the steps of the campanile.

Rotzi di Coporoni was standing on the far side of the square, in the shadows beneath a colonnade. He called out, 'Your friends have deserted you, shoe-maker. Botcchio and Dropsi went home once they thought we had gone. This time, otter, you won't be so lucky. You'll soon be making shoes in Hell for the feet of demons. My thieftakers will beat you to a pulp and I shall enjoy watching them. You've thwarted our plans this time, but there won't be a next time for *you*.'

The Thieftaker General could not keep the passion

out of his words. If he had intended to sound cold and hard, it was not working. His voice was so full of rage it spilled over and had him spitting venom onto the flagstones. Udolphus had indeed destroyed di Coporoni's plans, had indeed forced him into the choice of either banishment or death on the gallows. The big rat was so incensed with the otter he could not even think straight. All that mattered to him now was to get even, to have his revenge on Udolphus; only then could he consider how to evade the law and justice.

Behind him, Udolphus could hear Lucci frantically trying the handle of the closed door. The otter muttered, loud enough for his apprentice to hear, 'Stay in there, Lucci. Lock the door. There are thugs out here.' Then he took his pistol out of his pocket and made ready. 'I am a dead shot,' he called to the waiting thieftakers. 'I will certainly kill the first to approach me. And the second and third will have a great struggle, for I shall use this pistol like a shoemaker's hammer and break their heads. You may finally overwhelm me, but – but, my evil wrongdoers, who shall be the first to die?'

Those with the cudgels in their paws all looked at each other a little uncertainly. No one wanted to die, of course. But they were equally sure that they did not want this otter, who had robbed them of certain wealth, to escape with his life. It was just a matter of who was brave enough to tackle the tall, menacing otter and take that first shot.

Rotzi di Coporoni came out of the shadows. He

reached inside his coat and took out two objects that flashed in the sunlight. They were the dreadful Merino daggers, the glass knives that left their blades in the wounds. The thieftaker held these awful weapons, one in each claw, intending to bury both of them in the heart of his enemy, Udolphus Beck.

'I'll take the bullet, you lot pile in afterwards,' he snarled. 'I don't mind risking death to get even with that cockroach.'

The general began to stride across the flagstones, his ears twitching, his tail swishing and the big coat flapping around his ankles. At that moment there came a glugging sound from the drains. Within a short time the square was knee-deep in water. The waters rose rapidly, pouring in from the quays and wharves, spouting up from the drains, gushing through alleys and passageways to fill the great square. Thieftakers were all of a sudden fighting to keep their feet in the rushing currents that swept through the square, as they waded up to their waists in sea water.

'The *acqua alta*,' cried Udolphus. 'I am saved!'

The unraveller dived into the blessed waters of the lagoon. Water rats swim very well and the thieftakers plunged in after him. But water rats are no match for an otter when it comes to swimming. Not many mammals are, except perhaps dolphins and seals. Udolphus flashed away, dipping below the surface, twisting and rolling in a serpentine and sinuous fashion to evade his pursuers. Rotzi di Coporoni and his thieftakers had no chance of catching him. He moved with the swiftness of a barracuda through the submarine world of Vequince, weaving round the bases of columns, darting alongside the foundations of the houses, zipping between the legs of statues. He was a streak of darkness, a flash of white light.

The sea, recently wedded to the Duce and having been entreated to watch over its brethren, had come to the rescue of Udolphus. Perhaps it was just a freak of nature, this fortuitous phenomenon which had arrived in the nick of time to save the hero of Vequince. Perhaps it was nothing more than coincidence and good fortune. Or perhaps (and Lucci will swear this is the truth, even today) it was the sea responding to a cry for help. The ocean can be a very cruel element, but it can also be kind. Perhaps on this day, the day of its annual marriage to the Duce of Vequince, it was inclined to be generous and came to the aid of a good otter.

The pursuit was long and hard, but it only had one outcome. The otter escaped. When the waters subsided, Udolphus found himself at Signora Nelli's house. There he found Lucci, who had retreated up the stairs of the campanile and then later gone home. Udolphus changed into dry clothes and then went to the house of Admiral Grossa Belli, leaving with that able sailor all the names of the conspirators. He was pleased to learn that Roma Volecci was not the conspirator amongst the Council of Ten. Then the otter went home for a well-earned rest and a quiet evening with his friends.

\* \* \*

The morning after the attempted assassination of the government an official runner arrived at Nelli's house with the message that Udolphus and Lucci were to appear before the Council of Ten. Dressed in their best clothes, unraveller and apprentice went to the Ducal Palace to meet the rulers of the city. The pair stood before the Council, Lucci shaking like an aspen in the breeze. Udolphus noticed that there were still only nine of them.

Signor Chapaquida was missing.

Roma Volecci was there, looking very sober and sombre in his robes, but managing a wink when he thought he was unobserved.

'You are Herr Udolphus Beck, the Unraveller?' said a grizzled, grey-coated councillor with a crooked tail, a Volecci by his looks and bearing. 'And you, his apprentice?'

'We are,' said Udolphus.

Lucci merely gave a nervous little cough.

'Then the thanks of every citizen in this fair city of Vequince are yours,' stated the speaker. 'We have heard from one of our own, the distinguished Roma Volecci, and also from Admiral Belli and our own genius of music, Signor Viporatti. It seems you have been our saviour. We have one of our politicians, a member of this very council, in chains this day, having confessed to faking illness yesterday. A conspirator' – the elderly water rat spat the word out of his mouth – 'along with other plotters. We also have a confession from Signor Malacite, the alchemist, and Signor Pavolo, my own cousin. They have thrown themselves on the mercy of the Council of Ten and the king, the Duce of Vequince.' The speaker's face darkened. 'Foul, foul deeds have they wrought, and punishment must be theirs, despite their pleas. This city almost fell into the paws of such creatures, would have done so but for your expert unravelling, Herr Beck.'

'Thank you, signore,' murmured Udolphus. 'It was nothing.'

'It was certainly something, something great and grand, and for your services to us you are granted the Freedom of the City of Vequince, an honour which has never before been granted to a foreigner. Your apprentice, the young Lucci, will be groomed for the now vacant post of Thieftaker General. This is his reward. He is young but he has been well trained by you and will be given what we might call an "uncle" or a regent to assist him until he comes of age and can fill the position without assistance.'

'Thank you, signore,' croaked Lucci, his eyes round with disbelief. He looked up at Udolphus, who nodded gravely and prompted the longest speech of the young water rat's life. 'I – I will do my loyal utmost best to discharge my duties with honour. The Thieftaker General will no longer be despised and loathed throughout Vequince. From now on the post of Thieftaker General will be trusted by all as honest. I – he will carry out his duties of policing the city and in his performance will act without prejudice or bias.'

Applause came from the public gallery. Lucci looked up and was startled to see Sophia sitting there, beaming down on him with pride in her furry face.

She gave him a little wave with a gloved paw. He waved back, then realized he was still under scrutiny from the Council, and pretended to cough into his clenched paw, as if that was what he intended all along.

The councillor looked up from a document he was studying and gently smiled, as did all the members of the Council. 'My, my,' he said, 'that is a remarkable speech, coming from an orphan just lately from the streets. And a very worthy one, young Lucci. I feel we have chosen our future Thieftaker General well.' He shuffled papers in front of him and added, 'The previous general, may his eyes and liver rot, has not been seen since the *acqua alta*. He may be dead, he may have escaped to Florion or some other city. We do not know. It is a loose end which I personally would have preferred *knotted*, but there it is.'

So Rotzi di Coporoni had escaped justice, thought Udolphus. But then, nothing in life is perfect. There are no absolutely rounded endings to such circumstances. There are always dissatisfying sharp corners.

'If I may speak now, signore?' said Udolphus, gripping his three-cornered hat with his claws. 'There is someone else to thank.'

'Yes?'

'In your prison you hold a young jill water rat called Lucasta. It was she who first discovered the plot and raised the alarm. If it were not for her I would not be here. If it were not for her the city would be lost. I believe much of the praise given to myself and my apprentice should be hers.'

An officer of the Council leaned down and

whispered into the ear of the elderly Volecci, who then straightened and looked Udolphus in the eye. 'One of our members,' he said, 'Signor Roma Volecci, has already taken care of this matter by adopting the jill of whom you speak as his own daughter and heir to his personal fortune.'

'Thank you, Signor Roma Volecci,' murmured Udolphus, looking at the councillor in question. 'I am your servant.'

'No, Herr Beck,' replied the speaker, 'we are yours and for ever in your debt.'

As Udolphus had observed, there are no perfect endings. When the otter walked away from the Council, a Freejack of the city of Vequince, there was still a hideous prison with ugly things going on inside it. There were still foundlings and orphans scurrying about the streets, looking for something to eat. There were still criminals, still cockroaches in the sewers, still poverty-stricken and elderly citizens, still natural disasters poised behind the curtains of the horizon, still rogue wolves and bloodthirsty sharks.

One cannot change the world in a day. Some things should not be changed: wolves and sharks may be dangerous, but the world should retain some danger, or life becomes bland. Some things can never be changed: the world will never be completely free of criminals, no matter how hard society tries to clean itself. (Strange it is, thought Udolphus, that we have to campaign to keep from ridding the world of tigers, but find it impossible to rid it of murderers!) Some things need time to change them, and dedicated reformers, but it takes more than one otter, more than one jack's lifetime. Yet already Vequince was beginning to look at itself, as one jill left its jail and another jack had come up from the gutter to become head of police.

'Nelli,' Udolphus told his landjill, 'thank you for putting up with all my shenanigans. I shall be out of your fur in a few days, after a little holiday in this wonderful city of yours.'

'Oh, signore, you're welcome. I've never had such excitement. And to think – a Freejack of the city, under my roof! And you with that reward thing – that golden mask what Signor Roma Volecci gave you! Don't it shine like the sun, eh? Don't it dazzle you with its goldenness?'

Udolphus looked with great pride at the mask in his possession. Despite Nelli's enthusiastic description it did not 'dazzle' at all. The gold was old gold, dullish, gleaming tastefully in the light. It would please Udolphus's fellow Geraniums, who disliked flashiness and ostentation. Fashioned, of course, by Botcchio, the most significant maskmaker in the world, it was not one of your flamboyant character masks. It was not the friar Cocalino, or Zanni from the Commedia dell'Arte, or even the egg-throwing Mattaccino. It was the simple Citizen's mask: full face, plain in aspect, with two teardrop eye sockets and no mouth. One breathed through the two small nasal holes at the bottom of the nose. It was smooth and simple, but very refined and elegant. And very old gold. Priceless.

The great Viporatti came to see Udolphus, in case he hurried back to Geranium without saying goodbye.

'My dear signore,' said the musician, 'I shall dedicate an opera to you. I shall call it *Requiem for Udolphus.*'

A chill went through Udolphus at these words and he said, 'But – but I'm not yet dead.'

'Oh' – Viporatti laughed and waved a paw – 'you will be one day, and then they'll play it at your funeral and weep buckets, for the music will be so sad and moving.'

'I hope they'll be moved because they're upset.'

Viporatti waved a silken handkerchief. 'Oh yes, of course, but my music will send their souls soaring into the ether.'

They shook hands and parted.

As a reward for saving the city state of Vequince Udolphus was given the privilege of seeing the Fabulous Beast. He was taken to the great palace at the far end of the island. Within the palace was a formal courtyard garden of immense proportions, filled with works of art: statues of mythological creatures carved from marble.

There were orange trees, and myrtle hedges exhaling a wonderful fragrance, and fountains with water running down gutters of green obsidian. Within the boundaries of shrubs and marble was a huge camomile lawn, quartered by mosaic paths decorated with scenes of wild places: mountains, deserts, stormy seas, arctic tundras, forests, volcanoes.

Udolphus was taken with several others –

government ministers, important merchants – to the balcony which ran along the four inner sides of the house, supported by white pillars and over-looking the garden. Looking down from this vantage point, he saw a wonderful Beast, a creature of strange proportions and bizarre symmetry.

It was playing with a ball. The Beast knocked the ball back and forth. To Udolphus it seemed a game without any set rules or purpose. The Beast simply kicked the ball, ran after it, and kicked it again. Yet it seemed to be enjoying the activity, for every so often it let out a cry of joy. Its face shone with a huge smile and it chuckled to itself. This game lasted at least an hour, after which the Fabulous Beast simply left the ball on one of the scented lawns and walked around, studying visiting birds.

When Udolphus waved, the Beast stared up at him with an innocent face. Perhaps no one had taught it to respond to such a gesture, for after a few moments it simply turned away. Udolphus continued to watch the Beast, entranced by everything it did, though in truth it did not do very much except play its games and rest between times. There was an air of contentment about the garden, a sense of peace and goodwill.

Once the Beast laughed out loud, a snorting laugh at an absurd-looking bird which had flown in to peck at the oranges, and all the watchers on the balcony laughed too. Yet they looked at each other as they did so, ashamed of this show of bad manners on their part, since the bird looked rather offended by their unwonted attentions.

The otter came away from the experience profoundly moved. He knew the Beast was no prisoner, that it could leave whenever it wished to do so. This was despite the fact that Vequincians were convinced that all their golden luck was stored in that Beast; that without the Beast their trade would finally fail them, things would start to go wrong, the city would turn bad. He also knew the Beast had many companions, chosen from the populace, to keep it company. He was told the Beast had never complained of loneliness, despite the fact that it was unique and that there was and never would be any possibility of it meeting another Beast. Certainly the joy that Udolphus had witnessed while it was playing its game was not faked. It seemed a happy creature, its curiosity aroused by the visiting birds, and expressed full interest in all that went on around it.

Yet Udolphus left the palace with a feeling of infinitely deep sadness, an ache that was too strong to bear, even for his phlegmatic spirit. Something, somewhere had been lost, and though he did not know what it was, he wept for it. As he walked through the bustling crowds along the quays, the tears streamed down his face, fell onto his bodice and wet his chest. Those who saw him weeping noticed also from which direction he had come and turned away to allow him his unnamed grief in private. Many had been there, had witnessed, had felt the same terrible yearning, the same inexplicable sense of loss. The world was the world, but at some point it had been a different place, turning in a different time.

'Thank you, Udolphus,' Lucasta said, 'for all the help you have given me.'

'No, no,' replied the flustered otter, 'if it were not for you the city would be in the paws of tyrants. You have given me an unravelling which has been a wonderful experience. It is I who should thank you.'

'Will you be going home now?' asked the jill. 'Back to Geranium?'

'Oh, yes – I think so. A stroll over the mountains.' He looked around. 'This is a very beautiful city, a work of art in itself, but it is rather constricting. I'm beginning to yearn for the wide open spaces now – the mountains, the dark forests, the wide plains of Geranium. There is greenness here in the campos, but they are like little packets of greenery – there are no broad vistas, no big skies, no long and deep valleys.' He paused, then added, 'I shall miss the architecture. No other city has buildings like these, and if they do, they are few and far between. I shall treasure my time here in my dreams and think of you all very very often.'

Signora Nelli took out a kerchief and wiped her eyes. 'Oh, signore – we shall miss you too.'

With his backpack on his shoulders, Udolphus Beck made his way down to the quay, where his boat awaited. There was a small but special gathering waiting to see him off. Lucci was there, of course, paw in paw with his Sophia. And the great Viporatti. And even Admiral Grossa Belli had come to say goodbye. Viporatti had brought his violin and intended to play a 'farewell' tune as Udolphus was rowed away.

'Goodbye, Lucci,' said Udolphus. 'You have been my rock.'

'Master, when I'm a little older and have done my duty for the city I shall come and stay with you – if that's all right. I want to come on more adventures with you.'

'You must decide when the time comes, but I'm glad you said that. I'm glad you feel you want to be partners with a Geranium who has no sense of humour.'

Lucci smiled. 'Oh – you've got a sense of humour all right.'

There was a mist over the water when he left. A sea fog. Visibility was down to about a hundred yards. Much to the chagrin of the rower, he stood up in the boat and waved to his friends. Viporatti played a dirge on the violin, which had everyone in tears. Soon, soon, the mist swallowed the shoreline and they were all gone. Udolphus sat down and apologized to the boatjack, saying he had not intended to rock his vessel so.

'Oh, that's all right,' said the boatjack grudgingly. 'It's just I've got to be extra careful I don't run into another craft in this fog. It takes all my attention.'

'Of course. I quite understand.'

'So,' said the rower, pulling on his oar, 'you saved the city, eh?'

'I helped. There were others.'

'Ah, modest too. Geraniums are modest, ain't they? Now, a Vequincian would be shoutin' it from the rooftops.'

'Each to his own culture.'

'That's right, that's right. Now I don't—'

'LOOK OUT!' cried Udolphus in alarm, as they narrowly missed another rowing boat, which skimmed by them.

The boatjack expertly swerved his vessel away and avoided the collision. He let out an exhalation of relief. Udolphus gasped too, but it was not the near accident which had his heart pounding. It was the passenger in the other boat, whose eyes had also widened in shock and disbelief. They had passed each other, nose to nose, rodent and otter. Any closer and their whiskers would have brushed. Then both slim craft had slid into opposite banks of fog, like needles into cotton wool.

'Did you see who that was?' said Udolphus, still shaken. 'The passenger? I can't believe it.'

'Can't say as I did,' replied the boatjack. 'I was too taken up with missing 'im. Who was it then? The Archangel Gabriel?'

'No, someone from the other place.'

He said no more to the boatjack, but was indeed wondering if he had been seeing phantoms where there were none. They had passed each other so swiftly, how could he so sure? Yet there was no mistaking those vicious features, that heavy frame in the thick greatcoat.

Udolphus could have reached out and touched the nose of Rotzi di Coporoni.

# About the Author

Garry Kilworth was born in York but has travelled the world living in over 20 different countries. He now resides in Suffolk only yards away from a beautiful nature reserve and wild bird lake. His house was once a workhouse for paupers, 500 of whom are buried in unmarked graves in a daffodil wood at the bottom of his garden. He feels this is an appropriate dwelling for him considering his great-grandmother gave birth to his grandfather in a workhouse.

Garry has now written over 70 books, both for adults and children, but these days is concentrating on the latter. 'Kids,' he says, 'have soaring imaginations and I want to try to stay up there with them as long as I can.' He has won the World Fantasy Award, the British Science Fiction Association Award and the Children's Book of the Year Award.

His previous books for Random House Children's Books include the animal fantasy series, *The Welkin Weasels*.

# The Welkin Weasel *series*

The Monty Trilogy
*By Garry Kilworth*

'Thrilling and imaginative and reminiscent of Tolkien'
*Carousel* about *Welkin Weasels*

## GASLIGHT GEEZERS

Montagu Sylver is a famous weasel detective, intent on solving mysteries. Can he ferret out the truth when he learns that the anarchist Spindrick plans to blow everyone to smithereens with a fiendish bomb? Or find a lemming prince who vanishes almost as soon as he sets paw on Welkin soil?

Aided and abetted by his weasel companions, Monty is soon on the trail, but time is running out – especially when he becomes a fugitive from the law . . .

0 552 54704 2

## VAMPIRE VOLES

Muggidrear, the capital city on the island of Welkin, is in danger of becoming a vampire colony! Ghostly ships are arriving from Slattland, filled with coffins, and the vampire voles are becoming a real pain in the neck.

Montagu Sylver suspects that someone is deliberately sending the vampires across the seas to destroy Welkin for ever. With his trusty companions, he sets out for Slattland, determined to find – and destroy – their master.

Will Monty come whisker to whisker with the evil master vampire?

0 552 54705 0

## HEASTWARD HO!

Montegu Sylver is off to the East! Someone has stolen the priceless jade shoes of the Green Idol of the god Ommm, and the Great Pangolin of Far Kathay has asked Monty for his help.

From the moment Monty and his friends set paw on a steamship bound for the land of Eggyok, they face a hazardous journey – trekking across the desert, along the Silk Road to the roof of the world, and sailing up the Yingtong River. But things *really* get out of paw when Monty comes whisker to whisker with his old adversary, the evil lemming Sveltlana . . .

0 552 54706 9